CHRISTMAS IN WHISPERING PINES

"Why don't you tell me about some of your travels?"

Emma placed the dishes she was carrying on the counter. "I doubt that would interest you very much."

Clay put one long arm on the counter next to her and leaned around to look into her eyes. "It interests me."

Looking into the depths of his amber eyes, Emma felt as though she couldn't catch her breath. Her gaze traveled from his eyes to his mouth. He was grinning at her. A flirty, lopsided grin. Almost as if he knew she was thinking he was the most attractive man she'd ever laid eyes on. "Why?"

Clay's grin grew wider. "Do you always ask so many questions?"

"Only when things don't make sense," she replied.

She was truly a perplexing woman. "What doesn't make sense?"

"Why you seem to have an interest in me. That is, until Mrs. King always happens along. Are you the kind of man who simply enjoys flirting with women?"

"Why, Emma, do you think I'm flirting with you?"

What did he think he was doing pinning her to the counter and leaning down so close to her face that she could see the gold flecks in his beautiful eyes? "Aren't you?" If he wasn't a pastor, she might be inclined to pull his face to hers and give him a kiss he wouldn't soon forget. That would probably shock him all the way back to his pulpit . . .

Books by Scarlett Dunn

The McBride Brothers Trilogy
PROMISES KEPT
FINDING PROMISE
LAST PROMISE

The Langtry Sisters Trilogy
WHISPERING PINES
RETURN TO WHISPERING PINES
CHRISTMAS IN WHISPERING PINES

CHRISTMAS AT DOVE CREEK

Published by Kensington Publishing Corporation

CHRISTMAS IN WHISPERING PINES

SCARLETT DUNN

ZEBRA BOOKS
KENSINGTON PUBLISHING CORP.
http://www.kensingtonbooks.com

ZEBRA BOOKS are published by

Kensington Publishing Corp.
119 West 40th Street
New York, NY 10018

All Kensington titles, imprints, and distributed lines are available at special quantity discounts for bulk purchases for sales promotion, premiums, fund-raising, educational, or institutional use.

Special book excerpts or customized printings can also be created to fit specific needs. For details, write or phone the office of the Kensington Sales Manager: Attn.: Sales Department. Kensington Publishing Corp., 119 West 40th Street, New York, NY 10018. Phone: 1-800-221-2647.

Zebra and the Z logo Reg. U.S. Pat. & TM Off.
BOUQUET Reg. U.S. Pat. & TM Off.

First Printing: October 2018
ISBN-13: 978-1-4201-4452-9
ISBN-10: 1-4201-4452-9

eISBN-13: 978-1-4201-4453-6
eISBN-10: 1-4201-4453-7

10 9 8 7 6 5 4 3 2 1

Printed in the United States of America

Dedicated to Michael—
Your courage and resolve inspire me daily

Prologue

Kansas, 1872

"How did you get yourself in that predicament, little fella?" Clay Hunt waded out to the middle of the muddy creek bed until he was knee-deep in the muck in an effort to rescue a little calf not yet strong enough to free himself. "Your mama is right up there on the bank waiting for you." He wrapped his arms around the calf's legs and hoisted him in the air. "I know she told you not to go in there." It was a cold day with a crisp wind, and he felt the little calf shivering.

Once Clay made his way to the bank with the calf, he gently placed him on the ground next to his bawling mother. He patted the calf's head as he spoke to his mama. "You take better care of this little guy. He's a feisty little . . ." Hearing an unmistakable sound of a rifle report in the distance, Clay stopped talking and listened. One shot. He scanned the terrain in the direction of his house. Sound carried a long way on the range, and he didn't often hear gunfire. Turning toward his horse, he stopped abruptly when he heard what could have been two more shots.

These sounds were different, and Clay suspected they were fired from a pistol.

Jonas Meeker came galloping up on his roan. "Boss, did you hear that?"

Before Clay responded, he was already in the saddle. "Yeah. Came from the direction of the house."

"That's what I'm thinking," Jonas said.

They were riding fast, but suddenly Jonas slowed, motioning for Clay to do the same.

"What is it?" Clay yelled.

Jonas pointed to a trail on the plateau west of the ranch where horses were kicking up a streaming trail of dust. Both men knew without saying that riders were hightailing it out of the area fast.

"I expect Violet was signaling for us." Clay had taught his wife how to shoot his rifle, and he instructed her to fire three shots if she needed him. There had been only one shot, and that troubled him. Without another word, they gave their horses' full rein.

Clay and Jonas had been on the range since dawn rounding up strays, and they planned to head home in another hour for lunch. Before Clay left that morning, Violet told him to invite Jonas to lunch. She was preparing Jonas's favorite meal, and that included making a chocolate cake for dessert. Clay didn't have to twist Jonas's arm to get him to get to work that morning; the promise of chocolate cake was all the motivation he needed.

Jonas had worked for Clay for five years, and proved himself trustworthy and reliable. For the past two years, three younger cowboys also worked on the ranch. They were good men, but didn't possess Jonas's work ethic. For one thing, Jonas was an older man, and he knew everything there was to know about cattle ranching. His experience had helped Clay in a thousand different ways. Jonas wasn't inclined to go into town on a Saturday night and tie one on either, as the younger men were bent on doing.

The larger ranches paid better wages, making it difficult for Clay to employ younger men. He had to offer different perks, which prompted him to build a nicer bunkhouse, and Violet's cooking helped to lure men with healthy appetites. The men told him her fine meals were more appealing than having a few dollars on their monthly pay. They'd eaten in enough bunkhouses to know that the cooks didn't often stray from beans and bread. Violet was a wizard with her culinary skills on a meager budget, and she fed them a varied menu. Clay teased her that he had to work twice as hard since he married her so he wouldn't get fat.

The ranch house came into view and Clay's gaze searched the front yard for Violet and their six-year-old son. Seeing no one about, his heart started pounding, matching the thundering of his horse's hoofs.

He was several yards away when he saw his beautiful wife and son lying on the front porch. Both men jumped off their horses before they came to a complete stop. "Violet . . . Violet!" Clay dropped to his knees beside his wife and he saw blood covering the front of her dress. "Dear God," he muttered as he felt for a pulse at her neck. Nothing. He turned to his son with tears streaming down his cheeks. Like his mother, his young son had a bullet hole in his small chest. Clay's mind couldn't handle what he was seeing. He pulled his son into his arms and lifted his wife's head to rest on his knees. "Violet . . . Mark." His eyes searched their faces. They couldn't be dead—he couldn't believe they were dead. Clutching Mark to his chest, he rocked back and forth, repeating his name over and over. He then pulled his wife into his arms. Holding their limp bodies side by side, his tormented scream expressed an anguish so raw and deep it filled the void between heaven and earth.

Jonas was kneeling beside Clay, so shocked at what he saw, that he could hardly gather his thoughts. Hearing Clay's gut-wrenching wail brought him to his senses. He pulled his bandana out of his pocket, wiped his own tears away, and wrapped his arms around Clay. There were no words of comfort; they wouldn't come. He simply held Clay as he held his precious family.

They sat like that for a long time before Jonas came to grips with what had to be done. He needed to look around to see if he could make sense out of what happened. He wiped his face on his shirtsleeve, and said, "Boss, I'm going to have a look around."

Clay stared at Jonas, but he didn't respond.

Jonas recognized the signs of shock, and he gripped Clay's shoulder. "Boss, I want to see if I can figure out what happened here."

Clay's brain finally registered what Jonas saying. He nodded. "Yes. I need to know who did this. Let's carry them to the stable and we'll both look around." When Clay started to lift Violet in his arms, he saw something on her skirt. He reached down and picked up a playing card: the ace of spades with a hole in the center. Why a playing card was on his wife's skirt, he didn't know. It seemed unimportant at that moment, and he unconsciously stuffed the card in his shirt pocket. Clay carried Violet, and Jonas fell into step beside him with young Mark in his arms. Entering the stable, they placed the bodies in the buckboard. Clay swiped his hands over his face and turned toward the tack room. Jonas knew Clay was thinking about the saddle he purchased for Mark's Christmas present. Since the day Clay purchased that saddle, he'd looked at it every time he walked into the stable. Mark didn't think he was going to get a saddle this Christmas, and Clay could hardly wait for Christmas morning to see the surprise on his son's face.

Before Clay opened the door to the tack room, Jonas said, "Boss, leave it alone."

Clay hesitated at the doorway, braced his forearm on the frame, and dropped his head to the crook of his arm. He stood like that a long time before he turned around, and walked out of the stable with Jonas.

Both men kneeled down to closely examine the hoofprints in the dirt. Out of the mishmash of prints, Clay was able to see six horses had been there, and he committed to memory the small details of the individual prints.

"Three of them rode to the back of the house," Clay said, pointing to three sets of hoofprints leading around the side of the house.

When they reached the porch, Clay picked up the rifle and sniffed the barrel. It had been fired. The killers knew Violet had fired that shot to summon help.

Once inside the house, Clay noticed that his desk had been rifled through. The drawers were tossed on the floor, but Clay knew thieves found nothing worth taking. They weren't rich people, and like most folks during hard times, they'd struggled to keep their ranch going. Making their way to the kitchen at the back of the house, they stopped inside the doorway. Everything looked normal. The table was set, pans were on the stove, and there was a chocolate cake on the counter.

Clay had kept his loaded rifle on a shelf beside the back door when Violet was home alone. She could reach the rifle, but his son couldn't. He walked across the room and removed two boxes of cartridges off the shelf. Exiting through the back door, they saw the three sets of hoofprints. Six men had been at his home that morning, and they'd made certain his wife and son had no means of escape.

The barn, the stable, and the bunkhouse were intact, but the horses in the paddock were missing. He thought it was possible Violet surprised the killers as they were stealing the horses. Clay had put the horses in the paddock that morning, and now his beautiful young white mare was gone. He'd named the horse Moonrise, and he'd quickly developed a special bond with her. Moonrise was still young, but no animal had more heart. Clay had worked Moonrise hard the day before, and that was the only reason he wasn't riding her today.

"They took Moonrise," Clay said to Jonas.

Jonas knew Clay was crazy about that animal. "Boss, I'll follow these tracks for a spell." Jonas walked back to the front of the house and jumped in the saddle. He followed the trail to determine if they were traveling in the same direction where they saw the dust earlier. Sure enough, the dust they'd seen on the plateau was from the men who had killed Clay's family. He followed for some distance to see what direction they were headed before he turned back to the ranch. First things first. He needed to help Clay bury his family before dark. When he returned to the stable, he found Clay constructing a coffin for Violet. Before he picked up his tools to help, he walked to the bunkhouse to make some coffee.

"Boss, drink this." Jonas handed Clay a cup of strong, hot coffee laced with some whiskey. They shared their coffee in silence, and when they finished, they went about finishing the coffins, frequently stopping to wipe their tears away.

Once the coffins were constructed, they walked to the

buckboard to get Violet and Mark. Clay reached down and picked up Violet's cold hand. "Violet made your cake, Jonas."

Jonas stopped and stared down at the lovely woman who was much too young to be taken away. The last thing she did that morning was make him a cake. Such a simple statement, but it tore his heart out. He swiped at his tired gray eyes with his handkerchief. "Boss, I just don't know who would do such a thing." It was unimaginable how any man could kill a young woman and little boy. That was a whole different kind of meanness in Jonas's estimation.

"I'll find them." Clay brought Violet's hand to his lips. "I promise you, honey, I will find them." He noticed Violet's plain gold band was missing. Violet had told him many times, it was the most precious thing she owned. He'd had it inscribed with two simple words: *My love*. Her killer had it now. Clay vowed then and there he would hunt down these killers and exact justice for his wife and son.

Jonas couldn't say another word; he placed Mark's small body inside the coffin. He wished the other ranch hands were back from town in case those evil scoundrels came back. Yet he didn't doubt Clay could take on all six men at once and make it out unscathed. He hadn't seen Clay angry often, but he knew as sure as there was a God in heaven, these men would be in Hades by the hands of Clay Hunt, even if it took a lifetime.

Clay gently placed Violet's body in the coffin. He looked at her face a long time before he could close the lid. When it came time to close Mark's coffin, Clay couldn't do it. Jonas understood his feelings. It had to be the most difficult thing in the world to look upon their faces for the last time. He handled the task of closing Mark's coffin as he said a silent good-bye.

Long after Jonas walked to the bunkhouse, Clay stood over the graves. Jonas told him he'd have something for him to eat when he was ready, but Clay didn't think he'd ever be able to eat again. One of his greatest joys was sitting with his wife and son at the dinner table, eating the wonderful meal she'd prepared, and hearing his son talk nonstop. How could a man lose everything he loved in a matter of minutes? What would he have done differently that morning if he knew he'd never see his family alive again?

His mind drifted back to that morning. Like every morning, he'd told Violet he loved her and gave her a kiss. He'd ruffled Mark's hair, and told him to watch after his mother before he kissed him on top of his head. He could still hear Mark's reply in his innocent child's voice. "I will, Pa." Then he'd walked out the door, like every other normal morning. But this wasn't a normal morning. Why didn't God give him a sign his family was in danger? Why hadn't God protected his family? The *why* question seemed to follow every thought.

Clay joined Jonas in the bunkhouse, and they sat together over the meal, but neither man did little more than push the food around on their plates. Remembering the playing card in his pocket, Clay pulled it out and handed it to Jonas. "This was on Violet's skirt. What do you make of it?"

Jonas took the card and held it in the air and looked through the hole. "Someone shot that hole in there. I don't know why they would leave this behind." He shook his head in disgust. "How do you make sense out of men so mean?"

Clay stuffed it back in his shirt pocket and stood. "I'm going to get provisions together and go after them."

"I'll go with you, Boss."

"I need you to stay here, Jonas. Those young bucks can't run this ranch, and I'm leaving it up to you to keep it going. I don't know when I'll be back." He saw Jonas was about to object, so he placed his hand on his shoulder and gave it a gentle squeeze. "You know I'm right. It may be months before I return. I need you to handle things here for me. First thing I want you to do in the morning is go to town and tell the sheriff what went on out here. Tell him about the playing card, and see if he knows what it means. When I get to a town with a telegraph office, I'll let you know where I am, and I'll wait for your response."

"Boss, if you go as far as Denver, look up my cousin, Harper Ellis. You remember he stopped here last year."

"I remember him. It seems like you told me he rides close to the line," Clay said.

"Everything he does is above the law. He rides across the border to steal back cattle that has been rustled from their rightful owners. It ain't illegal, but maybe some of his methods might be a bit iffy. But Harper can be trusted. He's familiar with outlaws who hide out in Mexico. I'll send him a telegram and tell him about what went on here. If anyone knows the meaning of that card, it will be Harper."

As Clay and Jonas loaded his pack horse, Jonas said, "Boss, I know you'll look for Moonrise, and one thing I can guarantee, not another horse in the country will have your brand."

"That's for certain." Clay had named his horse after the name of his ranch. When Clay first started his ranch he'd slept outdoors for many nights before he'd built his house. His first night on the range, there was a half-moon glistening in the midnight sky, and he decided that night to name his ranch Half-Moon Ranch. When Jonas heard the name Clay had chosen for the ranch, he had the blacksmith forge a half-moon branding iron. Moonrise had his unique brand on his hind quarter.

The last item securely packed on the horse, Clay reached for the reins. He stuck his hand out to Jonas. "Jonas . . ." There was so much he wanted to say, but words eluded him.

Jonas took his hand, and took a deep breath in an effort to keep his emotions in check. "Boss, do you think you will be back for Christmas?"

Clay thought of his son's saddle in the tack room. "No, I don't want to be here at Christmas."

Jonas nodded his understanding. He hated to see Clay ride off alone to face these men. "Be careful, Boss. Your ranch will be here waiting for you to come home."

Clay pulled Jonas into his embrace. "Take care, Jonas. I thank you for everything." He turned away and led his horses to the gravesite. He stood silently over Violet's grave, reminiscing about the first time he'd met her. Emotions welled, and his voice faltered when he spoke. "Violet, I was the luckiest man on earth the day you accepted my proposal at the river. I'll never forget that day, and I honestly don't know what I will do without you. Thank you for loving me and giving me the best son in the world. I don't want to leave you, but I need to find the men who did this." He looked at the small grave beside Violet's. "Son, I love you." There were no more words. He mounted his horse and followed the trail of six killers.

Chapter One

Judge not, and ye shall not be judged; condemn not, and ye shall not be condemned; forgive, and ye shall be forgiven.

Luke 6:37 (KJV)

Denver, Colorado
December 1876

"Miss Langtry! Miss Langtry!"

Emma was signing her name to the hotel register when she heard someone zealously shouting her name. She turned to look over the throng of people who had trailed her inside the hotel in hopes of getting a glimpse at the famous opera singer. The crowd was held at bay by a thick red velvet rope separating the registering guests from the curious onlookers. Being five feet nine inches tall, Emma had no difficulty spotting the bespectacled young man pushing his way toward her. She acknowledged him with a barely perceptible nod of her head.

The young man smiled wide as he approached, and held out an envelope in her direction. Emma's dog, however, was not as welcoming. He moved his oversized muscled body between Emma and the stranger, and growled low, his warning to the young man that he was treading in dangerous territory if he took one more step toward his mistress.

Wearily eyeing the big beast, the young fellow waved the envelope like a banner of truce, all the while wishing he had a soup bone. "Miss Langtry, this came for you a few days ago. We've been holding it until you arrived. From the looks of the seal, we thought it was important."

Emma patted the dog on the head and murmured, "It's okay, Sweetie." The dog immediately stopped growling, sat on his haunches, and leaned into her leg.

"That was very kind of you to hold this for me." She pulled some coins from her reticule and dropped them in his open palm. "Thank you."

The young man passed her the envelope, and then pulled a notepad and pencil from his pocket. He cast a quick glance at the massive canine again and thought it best not to make a sudden move. "Would you sign this, Miss Langtry?"

"Certainly."

"My name is Jim."

Emma thought he was asking her to sign for the letter, but when she glanced down at the blank piece of paper, she realized he was requesting her autograph. Even though people of all ages had been requesting her autograph for over a year, she was still uncomfortable signing her name to a scrap a paper. After all, it wasn't as if she was president, or someone of major import to the world. She sang songs, something she'd done her entire life without expecting accolades or applause. But after her successful European tour, she was suddenly thrust into the limelight, and thanks to the posters plastered in every city, she was easily recognized. She'd entertained kings and queens in several countries with rave reviews, and when she returned home, she was surprised that her triumphant tour had preceded her.

As soon as she'd stepped off the ship, she'd been overwhelmed with requests for interviews from nearly every newspaper in the country. Unfortunately her notoriety also brought a total lack of privacy. In every town, people would be waiting for her stagecoach to arrive, just like today. The stagecoach was four hours late arriving in Denver, and much to the dismay of her fans, she didn't have time to sign autographs for the people who had waited all day. She wouldn't even have time to practice for tonight's performance with Carlo Palladino, the Italian tenor who accompanied her, and Andre Hoffman, their pianist.

"I'm a big fan. I'm coming to see your performance," Jim said, staring in awe at the tall, striking woman with clear blue eyes.

Emma smiled, thankful the young man provided her with something to write on the piece of paper beside her signature. *Jim, I hope you enjoy the performance. Emma Langtry.* "Here you go."

"Emma!" A voice every bit as deep as Carlo's called out to her. She turned to see Morgan LeMasters, her new brother-in-law, walking down the staircase.

Emma waved to him to let him know she saw him over the multitude of people swarming her. Without a glance at the telegram, she shoved it in her reticule.

Morgan had no problem parting the crowd as he walked through. His size, combined with his air of authority, made people automatically give him a wide berth. When he reached Emma, he spared a brief glance at the dog by her side, and said, "The women are in our room getting dressed. They were worried you wouldn't arrive on time."

"I was worried as well." She introduced Carlo and Andre to Morgan before she made plans to meet them at the Grand Crystal Hall in one hour. "I want to spend a few minutes with my family."

"I trust this gentleman will look out for you," Carlo said.

Eyeing the large, barrel-chested man, Morgan was about to give him a piece of his mind if he was questioning his ability to protect his sister-in-law.

Emma saw the look on Morgan's face, and patted his arm. "Don't get your dander up. Carlo is the one who handles any ruffians we may encounter if he thinks Sweetie can't handle them."

Emma's words did little to appease Morgan, and he fixed Carlo with a hard stare. "Have no concern over her welfare."

Carlo inclined his head, indicating his approval of Emma's brother-in-law. "We'll see you at the hall."

Somewhat placated, Morgan turned back to Emma. "Who's Sweetie?"

Emma stroked her dog's head. "He's Sweetie."

Morgan arched his brow at the large dog, and as if on cue, the dog nudged his way between Emma and Morgan.

"Let's go upstairs." Morgan led the way to the staircase where Clay Hunt and Jack Roper were waiting to be introduced. "You remember Sheriff Jack Roper, don't you?" Morgan asked.

Emma smiled at Jack. "Certainly. Granny's last letter said you are also now my brother-in-law."

"Yes, ma'am," Jack said.

"It's good to know there are two men in Whispering Pines smart enough to know good women when they see them," Emma quipped.

Morgan laughed at her outspoken thoughts. He clasped

Clay's shoulder and said, "This is Clay Hunt, our new pastor in Whispering Pines."

Emma's first thought was Granny's description in her letters of the pastor was right on target; he was handsome. She'd also mentioned he wasn't married. "Granny mentioned you in her letters. She has been very impressed with your sermons."

"Knowing your grandmother as I do now, I'm certain she was being generous in her praise." Clay was impressed by Emma's self-assured manner in the midst of the crowd pushing and shoving their way to her. She didn't appear to be the least bit ruffled by the commotion surrounding her. Granny had told him her eldest granddaughter was a lovely woman, but she'd failed to mention how tall she was. With her hair piled high in an elaborate fashion, she was almost as tall as he was, and he was two inches over six feet. She didn't look a thing like her sisters either. The only trait all three sisters shared was their bright blue eyes. He directed his attention to the dog at her side. The creature was the tallest, mangiest-looking dog he'd ever seen. His gray wiry coat was standing on end as if it had no particular pattern. He'd watched the dog when the young man handed the telegram to Emma, thinking the boy would be lucky if the mongrel allowed him to walk away with his arm still attached.

"It sounds as though you know Granny quite well." Granny's last letter said Pastor Hunt could deliver sermons that were both educational and inspirational. In her experience, that was a gift not common to all preachers. Emma was looking forward to hearing his sermons, and she thought it was a bonus that he was easy on the eyes. He was tall and lean, with golden honey eyes that she imagined melted some female hearts around town.

Clay's gaze shifted back to the dog whose head reached Emma's waist. "What's his name?"

"Sweetie." Emma stroked her dog's head again to let him know they were among friends and he had no reason to be on guard.

Clay tried not to laugh. "Sweetie? He didn't look so sweet when that young man approached you."

Emma smiled. "His name is really Rufus, but he only responds to Sweetie. He is quite protective of me."

"Good to know," Clay said, holding his hand out to the dog for him to sniff. This was definitely an animal he'd want as a friend and not as a foe.

Sweetie sniffed for a long time, and once he decided Clay was no threat, he sat down on his foot.

Clay noticed the dog smelled better than he looked. "He smells good."

"He loves to bathe in my toilet water." Emma eyed her dog leaning into Clay's leg. That was his way of letting her know he liked Clay.

"Make way," a burly man called out, carrying a huge trunk on his shoulder, followed by three men carrying similar trunks. "What room number, ma'am?"

Instead of revealing her room number to everyone in the lobby, Emma said, "Please follow us." When they reached the rooms, she turned to Morgan. "Where is your room?"

"Right across from yours. We are all on this floor."

"Perfect. I'll be over in a moment."

Once the men placed her luggage near the wardrobe and left the room, Emma quickly washed her face and brushed her hair. She wanted to say hello to her family before she bathed and dressed for tonight's performance.

She hurried from her room with Sweetie on her heels, and knocked on the door across the hall. Granny opened the door and burst into tears as soon as she saw her granddaughter.

Emma wrapped the tiny woman in her arms. "Don't cry, Granny. I will start blubbering like a foolish woman."

Granny pulled away a few inches and looked her up and down. "You look just beautiful."

Rose and Addie hurried to the pair of crying women, and wrapped their arms around them.

"Let's close the door before we let all of the heat out of the room," Rose said, ushering them inside to sit in front of the fireplace. Noticing the dog staying close to Emma's heels, she said, "Who is this?"

Emma introduced Sweetie as Rose poured some water in a bowl for the dog. When Rose placed the bowl on the floor, Sweetie nudged her hand in appreciation before he started lapping at the water.

As he drank, Granny stroked his bristly coat. "He looks like a great protector."

"The best." Emma knew there was no need worry about Sweetie being aggressive with Granny and her sisters; he had a sixth sense about the people she cared about. Not only that, but he was a big softie when it came to women.

"Did he go to Europe with you?" Granny asked.

"Actually, I brought him home from Europe. I guess you could say he adopted me."

To make Emma's point, Sweetie finished drinking his water and positioned his large body as close to Emma as he could get without crawling into her lap.

Rose handed Emma a cup of tea. "What do you mean he adopted you?"

"I saw him wandering alone on the streets in Paris, filthy and starving. I took him to my hotel, bathed him, fed him a big juicy steak, and we became best friends. When it was time to come home, he came with me. I swear he grew a foot on the voyage home." Emma hadn't realized how large he was going to be, but it wouldn't have made a difference. Sweetie had stolen her heart from the start, and he was hers after that first night. He'd turned out to be the best companion she could imagine.

"Well, he certainly smells luscious," Addie said.

"I bathed him in toilet water that first night at the hotel, and now he demands it. If I don't pour some in the water, he gets cranky, and no one wants to see Sweetie cranky," Emma said.

Envisioning that big dog in a tub of perfumed water made the women laugh.

"I'm so happy you are here. We've missed you so much. We were so worried when the stagecoach was late," Granny said.

"It was nothing serious, just a delay at a way station." Emma glanced at her sisters. "You both look wonderful."

"We are well," Addie said.

Granny pulled her handkerchief from her sleeve and wiped her eyes. "I can't tell you how it does my heart good to see all of my girls at home."

"I wish you never had to leave, Emma," Rose said.

Emma laughed. "I just got here, so let's not talk about me leaving. I only have a few minutes before I need to get dressed, so quickly tell me all of your news. When is your baby due, Rose?"

"I have a few months yet. I hope you are home then."

"I have a performance in San Francisco after the first of the year, but I'm here now for the whole month," Emma said. "I will ask Andre if we have time to come home after our San Francisco performance before we go back East."

"I do hope so. It will be a joy to have you home as long as possible," Granny said.

Emma reached out and squeezed Granny's hand. "Yes, it would be wonderful." Emma had missed being home over the years, but it wasn't until she saw Granny that she'd realized she missed her family much more than she wanted to admit. Before she became maudlin, she turned to Addie.

"Where are your children? I can't wait to meet them. I think it's wonderful that you and Jack adopted them."

"The children are excited to meet you. They are at the ranch with Joseph Longbow and Morgan's foreman, Hank Murphy. You remember them, don't you?"

"Of course, I do. Joseph was always patient and kind to us as children. And if my memory serves me correctly, we all thought Hank Murphy was almost as handsome as Rose's husband."

"He still is," Rose said. "I'm amazed he's still single."

"He has some competition with our new pastor, Clay Hunt," Addie said. "Wait until you see him, Emma."

"I met him downstairs." Emma didn't mention that for the first time in her life she actually felt shy in the presence of the tall dark-haired pastor. "Why did the men leave?"

"They said they'd give us some time together. They probably went to see Marshal Holt and Sheriff Trent. They are coming to the performance too."

"You didn't say if you found the pastor attractive." Addie's gaze slid to Granny to see if she was listening.

Emma noticed everyone grinning. "What's going on?"

"We were just curious if you think Clay is handsome," Rose replied.

Emma's gaze swept over each woman. "You three are up to something. What are you not saying?"

"Granny thought you and Clay would make a good match," Addie admitted.

Emma's mouth dropped open. "Granny, surely you didn't say that to him." Knowing Granny as she did, she wouldn't put it past her to tell the pastor exactly what she thought.

Granny took a sip of tea. "I may have mentioned it to him."

Addie and Rose started laughing.

Emma rolled her eyes at Granny. "No wonder he kept staring at me as though I had two heads."

"Nonsense. He was staring at you because you are a beautiful woman," Granny replied.

"I haven't changed in five years, Granny. I don't have Rose's beauty, nor Addie's curves. Most men find me too tall, too skinny, and too direct."

"Only insecure men would be intimidated by you. That's why I think Clay and you would get along well."

"Are you saying he's that kind of man?" Emma asked.

"Well, some of the congregation at church voiced their concerns about him . . ." Granny was interrupted by a knock on the door.

The door cracked open, and Morgan said, "Are you ladies decent?"

"Of course. Come in," Rose replied.

Morgan, Clay, and Jack entered the room with U.S. Marshal Holt and Sheriff Trent behind them.

After Morgan introduced Emma to the two men, he said, "Marshal Holt stayed at the farm while he was recuperating."

"It's nice to meet you both." She looked at the marshal, and said, "Addie told me all about your ordeal in her last letter. I'm happy to see that you recovered nicely."

"Your grandmother is an excellent doctor," Marshal Holt said.

"Marshal Holt stayed in Denver just to hear your performance tonight," Granny said.

Emma smiled at him. "That's very kind of you. I do hope you will not be disappointed." Emma noticed Sweetie got up and walked to Clay, and the pastor rubbed his ears in the specific way Sweetie preferred.

"I saw one of your performances back East. It was a real pleasure," Marshal Holt said.

"The whole town has been looking forward to this night," Sheriff Trent said. "Since your posters went up, you've been the talk of the town. I'm amazed Morgan was able to get rooms in the hotel."

"I sent a telegram to the hotel as soon as we found out the date Emma would arrive," Morgan said.

"But how did you get the rooms directly across from mine?" Emma asked.

"When we arrived, the clerk said he couldn't give us the room across from yours, so I threatened to shoot him," Morgan quipped.

Rose's eyes widened in surprise. "You didn't!"

Morgan winked at her. "No, I didn't need to. Jack threatened to put him in jail."

Addie gaped at her husband. "Did you?"

Jack grinned. He didn't bother to deny the truth.

Granny laughed at the two men she considered her sons. "You two are a pair of knaves."

Clay stood back, watching the men tease their wives. It warmed his heart to see the love they had for the women. It reminded him of a time in his life when he'd been that happy. He glanced at Emma, and at the very same time, her eyes met his, but she quickly looked away.

"You ladies look beautiful," Morgan said.

Jack walked to his wife and stared at the gown she was wearing. "Morgan's right. I've never seen four prettier ladies in my life." He sounded pleased, but his expression said something else. It seemed to him that his wife's dress showed too much of her voluptuous figure.

"You're gawking, honey," Addie whispered.

"I expect every man in Denver will be gawking," Jack muttered. He had yet to learn the fine art of patience when he saw men drooling over his shapely wife. She was always tastefully dressed, but the problem was, there was simply no

way to hide her curves. Unless he placed a feed bag over
her, men were bound to gawk. He glanced at her buxom
figure one more time, and thought the feed bag idea may
have some merit.

"Granny, you look so pretty, I expect Jack and I will be
fighting off suitors tonight," Morgan said.

Granny slapped his arm. "You are a silver-tongued
devil, but I love you more for it. I'd say you're spending too
much time with Jack. I thought he had cornered the market
on nonsense, but I may be wrong about that."

"You know you love me as much as Morgan," Jack
teased.

"You're both full of nonsense." Granny hoped Emma
would find a man as fine as her two sons-in-law. To her
way of thinking, Clay fit the bill. Now all she needed was
cooperation from both parties. Nothing would make her
happier than to have all of her granddaughters living in
Whispering Pines, and giving her many great-grandbabies.

"What time should we leave? There's quite a line forming
all the way down the street," Morgan said.

Emma looked at the clock on the mantel. "Oh, my heavens, I must get ready. Wait for me so you won't have to
stand in that line. I have reserved a box for you." She
glanced at the marshal and the sheriff, and added, "There
are enough seats for everyone."

Chapter Two

The men were following the women on the sidewalk as they walked to the Grand Crystal Hall. Just as Jack expected, the women captured the eye of every man walking by, and he glared at each and every one.

Morgan noticed too. "I'd say the Langtry sisters garner a lot of attention."

"I think we can teach them some manners," Jack grumbled.

"No harm in looking at pretty ladies, as long as all they do is look," Clay told them calmly.

"Says the man who is not married to one of them," Morgan said.

"Yeah," Jack agreed. "You'll feel differently when it's your wife men are gawking at."

"I don't think they mean any harm," Clay said. There was a time he knew exactly how Morgan and Jack felt. His wife was a beauty, and it had rubbed him the wrong way when men would ogle her. Now he'd give the world to have her back so men could look at her.

Jack and Morgan exchanged a look that said, *Wait until it happens to him again*.

"Have you seen the Grand Crystal Hall yet?" Emma asked her grandmother.

"No, we haven't, but Jack told me all about it," Granny said.

Morgan elbowed Jack in the ribs and muttered, "Uh-oh."

The words barely left Morgan's mouth when Addie turned around to look at her husband. "You didn't tell me you have been there."

"I haven't, but the marshal and sheriff told me all about it," Jack said.

"Have you been there, Morgan?" Rose asked.

"No, ma'am. But I hear it lives up to the name."

Sheriff Trent grinned at the men, but he didn't dispute their account. "It is a beautiful place."

They reached the hall, and Granny remarked that it took up more space than any six buildings combined in Whispering Pines. Once inside, the women turned in complete circles to admire the lavish décor of the enormous room. Huge crystal chandeliers throughout the room were glittering like diamonds, and provided a soft golden romantic glow over the opulent interior. One would never know the time of day for the deep red velvet drapes covering the windows, blocking all of the light from the outside. Expensive Persian rugs covered the hardwood floor, and large upholstered settees and chairs were artfully arranged along the walls for more intimate conversations. A massive staircase in the center of the room led to the balcony seats. A long, highly polished mahogany bar spanned the back of the room. Adorning the back wall was an enormous mirror which allowed the patrons lined up at the bar full view of the room. In front of the bar, there were several gaming tables, already filled with players hoping to beat the house. On one side of the room a floor-to-ceiling velvet curtain concealed the stage. People were already seated in the chairs facing the stage, and applause erupted when they spotted Emma in the room. She bowed politely, and turned back to her family.

"This is a beautiful place," Granny said.

Emma pointed to the balcony and said, "I reserved seats up there for you. You should have a good view of the entire stage."

"Emma, we plan on eating dinner at the hotel after the performance. Invite the gentlemen we met earlier," Morgan said.

Emma was grateful to Morgan for including her friends. "I'm sure they would be delighted to join us. Carlo loves a party."

Granny kissed Emma on the cheek. "Good luck, honey."

Emma glanced at Clay and asked, "Would you mind taking Sweetie with you? He seems to like you."

"Of course. I told him I rather he be my friend than my enemy." Clay watched Emma talk to the dog and explain he should go with him. He had a feeling the dog understood Emma's instructions. As she walked away, Sweetie stayed with Clay without hesitation.

Within minutes after they took their seats, Granny leaned forward to view the crowd below. "There's not an empty seat to be found." As they waited, the women waved to people they knew from Whispering Pines. Granny pointed out to Clay all of the church members in the crowd to put his mind at ease. Some of their parishioners were not keen on their pastor attending the event since it was being held at the Grand Crystal Hall, where there was gambling and drinking.

The curtain on the stage parted, the conversations ended, and a rousing thunderous applause filled the room.

* * *

Granny was still gushing over the performance when they sat down to dinner at the hotel. "Carlo, you have a beautiful voice, and Andre, you are a very skillful pianist."

The two men were instantly charmed by Granny. "Thank you. Your granddaughter makes our job much easier. She sings like an angel," Carlo said.

"That is exactly what we told her when we were young," Rose said. "I daresay it is much more entertaining to sing for so many people. I'm afraid Addie and I didn't appreciate Emma's talent as much as we should have."

"She told us you would listen for hours," Andre said.

"How did you meet Emma? From your performance, one would think you've been together forever," Granny said.

"Andre had accompanied me before he came to America. Once he found Emma in America, he said he knew we belonged together," Carlo said.

"The three of you are perfect together; it must have been destined," Granny said.

"Thank you," Andre said. "It is my honor to accompany your granddaughter and Carlo."

Clay wondered if Emma was in love with Carlo or Andre. Both men were quite striking in appearance, and obviously men of accomplishment. He could understand how close they would become traveling the world together. "Do all of your performances draw such a crowd?"

"Since our tour of Europe, the crowds have been overwhelming," Emma said.

"Emma, have you told them what a hit you were in Europe?" Carlo asked.

Everyone turned their eyes on Emma. Emma gave Carlo a pointed look. "I told them our tour was very successful."

Carlo arched his brows at Granny. "Did your granddaughter tell you that we performed before kings and queens?"

"Why, Emma! You didn't tell us that," Granny exclaimed.

"Carlo, why don't you tell them about the wonderful cities we have seen," Emma suggested, hoping to avoid the conversation she knew Carlo would broach.

Carlo didn't need further coaxing. He mesmerized them with his deep voice and animated gestures, relating tales of the many castles they'd seen, and the palaces where they had performed. But he managed to find a way to mention the prince who had become smitten with Emma in France. "The prince wooed her to no avail. He was heartbroken when she left France." He gave Emma a mischievous grin. "But alas, I'm afraid Andre had already arranged performances in America, and Prince Charming was left alone at the dock."

Addie asked the question on everyone's mind. "Is he your Prince Charming?"

"Carlo is exaggerating as usual. Not only is he a brilliant tenor, he is an accomplished actor. And if he doesn't watch it"—she kicked him under the table—"Sweetie will eat his steak."

"Ouch." Carlo groaned and leaned over to rub his shin under the table.

Emma gave him a look that clearly stated she was going to strangle him when they were alone.

"Is he truly a real prince? Did he speak English, or do you speak French, Carlo?" Granny asked.

"He is indeed a very royal French prince. He told me he was tutored in English as a young boy," Carlo said, smiling from ear to ear. He leaned to Granny's ear, and said in a lower tone, "When we were departing, the prince told me in the strictest confidence that he intended to come to America to pursue your granddaughter."

Emma wished the floor would open up and swallow Carlo whole. Naturally, with his perfect theatrical voice, everyone at the table heard what he supposedly whispered to Granny.

"If the prince comes to America, I'm sure it will be to hear us perform, and not to court me," Emma said.

"Us?" Carlo said. "Prince Henri d'Evereux only has eyes for you, dear Emma. I doubt he even knows I am a tenor, much less sharing the stage with you. I would not be surprised if we see him in San Francisco the first of the year."

Even though Andre found Carlo's antics amusing, he took pity on Emma, and he changed the conversation. "Although I haven't had time to discuss this with Carlo and Emma, we have been offered an opportunity to have two more performances in Denver. After our performance tonight the owner of the Grand Crystal asked if we would be staying in Denver for a while. He said we could select our own dates." Andre's gaze shifted from Emma to Carlo. "What do you think? He made us a very generous offer."

"If my family doesn't mind. I promised them I'd spend the entire month in Whispering Pines. Carlo may have other plans too," Emma replied.

"We would love to come to see you again," Rose said. "What do you think, husband?"

"If the weather holds, which is always something we have to consider in December," Morgan said.

"Carlo?" Andre asked.

"I had planned to go on to San Francisco, but for no

particular reason. Since the offer is a generous one, and this is a lovely venue, I say we schedule the dates."

"Are all of the places you sing as nice as the Grand Crystal Hall?" Clay asked.

Emma turned her attention on the handsome pastor. While she found him very physically appealing, there was something about him that seemed quite sad. She didn't know if he was shy, or just the type of man who didn't have much to say. "No, we have performed in older, smaller saloons. But the people enjoy the performances as much, if not more, as the patrons of the Grand Crystal tonight. They're always appreciative to hear something they've never heard before."

"We feel it is our duty to bring our music to everyone, no matter their position in life," Andre said.

"Noblesse oblige," Clay said, thinking the Frenchman spoke as a man of privilege.

"Not at all. We are not from advantaged backgrounds. We don't hold the opinion that our performances should only be enjoyed by nobility. It makes us happy to share the music with those who may never have another chance to hear opera." Andre smiled, and added, "Of course, we charge nobility substantially more."

Granny noticed Clay had been very quiet tonight, and she suspected he was concerned over the parishioners in the church who objected that he attended tonight's performance. "I think it's wonderful that you bring joy to the ordinary people, just as you do for kings and queens. I noticed several people from Whispering Pines were in attendance tonight."

Morgan understood Granny's comment was made to put Clay at ease. "Jack and I told Clay he didn't need to worry about the congregation. There were just as many people from the church in attendance as there were those who stayed home."

"Why should anyone object to you attending our performance?" Carlo asked.

"A lot of folks view the Grand Crystal as a saloon," Clay responded.

"I do not understand. Do they think when you walk into a saloon, you can't resist gambling and drinking?" Carlo asked.

Clay contemplated Carlo's question. It was a good question to put to his parishioners. "Perhaps they think it is difficult to resist temptation."

"You shouldn't have come if it was going to create problems for you." Emma didn't understand people being so narrow-minded. His hesitation to attend was understandable since he was new to Whispering Pines and he would naturally worry about offending members of the church.

"I can handle any objections, and I enjoyed the performance." Clay wasn't being diplomatic; he felt blessed to hear Emma sing. Her voice evoked emotions in him he thought he'd buried long ago. "I am curious if some of the places get a bit rowdy where you perform."

"Yes, there have been a few times the local sheriff found it necessary to escort men off the premises. We don't mind singing wherever we are invited as long as the audience can enjoy the performance. It's thrilling to see their faces, and to know for one night we've taken their minds off their troubles."

"I'm certain that joy lasts for more than one night. It's an experience they will recall the rest of their lives," Rose said.

Clay agreed with Rose. Emma's performance was one he would never forget. He understood what Carlo meant when he said that the prince didn't even know he shared the stage with her. She definitely had a gift, and she commanded all of the attention. His eyes had only been on her.

Once dinner ended, Carlo and Andre excused themselves, but everyone else stayed in the restaurant to talk.

Morgan nudged Jack, and nodded toward the entrance of the restaurant. "There's Judge Stevens."

"Who is Judge Stevens?" Emma asked.

"Your brother Frank married his daughter," Jack replied.

"Is that the judge who dropped all of the charges against him?" Emma asked.

"That's the one," Morgan said.

Emma recalled Granny's last letter to her. "Granny, didn't you say Frank's wife was killed during a bank robbery?"

"Yes, she was. They were only married for a few weeks."

"Does anyone know where Frank is now?" Emma asked.

Everyone looked at Sheriff Trent. "Last we heard, he was still looking for the judge's girlfriend, Leigh King."

"Why is Frank looking for his girlfriend?" Emma asked.

"That's a long story," Morgan said. "Let's talk about this tomorrow. It's late, and we have to leave early in the morning. We'd best retire for the night."

Morgan started to stand, but Jack put his hand on his arm to keep him in his seat. Morgan gave Jack a quizzical look.

"Frank just walked through the door, and he's headed for the judge's table," Jack said.

The table went silent, and everyone turned to see Frank Langtry stroll through the restaurant as though he were the conquering hero returning home. When he reached the judge's table, the judge stood and embraced him.

Rose gripped her husband's hand. She still feared Frank would make another attempt to kill Morgan.

Morgan put his arm around her shoulders. "It's okay, honey, nothing is going to happen."

"What I wouldn't give to hear that conversation between Frank and the judge," Sheriff Trent said.

"I wonder if he found the judge's girlfriend," Emma said, staring across the room at her eldest brother. She still had a difficult time believing he was an outlaw. After what Rose and Granny told her about the crimes he had committed, she couldn't understand why he wasn't in prison.

"I think it's time we call it a night," Morgan said.

Jack leaned to Morgan's ear and whispered, "You think we can get out of here without Frank seeing us?"

Morgan shrugged. "If Frank says anything, he'd best keep it civil."

They made their way to the lobby and were almost to the staircase when they heard a voice behind them. "Well, well, if it isn't Morgan LeMasters with my family," Frank remarked.

Morgan turned around to face him. Jack, Clay, Sheriff Trent, and Marshal Holt moved to stand beside him.

Frank looked at the one face he didn't immediately recognize. Clay Hunt. "I think I've seen you somewhere before."

"I almost witnessed your hanging that morning in Kansas a few months back. Fortunately for you, Rose happened along on that stagecoach."

Frank grinned. "Oh, yeah, you're that man who didn't carry a gun. Things might have turned out different that day if you did."

"A gun is not the answer, Frank," Clay said.

"No? I was mighty glad that other fellow traveling on that stagecoach had that derringer." Frank smirked at

Morgan. He knew it had to gall Morgan that he'd been able to get the drop on him with that passenger's derringer.

"You will be held to account for your actions that day. You left your own sister while she was unconscious and in bad shape," Clay said.

Frank threw his head back and laughed. "In case you haven't heard, the judge has dropped all charges against me."

"I'm not talking about the law holding you accountable. You'll receive another kind of judgment when your days on Earth are done," Clay countered.

Frank stared hard at Clay. "I get it, you're a Bible thumper. I was raised by a bunch of Bible thumpers, and I've had my fill of your ways." His eyes slid to Granny. "Preacher was always spouting words from the Bible, and I ask you, where did that get him?" His gaze darted past Morgan. "Do I see my famous sister behind you?" He made a move to step around Morgan, but Morgan blocked his path. "I guess you've turned her against me too, haven't you, LeMasters?"

"I don't have to turn anyone against you, Frank. You've done that all by yourself."

Emma stepped forward until she was nose to nose with Frank. "What do you want, Frank?"

"I just wanted to say hello to my famous sister."

"You've said it, now we'll say good night." Emma started to turn around, but Frank wrapped his hand around her arm, holding her firmly her in place.

Almost as fast, Clay grabbed Frank's arm. "Let her go."

"Back off, Bible thumper. I just want to talk to my sister for a minute."

Clay didn't release his arm, and Sweetie darted to Emma's side and started growling at Frank.

Emma wasn't intimidated by Frank; she stared him in

the eye. "I have nothing to say to you, Frank. After what you've done to our family, I'm surprised you'd show your face around us."

"Don't believe everything you hear about me." He glanced from Emma to Morgan. "Someone has been telling you lies about me."

"My family wouldn't lie to me about you," Emma countered.

Frank laughed. "You don't see me in jail, do you?"

"You should be in jail," Emma replied. "And if you don't release my arm, Sweetie will gladly remove yours at my command."

Frank glanced down at the snarling dog, and seeing his teeth were bared, he released Emma's arm.

Only then did Clay release his hold on Frank's arm.

"Maybe I'll hear you sing another time." Frank turned around and walked back into the restaurant.

"It's hard for me to believe that after all he's done, he is still walking around a free man," Clay said.

"There's not a thing we can do about it. The judge dismissed every charge against him," Sheriff Trent said.

"Our only hope is to be able to find his gang and see if they will implicate him on the bank robbery. We've sent wanted posters to every sheriff from Montana to Mexico." Marshal Holt reached inside his pocket and pulled out three posters and handed them to Jack. "Here you go. I'm sure you recognize these men."

Jack unfolded the posters and looked at them before he handed them to Morgan. "Yep, we know them."

"These are the same men we were going to hang along with Frank after trailing them from my ranch," Morgan said.

"The bank president and the clerks can identify them. The marshal came up with the idea to send these posters out hoping when Frank's gang sees them they'll figure out they are going to be charged with all of the crimes. They weren't granted a pardon along with Frank. We all know Frank may not have been in the bank during that robbery, but he was involved," Sheriff Trent said.

"Divide and conquer," Clay said.

Marshal Holt smiled. "Yeah. Maybe if we work a deal with them, they'll sing like birds, and give us some new ammunition to charge Frank with something."

"But Frank is as thick as thieves with Judge Stevens. He's not hanging around here for no reason, and I can't see the judge changing his mind," Morgan said.

"I worry more about how close he is to the judge's sister, Ruth. She's the richest woman in Denver, and I hear Frank is going to work for her," Sheriff Trent said.

"Work for her?" Emma asked.

"She owns the gold mine in Black Hawk," Sheriff Trent answered.

"That's less than a day's ride from Whispering Pines," Rose said.

Morgan heard the fear in his wife's voice. "Honey, don't worry about Frank. I think he's forgotten about killing me." Morgan didn't believe a word he'd just said to his wife, but he didn't want her worrying.

Emma saw the look between Jack and Granny. No one was buying what Morgan was saying, but she kept that thought to herself. Considering Rose's condition, Emma thought Morgan was just looking out for her welfare.

"I got a lead on Taggart and Culpepper, so Sheriff Trent and I are taking off in the morning," Marshal Holt said.

"Where are they?" Jack asked.

"I got a telegram saying they were spotted near Purgatory Canyon." Marshal Holt pulled a playing card from his pocket and held it in the air for the men to see. It was an ace of spades with a bullet hole in the center. "This was found on a rancher lying dead on his front porch near Purgatory Canyon. This is the calling card of those two killers. We've found these on dead bodies from Kansas to Colorado."

Clay reached for the card and examined it closely. He'd carried a card just like it in his pocket for several years. "These are the men you've been chasing?" He remembered Morgan and Jack had told him the marshal was chasing two outlaws when he arrived in Denver, but he hadn't realized it was Culpepper and Taggart. Those two names were carved on his very soul.

"Yeah, Joe Culpepper and Win Taggart. Did you ever run into them?" Marshal Holt asked.

Just hearing the names Culpepper and Taggart brought back such painful memories that Clay could barely hide his emotions. "I know of them."

Morgan noticed the hard edge in Clay's voice, and he glanced at Jack. Jack's expression said he'd noticed the same thing. They were aware that Clay had trailed these two killers before he became a pastor.

"They've done a lot of killing." Clay didn't mention he'd chased Culpepper and Taggart for a long time, but lost their trail in Deadwood. It was Culpepper and Taggart, two men of the murderous group who had been on his ranch that fateful day. They were the remaining two who had evaded him. He'd caught up with Jonas's cousin, Harper Ellis, and he told him the names of the killers that left their custom-made calling card each time they murdered someone. "Be careful, Marshal. Their reputation precedes them."

"So does yours, Pastor Hunt," Marshal Holt said.

Everyone grew quiet. Morgan and Jack exchanged another fleeting look. They'd known about Clay's past, but they hadn't discussed his affairs with anyone.

The marshal and Sheriff Trent were friends of Morgan and Jack, but Clay didn't think they'd discussed his business with them. Clay looked the marshal in the eye. If the marshal thought he was going to spill his guts about his past, he was in for a long wait. He'd sought his forgiveness, and it wasn't from Marshal Holt.

Marshal Holt clapped Clay on the back and said, "I hear about your sermons from all over the territory. Next time I'm in Whispering Pines I plan to visit your church. I was laid up with a bullet hole last time I was there."

"I'd like to see you in church. There's no better place to find peace, or at least, as much peace as one can find in this world." Clay wondered if he'd ever find peace over losing his wife and child in such a senseless, brutal murder. Sometimes he thought he'd finally found it, but then there were times, like tonight, when he heard the names Culpepper and Taggart, that the past caught up with him all over again.

Granny thought they needed to end the evening on a lighter note. Something had dampened Clay's spirits, and she wanted the night to be a happy one for all. "He's the only pastor that I've heard who can hold a candle to my dear husband. We are truly blessed to have him."

Clay smiled at Granny. "I'm the one who was blessed to find such a welcoming community." He'd been thankful to find a home like Whispering Pines, but now he questioned if he was the right man for the job. As soon as he heard the names Culpepper and Taggart, the memories he'd tried to bury surfaced without warning.

"We'll see you when you return. Be careful. There all sorts of varmints hiding out in Purgatory Canyon," Morgan said.

The marshal shook Clay's hand. "I'll see you when I come through Whispering Pines."

"I must admit I'm tempted to go with you to Purgatory Canyon, but I have a different calling now," Clay replied. Though it had been a long time since he'd ridden away from the graves of his wife and son, at that moment, it felt like it was only yesterday. He'd repented of his sins, and turned his life around, but he couldn't deny he had an urge to strap on his guns and hunt those men down. God help him. It seemed to be a constant struggle to be a better man when the past kept rearing its ugly head. He didn't know if it was a test of his faith, or if it was his lot in life not to be able to put the past behind him.

"If what I've heard is true, I can understand." Marshal Holt was aware Clay Hunt had a reputation, but no one had ever seen him commit murder. Bystanders always said he killed in self-defense, and that wasn't a crime. Knowing that Morgan LeMasters and Sheriff Roper were in Clay Hunt's corner went a long way with him. As far as he was concerned, Morgan and Jack were two of the finest men he'd ever met, and if they thought Clay was a good man, he wouldn't question their word. The entire family had done nothing but sing the pastor's praises when he was recovering at Morgan's ranch.

Chapter Three

"You have no idea where Leigh went?" Judge Stevens asked Frank.

"No, sir, I lost her trail in St. Louis. If she took a train east, she didn't travel under her given name." Frank was such an accomplished liar that he was confident the judge would never figure out that his girlfriend, Leigh King, was actually living with him in Black Hawk. The judge had no idea his own sister, Ruth, was an accomplice in Frank's scheme. Ruth had convinced Frank into managing her gold mine in Black Hawk, and she'd wanted to get Leigh far away from the judge, so together they hatched the plan. Even Frank had to admit that Ruth was even more ruthless than any outlaw he'd ever seen when she was determined to have her way, and he admired her for that. The way he saw it, they made the perfect team. Frank had no reason to complain about life at the moment; he was making a killing pocketing gold nuggets in addition to the sizable salary Ruth was paying him. He prided himself on creating his own fortune. After all, if he hadn't had the foresight to marry the judge's daughter, his future would not have been as promising. He wasn't going to mess up a good thing, and he was determined to stay on Ruth's good side.

Ruth was the wealthiest person in Denver, perhaps in all of Colorado, and she had no children to inherit her money. Now that her only niece was dead, Frank felt certain Ruth would make him a wealthy man one day. It didn't matter to him that she'd had only taken him under her wing because of her niece. Once Charlotte was killed, Ruth had turned to him. Like Charlotte, Ruth believed all of his lies, and she'd used her influence with the judge to have all charges against him dropped. When Ruth guessed the true nature of his relationship with Leigh, she hadn't turned against him. She merely said her own dear husband hadn't been faithful, but as long as he was discreet, she had tolerated his transgressions. Ruth was a pragmatic woman, and she was willing to overlook a man's peccadilloes, as she called them, as long as she had everything she wanted. Indeed, Ruth had everything she wanted, and Frank wanted some of what she had. She'd even given Frank ten thousand dollars in gold to pay Leigh off when the time came for him to send her on her way. Naturally Ruth had one stipulation: Leigh had to agree to stay away from the judge forever. There was no way Ruth would allow her brother to embarrass the family name by marrying a much younger woman of no social standing.

"I don't know where we go from here," the judge said.

"I think this is a dead end, Judge." Frank wanted to encourage the judge to go back to Colorado City and forget about searching for Leigh. "Maybe it's time to forget about this."

The judge dropped his head in his hands. "I just can't. I can't forget her. I survived that heart attack just thinking about Leigh and how wonderful our reunion would be. She never forgave me for not telling my daughter about our relationship. I know that's the reason she left." He looked up at Frank. "My sister said you had no indication that

Leigh was unhappy, or that she wanted to leave town. Is that right?"

"No, sir, I had no reason to believe she was going to leave. I went to visit her that day in the hotel and she was gone. She didn't leave anything behind. At first, I figured she missed you and decided to catch a stage to Colorado City." Frank almost laughed aloud at his own lie. Truth was, Leigh was afraid the judge would return before they left Denver.

"I'm going to St. Louis and see what I can find out. I've already contracted a Pinkerton detective, and thanks to you, we will know where to start. I'll have him meet me in St. Louis."

Frank didn't like the sound of a Pinkerton detective on the chase for Leigh, but at least the detective would start looking many miles from where she was living. It didn't seem likely that anyone would find her in Black Hawk. When he and Leigh first arrived in Black Hawk, he'd insisted she not reveal her real name to anyone. Everyone at the mine thought her name was Ellen, and since the judge had never been to Black Hawk, Frank felt they were reasonably safe. "Judge, I hate to say this, but it's possible she met up with another man. Have you considered that might be the case?"

The judge shook his head. "I refuse to believe that. We were happy together. I do admit that Ruth has said the same thing to me. But as you know, Ruth disapproved of my relationship with Leigh from the start. She would say anything to turn me against Leigh. All that matters to Ruth is keeping up appearances for the family name. The blasted woman has never been in love. She loved her husband's money, not the man." He shook his head. "If she loved someone as I love Leigh, perhaps she would understand."

"If Leigh did meet up with someone, perhaps she is

using his name." Frank didn't want to overplay his hand. When the judge didn't respond to his speculation about another man, he added, "I'm real sorry I didn't have better luck, Judge."

"Frank, you've done more than any other man would have done. I appreciate that you were on her trail so quickly once you found out she'd left. I think the information you provided will help the Pinkerton man find her. No one has done more for me, and I won't ever forget your loyalty."

"I didn't tell you before, but I did try to soften Ruth's opinion of Leigh. I told her Leigh was a nice woman, and that you deserved some happiness in life," Frank said.

"Ruth is too set in her opinions. She doesn't understand it is quite common for older men to court much younger women." The judge didn't care one way or the other if Ruth accepted Leigh or not, it just made his life easier if he didn't have to hear her harp about it incessantly.

"Maybe we should find Ruth a younger man," Frank said. Truth was, Frank was only half joking. He'd often thought Ruth was a very attractive older woman. She was educated and worldly. Frank enjoyed teasing her, even flirting with her. He imagined many a younger man might show an interest if they knew the possibilities of unimaginable wealth.

"That'll be the day." The judge laughed, and dismissed the thought entirely. "Ruth tells me you've agreed to work at the mine?"

"Yes, sir. I'll be heading there in a few days."

"Good. I hope you don't mind if I contact you there if I need you."

"Not at all. I'll do anything I can to help. Just send me a telegram at the mine."

"I guess you'll be staying with Ruth tonight. But in the

future, you can stay with me at the ranch now that the house is complete." After his daughter married Frank, the judge had planned on marrying Leigh and living on his new ranch. He'd planned on retiring in a year, and he'd looked forward to taking Leigh on a European tour.

"I'd love to see your place. Since you are leaving for St. Louis soon, I'll stay with you the next time I come to Denver." Frank planned to stay in Denver as long as Ruth wanted him to stay. Now that the judge was leaving town, he hoped his stay was a long one. The more time he could spend with Ruth, the better.

"I'll send a telegram in the morning to see if the Pinkerton detective has arrived in St. Louis, and make my plans accordingly."

Ruth was sipping on brandy in her library waiting for Frank. She invited him to pour himself a drink and join her in front of the fire. Once Frank took a seat, he related his conversation with the judge.

"You're certain he has no idea that woman is staying with you in Black Hawk?" Ruth asked.

"I told him I lost Leigh's trail in St. Louis, and he said he was leaving to meet the Pinkerton detective there."

Ruth pursed her lips in disapproval. "He told me he was going to hire that Pinkerton man. I told him if the girl wanted to come back, she would of her own accord."

"It doesn't look like he's going to give up searching for her anytime soon. If that detective doesn't find anything in St. Louis, I'm not certain that will put an end to his search. He seems determined," Frank said.

"You'd think after his heart attack he'd stop all of this foolishness. It seems his infatuation has only increased. That woman is all he talks about. Honestly, I'll be happy if he does go to St. Louis for a while. I'm sick and tired of hearing him lament over her. I told him she probably found a younger man and is long gone by now."

"I suggested the same thing, but he refuses to believe that is possible."

Ruth couldn't help but smile at the irony of the situation. "In a way, that is exactly what happened. She certainly developed a fondness for you rather quickly and left him without a thought."

Frank chuckled, and held his brandy glass in the air. "I am a younger man."

Ruth nodded. "You're not in danger of losing your heart, are you, Frank? I don't intend to besmirch Mrs. King, but I do think she was only interested in my brother for his money, and the kind of lifestyle he could provide. She saw a life full of riches, and if he didn't live much longer, she'd be set up as the wealthy widow and have her pick of any man she wanted. I don't want you to get duped by her. You know, women can be quite deceitful if the circumstances warrant."

"You don't have to worry about me, Ruth. I'm not like the judge, and as we discussed, when I tire of her, I'll give her the gold so she can set herself up somewhere far away from here."

Ruth eyed him for a full minute before she nodded. "Good."

Frank grinned at her. "What about you, Ruth?"

She gave him a quizzical look. "What about me?"

"Do you ever think of finding a younger man?"

Ruth couldn't say she was surprised by his audacity. Actually, she liked that about Frank. "Do you have someone in mind?"

"You're an attractive woman, Ruth, with many good

years ahead of you. I don't think an older man could keep up with you."

Ruth inclined her head at that statement. "You are right about that. My husband couldn't keep up with me. But a younger man who would be interested in me would only be interested in my wealth."

"Would that be so terrible, if you both enjoyed what life had to offer?"

Ruth didn't respond. She thought Frank might be toying with her, and she was too smart to fall into a trap of his making. Younger women might succumb easily to his charms, but she was older and wiser. Still, there was a part of her that enjoyed his flirting. "Are you flirting with me, Frank?"

Frank winked at her. "Yes, ma'am, I am. You're a beautiful woman, Ruth. Money or not, a man would be lucky to have you on his arm."

Ruth inclined her head at the compliment. "That's one of the problems with wealth, Frank. An affluent woman can never be certain a man wants her and not her money."

They sipped their brandy in silence, and when Frank asked if he could refill her glass, she agreed. She had other matters to discuss with him. "I went to the Grand Crystal Hall tonight to hear Emma Langtry. Are you related?"

"She's my eldest sister. I saw her at the restaurant with my other sisters tonight."

"So there's bad blood between all of you?"

"Yes, ma'am. I'm afraid Morgan LeMasters has turned my whole family against me."

"What a shame. Your sister is very talented, and she is quite an imposing figure of a woman. It was a most enjoyable evening. Have you heard her sing?"

"Not since we were kids. She was always singing back then." Frank had never really paid attention to Emma's singing. He couldn't believe a woman would be paid to sing, but he figured it was a probably a good thing she could earn money with her voice since he never expected her to find a husband who could tolerate her outspoken manner. She had never been one to hold back her thoughts. He could never charm Emma like he could Addie and Rose.

"Some friends of mine heard her sing in Paris, and they said she was quite a sensation. It sounds like she is on her way to becoming a prosperous young woman."

Frank arched his brow in surprise. "Really? A woman can make a lot of money singing songs?"

Ruth laughed at his doubting expression. "They can if they have her talent. She's traveled all over Europe and performed for royalty. The man who manages her tours is a well-known pianist in his own right, and from what I've heard, he's also an excellent businessman."

"I find it surprising," Frank admitted.

"Don't you know that culture is coming to the West, Frank? That is why I invested as a silent partner in the Grand Crystal Hall. We will have theater troupes and stars like your sister coming here from all over the world to perform."

Ruth was always surprising Frank with her business acumen. "I didn't know you owned part of that operation. I haven't been there."

"I don't advertise my investments. My partners are the operators, and they are making a tidy profit. Gambling is almost as profitable as gold."

"Is gambling the only entertainment in that fine establishment?"

Ruth finished her brandy. "Are you asking if we have girls serving the drinks?"

Frank tossed back his brandy and chuckled. "Yes, ma'am, that's exactly what I'm asking."

"Yes, there are girls serving drinks and they also dance with the customers. I understand my partners are hiring the prettiest girls they can find. Judging by the profits from whiskey, I'd say they are doing a fine job. We also have private dining rooms on the second floor, and while I haven't had dinner there yet, I understand they serve some of the best steaks in the West."

"Then we will have to go to dinner there tomorrow."

"That would be lovely." Ruth didn't often get out at night, and it would be nice to go to the Grand Crystal Hall when no one was expecting her. Even though she preferred to be a silent partner, she still wanted to see how her partners operated the business day to day. "When do you plan to return to Black Hawk? I don't imagine it's too safe leaving Mrs. King alone for long."

"I took her to Whispering Pines. She's staying at the hotel there. No one knows her, and I told her I'd be back in a couple of days." Frank wanted to meet up with his gang, but when he rode into town and saw wanted posters on Dutch, Reb, and Deke in the window of the saloon, he knew he should forgo meeting them. The posters stated there was a thousand-dollar bounty for each man involved in the Denver bank robbery. While Sheriff Trent and Marshal Holt might suspect that he'd planned the robbery, they couldn't prove it. The bank president was shot, but he'd survived. Frank figured the man could testify against his gang, but they had nothing on him. The sheriff and the marshal had no way of knowing one of the men they were looking for was dead. Reb had been killed by two outlaws, Win Taggart and Joe Culpepper.

After the bank robbery, Frank had met up with his gang outside of Whispering Pines to split the money, and as chance would have it, Culpepper and Taggart happened on them in the middle of the night and took them by surprise.

Culpepper and Taggart had taken the loot from the bank robbery, and killed Reb in the process.

Corbin Jeffers was the only member of the gang who didn't have his mug on a wanted poster. He'd been waiting at the back of the bank with the horses, so no one got a look at him. With a bounty on his gang, Frank didn't want to go anywhere near them if they got caught. He couldn't afford to be implicated in that robbery now that the judge had all previous charges against him dropped. With Ruth's gold mine, he had a more profitable way to make money than rustling and robbing banks. He planned to get rich off of Ruth's gold. Once he had enough money to take him anywhere he wanted to go, he'd do the one thing he'd wanted to do for as long as he could remember: kill Morgan LeMasters.

Chapter Four

New Mexico Territory

Corbin Jeffers walked into Rustler's Saloon, along with his friend, Harper Ellis. He spotted Deke Sullivan and Dutch Malloy sitting at the back of the room and headed in that direction.

"Look who I found walking into the hotel," Corbin said when he reached the table.

Dutch held out his hand. "Harper, good to see you." Dutch had known Harper for over ten years, but he hadn't seen him in a couple of years. He pointed to a chair, and said, "Have a seat."

Deke shook hands next. "Where have you been keeping yourself?"

"I've been up in Denver visiting my sister for a spell. Made enough money off my last job to hold me over for a while. But it was starting to run low, so I thought I might ride on down to Mexico and try to find some horses rustled from Calhoun's spread. He's offering to pay a fine reward, and I wanted to get out of Colorado. It's just too dang cold."

"I know what you mean. The older I get, the less I like

the snow," Dutch said. "Have a drink with us to warm your old bones." He raised a hand for the saloon girl. When she turned his way, he said, "Bring us another bottle and two more glasses."

Harper settled back in his chair. "Whiskey sounds good right now."

"How is your sister and her kids? Did her no-account husband ever come back?" Dutch asked.

Harper shook his head. "No, sir, he didn't. He'd better hope I never run into him. My sister and those kids have it rough. I do what I can to help them out, but it's tough on her with four kids to raise by herself. She takes in laundry, does some sewing for women, and just about anything else she can to feed those kids. She always asks about you, Dutch."

"Your sister is a sweet little thing, and pretty too. I never could figure a man running out on her," Dutch said.

"She's still a handsome woman, but I don't reckon no fellow wants to take on a woman with four kids. She's twelve years younger than me, and she still looks like she's a young girl."

"Just how old are you, Harper?" Dutch asked. "You've got a head full of white hair now, and it wasn't that long ago, it was black."

Harper ran his hand through his hair and chuckled. "I'm almost fifty."

"Dang, you are getting old," Corbin said.

When the laughter died down, Harper leaned close to Dutch and said, "I stopped here thinking I might find you boys."

"Why are you looking for us?" Dutch asked, thinking Harper might need their help on a job.

Harper reached in his coat pocket and pulled out some papers. Once he unfolded them, he glanced around to make certain they had some privacy. Seeing no gawkers were sitting nearby, he placed three posters on the table.

The three men leaned over and looked at the posters. Staring back at them were rough drawings of Dutch, Deke, and Reb on wanted posters. There was a bounty of a thousand dollars for each man, wanted for bank robbery, attempted murder, and rustling.

Dutch gulped back a shot of whiskey. "Where did you get these, Harper?"

"Denver. I had a feeling you boys would be holed up here, and I wanted you to know about this."

Harper folded the posters when the waitress brought the fresh bottle of whiskey. Dutch was quiet as he poured drinks all around.

When the waitress walked away, Harper said, "I've known you a long time, Dutch, and this poster said you are wanted for attempted murder. You're not a man who has ever killed anyone, or been accused of attempted murder as far as I know."

"You're right, Harper, I've never killed anyone, and I didn't this time. Deke didn't either. It was Reb who shot that fellow, and Reb's dead. You remember Reb?"

"Yeah, I remember him. Who shot him?"

"Two hombres by the name of Culpepper and Taggart. You ever heard of them?" Dutch asked.

"I know of them. Killers," Harper stated matter-of-factly. "How come they shot Reb?"

"We was hiding out in an old shack near Whispering Pines, and they got the drop on us in the middle of the night. They were planning on hightailing it outta there with everything we had, and Reb went for his gun," Deke said.

Harper gave Dutch a hard look. Dutch said he didn't kill anyone, but he didn't say they hadn't robbed a bank. "Did those two hombres take the loot from the bank robbery?"

"Yep." Dutch didn't hesitate to tell Harper the truth. He'd known Harper a long time, and even though he wasn't an outlaw in the usual sense of the word, he trusted him. Harper rustled, but he rustled cattle and horses that had already been stolen and taken into Mexico. Ranchers hired Harper to find their property and return what was stolen by any means necessary. Harper was never wanted by the law, and he was respected by both outlaws and law-abiding citizens. Most of the time Harper worked alone unless the job was too large; then he hired men he trusted. No one asked questions about what he had to do on the other side of the border to return the property to the rightful owner. Everyone knew Harper was a man who could keep his mouth shut, and mind his own business. Dutch had often thought if he'd been smart, he would have partnered up with Harper years ago.

"So you boys did all of the work, and Culpepper and Taggart benefited."

"That's about the size of it," Deke said.

"We've been waiting here to meet up with Frank Langtry," Dutch said.

Harper shook his head at Dutch. "You mean to tell me you boys are riding with Langtry?"

"Yeah, we rustled with Frank on LeMasters's land. Darn near got us lynched," Dutch said.

"Dang, Dutch, I thought you were smarter than to ride with that no-account son of a gun. And you have to be plumb loco to rustle on Morgan LeMasters's land. I hear he's as mean as a rattler when you cross him," Harper said.

"I wish I had been smart enough not to listen to Frank. And you're right about LeMasters. He had the ropes around our necks, but we lucked out when Frank's sister happened by. She talked LeMasters into taking us to jail."

"How'd you get out of that mess?" Harper asked.

"It's a long story, but there was a stagecoach accident, and Frank had been riding inside the coach with his sister. Anyhow, he got the upper hand on LeMasters, and we got away."

"So you didn't learn your lesson, and went in with him on this bank robbery?" Harper could hardly believe what he was hearing.

"Yeah, we thought we was going to make a killing," Deke said.

"You're gonna make a killing all right, but it'll more than likely be your own. You don't see a poster on Langtry, do you?" Harper tapped the folder posters with his fore-finger. "Frank will always take care of himself. And where was Frank while you boys were robbing the bank?"

"Frank had the robbery planned out so he wasn't inside the bank. He was the one who created a diversion while we were inside the bank," Deke replied.

"You boys got the raw end of this deal," Harper said.

"Yeah, and we sure can't hole up here any longer wait-ing on Frank." Dutch pounded his fist on top of the poster that held his likeness. "Now that these posters are every-where, we'll have bounty hunters running us to ground."

"What'd you hear in Denver about the robbery?" Deke asked Harper.

"I heard two women got shot along with the bank pres-ident. The president lived and so did one of the women."

"We thought Frank might be in jail and that was the reason he's hasn't made it here," Corbin said.

Harper shook his head. "Nope. I heard he's going to work at the gold mine owned by that rich woman in town."

"The one with that house on the hill?" Corbin asked.

"That's the one. My sister tells me that woman has more money that Croesus."

"She's related to Judge Stevens. Frank married the judge's daughter, and she was the one who died in the robbery."

"Reb killed a woman?" Harper asked.

"No, the bank president shot at Reb, but instead of hitting Reb, his bullets went through the window. The girl was hit and died on the spot."

"My sister said two women were shot," Harper said.

"The other one was Frank's girlfriend," Deke said.

Harper was trying to follow the story. "Let me get this straight. Frank was outside the bank with his wife and his girlfriend at the time of the robbery?"

Dutch laughed at Harper's confused expression. "That's right. Frank took up with the judge's girlfriend before his wife was killed. The judge didn't know what was going on right under his nose."

Harper shook his head. "This is some story. Frank always was one sorry human being. I heard the judge had a heart attack."

"Is he dead?"

"No, he survived," Harper said.

"Frank was supposed to be here a few days ago. We were beginning to think they figured out the robbery and arrested him," Deke said.

"He's probably in Black Hawk at that gold mine." Harper looked at each man. "And I reckon since his mug ain't on a wanted poster, he'll steer clear of you boys."

"Frank said he was in tight with that rich woman. She's probably giving him all the money he needs," Corbin said.

"Yeah, and here we are with no more money, and our faces on wanted posters," Deke said.

Dutch stuffed the posters in his pocket. "I guess we're going to be looking over our shoulders from now on."

"I think we will be safe enough here," Corbin said.

Dutch laughed. "Do you think that these outlaws in here

wouldn't turn us in for a plug nickel, much less a thousand dollars?" Dutch didn't wait for an answer; he looked at Harper and said, "Are you set on going to Mexico, or could you be talked into taking a detour that could prove to be more profitable?"

Harper cocked his head. "What do you have in mind?"

"Seeing as how we need to lay low, I'd like to take a trip to Purgatory Canyon. I have a feeling Culpepper and Taggart are hiding out there."

"We owe them for robbing us. That's for sure," Deke said.

"At least they didn't kill us like they did Reb," Corbin said.

Dutch shook his head in disgust. "Yeah, let's be sure to thank them when we see them."

"I've never been to Purgatory Canyon, but I hear it's not a safe place to go," Harper said.

Dutch pointed to Deke and Corbin. "We know Purgatory Canyon like the backs of our hands."

Deke nodded his agreement. "Dutch is right. We know that terrain better than anyone, and we've met up with a lot of outlaws in there. We ain't never seen Culpepper and Taggart there, so we'd have an advantage of knowing the lay of the land."

"What makes you think they are there now?" Harper asked.

"They were being chased by U.S. Marshal Holt. Where else were they going to go? We made friends with that old codger, Indian Pete. He's lived in that canyon his whole life and he's about eighty years old. If Culpepper and Taggart are hiding out in there, Indian Pete will know. All we have to do is take him a bottle of whiskey and he'd lead us to where they are hiding out."

"I don't think Culpepper or Taggart could take us in a fair fight," Deke said.

"Who said it would be fair?" Dutch said. "We'll get the drop on them, just like they did on us—in the dead of night. And I hope they're as drunk as we were."

"If I go with you, what's in it for me?" Harper needed to make some money to help his sister out with her kids.

"We got forty thousand dollars in that robbery. Of course, that don't mean there'll be that much left. But whatever we get back, we'll split four ways."

Harper swirled the whiskey in his glass as he considered Dutch's offer. He might be taking a risk trying to find two killers who may have already spent some of the money. On the other hand, even if there was only fifteen thousand left, he'd have to work months to make that much money. What the doctor in Denver said played in his mind. *You've got cancer, Mr. Ellis, and I'd be surprised if you last another year. You should get your affairs in order.* Harper knew he didn't have much time to waste. Even if his take was five thousand dollars, it'd go a long way to making sure his sister and her four kids had something besides a life full of heartache.

Still, he wasn't keen on breaking the law. He figured how he'd chosen to earn a living was the best of both worlds. He always thought he understood an outlaw's mind. The one thing he had in common with them was he'd always thrived on the excitement of taking chances and living on the edge. Yet he also thought like a lawman. He believed in right and wrong, but where he parted company with the law was how he'd chosen to mete out justice his own way. He wasn't one to wait around on a court of law. If the ranchers had waited around for some judge to do something about their stolen property, they'd be waiting until daisies covered their graves.

"You don't think the three of you can take Culpepper and Taggart?" Harper asked.

"I've thought about where they could be hiding out in there, and it would be better if we had four guns," Dutch said. Dutch was also figuring that Corbin was pretty much useless with a gun, and Harper was a pretty good shot.

"What about the marshal? What makes you think he won't go to Purgatory Canyon?"

Dutch shrugged. "He could, but most lawmen who made that choice have ended up dead."

"Have you boys thought about getting that money back and then turning yourselves in?"

"Why do you ask that?" Dutch asked.

Harper figured he owed it to Dutch to offer a different point of view. He'd lived longer, and he'd seen his fair share of mistakes made by outlaws. Dutch, Deke, and Corbin weren't bad men; they'd just started off in life without a prayer. Maybe they could benefit from his knowledge, or maybe not. It was up to them. What was that old saying about leading a horse to water? "If the law catches up to you, that money might be your only bargaining chip. If, as you say, Frank is in with Judge Stevens, I don't think he'll have a problem pointing the finger at you for all his crimes. You'll be the one swinging from a rope and not Frank."

Chapter Five

Clay had intentionally ridden his horse behind the buckboard on the ride back to Whispering Pines early Sunday morning. Sweetie leaped from the buckboard to run beside him. The ladies were talking nonstop, and Clay could hear some of their conversation, but he didn't participate. It wasn't like him not to be sociable, but he had a lot on his mind that he needed to sort out. Weighing heavy on his mind were the members of the church. He didn't feel he should apologize for going to the Grand Crystal Hall, but he'd still have to find a way to mend fences with some of the parishioners who'd disapproved of his actions. Carlo had asked him an interesting question, and it was one he intended to pose to the congregation tonight. *If* they showed up for the late service.

His congregation wasn't the only thing on his mind. As soon as he'd heard that Marshal Holt and Sheriff Trent were leaving to trail Culpepper and Taggart, he'd been thinking about the man he was a few short years ago. He no longer had the desire to kill men as he did in the past, but he felt the need to see for himself the kind of men who had gunned down his family. The other men who had ridden with the gang had pinned the murders on Culpepper and Taggart. Of course, they were all killers and probably trying to save their own hides when he'd faced them in gunfights, but Clay thought they had told the truth in the end. The question on Clay's mind this morning was why he wasn't able to forgive them. The Good Book said if he wanted forgiveness, he had to forgive. But how could he get to a place of forgiveness for men who'd committed such evil deeds? The Bible also said one sin was no greater than another. That was another tenet he had difficulty understanding.

Until last night, he'd thought he had moved on from his past. Now he wasn't as certain. Physically he'd moved on. He'd left behind the graves of his family, and the ranch he loved and built with his own two hands. But his locale wasn't the issue. His soul was. Forgiving men for their sins was an easy sermon to preach, but it was a different thing altogether when faced with forgiving men who'd committed the sin against the ones you loved.

"He doesn't talk very much," Emma said.

Seeing the direction of Emma's gaze, Granny said, "You're talking about Clay."

"Yes. He hasn't said two words this morning."

Morgan and Jack heard the conversation. Jack turned around and said, "He's not so quiet from the pulpit. I think he's worried about what some of the folks will say tonight at church."

"I'm not convinced that's all that's on his mind," Granny said.

"He shouldn't be worried at all about going to the Grand Crystal last night. Half of the church members were there," Jack said.

"He's worried about the other half who weren't there.

They made their voices heard, and didn't approve of him going to a place where alcohol was served." Morgan had told Clay not to be troubled about their opinion. He'd learned long ago you couldn't make everyone happy. He figured as long as you were doing the right thing for the right reasons, you had no reason to worry. Unless you didn't have the strength of character to avoid succumbing to the temptations of such establishments. He knew Clay was a man of admirable character, and he had no such problem.

"Granny, were you concerned what people would say about you going to our performance last night?" Emma asked.

"Heavens, no. I loved the place, and no other place could accommodate such a large crowd. I've been around the church all my life, and when I've doctored folks, I can't tell the saints from the sinners. The good Lord has told us not to judge others, and we all should remember that directive. Clay has good intentions, and he doesn't want to disappoint anyone. When he gets to be my age he'll learn you can't please everyone. We should leave it up to the Almighty to do the judging. He's had a lot of practice, and He can certainly do it without any help from the likes of me. I think a few folks are being judgmental, but others see it as their duty to steer their brothers from temptation."

Emma leaned over and hugged her grandmother. "Oh, Granny, I wish more people thought like you. You always understand both sides of a situation. I hope the folks who objected will not hold it against the pastor."

Jack and Morgan exchanged a glance. They knew some of the church ladies would be in high dudgeon with Clay this evening. They were staunch in their beliefs about the evils of socializing in venues where alcohol was served, and not even the talented pastor would change their views.

But Granny was right; they were good people, and they were to be commended for sticking to their beliefs.

"Do you think Clay's sermon will be on judging others?" Morgan asked.

"I'm betting it will be on the wages of sin after seeing all of those gaming tables full last night. And they sure had a lot of people coming and going out of those rooms upstairs," Jack replied.

"What rooms?" Rose asked.

Morgan elbowed Jack. "Yeah, Jack, what rooms?"

Jack hadn't realized the women didn't see everything he'd observed on the second floor of the establishment last night. There was a large sign that clearly stated that the private rooms were for conversation only. He'd heard about high-class establishments that employed well-educated young women to entertain men with diverse conversation, but he'd never personally frequented such a place. He'd also heard the rules were strictly enforced, and if a man got out of line, they were quickly escorted off the premises by the law. "The rooms on the second floor are where people can have private conversations."

Morgan arched his brow at him, thinking by his vague response the women would think he meant something totally different.

"That better not mean what it sounds like, Jack Roper," Granny warned.

Jack rolled his eyes, thinking Granny saw right through his response.

"Don't roll your eyes at me, young man," Granny said.

Morgan laughed.

Jack's deputy, Webb, had told him Granny had eyes in the back of her head, and he was beginning to believe it. "What makes you think I rolled my eyes at you, Granny?"

"I know you, Jack Roper." Granny was smiling, but Jack didn't need to know that.

"You are teasing about these conversation rooms, aren't you?" Addie asked Jack.

Jack turned to look at his wife. "No, honey, I'm not. These kinds of"—he almost said "saloons" but he caught himself—"entertainment places hires well-educated, pretty ladies to have conversations with men in private rooms."

"And how do you know having *conversations* are what they are doing?" Addie asked.

"There was a sign at the top of the stairs directing folks to the *conversation* rooms." Jack was smiling at his own clever retort.

Rose was incredulous. "Are you telling me men pay good money to converse with women when most of them have wives at home?"

"It's been known to happen," Jack replied.

Morgan was enjoying the grilling Jack was receiving. He should have known better than to open his big mouth.

"Morgan, did you know about this? You've spent a lot of time in Denver. Have you been there?" Rose asked.

Morgan was handling the team, so he didn't turn around, but he didn't need to look at his wife to know by her tone that she wasn't pleased. "No, I haven't been there. I believe I told you that last night." He wasn't about to mention he'd been in a place like the Grand Crystal Hall years ago in San Francisco. The women were indeed beautiful and intelligent. But if a man didn't have a sizable bank account, they didn't make it to the conversation rooms. Before men were even allowed in the club, they had to provide a recommendation from another member. The Grand

Crystal Hall wasn't quite as elite, but he figured the same rules applied.

"One would hardly think a man would pay for conversation when they can talk to their wives, or if they are not married, they could talk to the women at church," Addie said.

Morgan shot Jack a quick glance, trying to stifle his laughter. Jack was trying hard to keep a straight face.

"It all sounds very fishy to me," Rose said.

"I've sang in a few places that have the same kind of conversation rooms." Emma thought if her sisters knew of some of the places she'd performed, they'd die of fright.

"What respectable woman would work in such a place?" Rose asked.

"Some of these gals are from prominent families, have traveled the world, and are able to converse on many subjects," Emma replied.

"Why would good families allow their daughters to work in such establishments? And why would such educated women even want to do that?" Rose asked.

"I'm sure those women are of age," Granny said. "Perhaps their families have no say in the matter. Everyone makes their own choices. Many younger women are easily influenced by what they might think is a more interesting life, and their heads are turned by the flattery of wealthy men."

"Perhaps they are trying to find wealthy husbands," Addie said.

"I think it's disappointing that young women don't learn to make their own way in a respectable profession," Rose said.

"The respectable positions don't pay as much, and they

are not that easy to come by unless you live in larger cities," Emma said.

"True enough," Granny said.

"And don't forget, many people think my profession is not respectable," Emma reminded them.

"Why in heavens not?" Granny asked.

"For the simple reason we perform in what people think are unsavory places. They judge me based on that fact alone. Just like your pastor has found out."

Morgan and Jack were thankful the conversation took a different direction.

But Rose wasn't ready to let the subject drop. "Husband, would you ever visit a *conversation* room?"

Morgan heard the skepticism in her voice. He had a feeling she didn't believe that the conversation rooms were there for talking only. "I don't need to, I have you."

"But what if you didn't have a smart, beautiful wife?" Emma teased.

Morgan hesitated, trying to think of a diplomatic response. "I'm a smart man. I waited to marry until I found the woman of my dreams."

Even no-nonsense Emma thought Morgan gave the perfect response. "Rose, I'd say you have yourself a winner."

"I'm just as fortunate," Rose replied.

The men were thankful they were almost home, and even more grateful when the women's conversation turned to fashion and other topics that men tuned out.

Clay walked toward the pulpit with a hint of trepidation. A quick glance at the crowd told him a few of the folks who were against him going to Denver last night were sitting in their usual places. There was a chance they might not like his sermon tonight, but he prayed they received it in the way he intended. Perhaps they might even share the sermon with those who decided not to attend. The room was silent as he placed his Bible on the stand, and pulled his notes from his jacket pocket. He glanced around and saw Granny sitting beside Emma, along with Morgan, Jack, and their wives sitting in the first pew. He knew they were worn-out from traveling, and he appreciated that they had ridden back to town to offer their support.

He took a deep breath, tucked his notes in his jacket pocket, and asked God to give him the right words.

"As you know, last night I was in Denver and that is the reason we are holding a late service. I had the distinct honor and privilege of hearing Miss Emma Langtry perform, along with the famous Italian tenor, Carlo Palladino, and their very accomplished pianist, Andre Hoffman." He looked at Emma, and said, "We are also fortunate to have Miss Emma Langtry in our congregation tonight." His gaze briefly slid to Sweetie lying peacefully at Emma's feet before he locked eyes with her again.

Emma met his gaze. There was something about the way he was looking at her, as if he was trying to say something without words. Their eyes locked for several beats, and people began to glance around, wondering if Clay had forgotten what he was about to say.

Clay cleared his throat. He didn't know what had just happened, but when his eyes met Emma's, he didn't want to look away, but he had to continue. "It's been said that when we hear angels sing, it will be the most beautiful sound we have ever heard. I've never been fortunate to hear actual angels singing, but I think I came as close last night to hearing an angel sing, at least until my time on Earth is done. I'm so thankful Granny Langtry and her family invited me along on that trip to Denver." He glanced Emma's way again. "I've never heard more beautiful sounds as I heard in the Grand Crystal Hall last night. I think everyone in our church would appreciate the performance of Miss Langtry. The evening didn't end with the performance. Afterward, we had a pleasant dinner at the hotel, and we had a wonderful discussion with Mr. Palladino and Mr. Hoffman. I learned that they have performed in front of royalty all over Europe." Clay glanced over the crowd to make certain they were listening. "Carlo, this intelligent, talented man, made a comment that forced me to look at things from a different perspective. I understand the concerns of many about lending support to places where the values of the church are not upheld. But there is another side to that argument. Where better to find lost sheep if not in places where they may be found? They won't be under the shepherd's watchful eye. And if we are to live by example, shouldn't that example also be displayed in the very places where love and compassion may be lacking? Just this morning, I overheard a wise woman say that passing judgment was not her job; she would leave that up to the Lord. We could all benefit from this point of view." He hesitated again, and took a moment to open his Bible before he looked at the faces again. "I am not a perfect man. We all have done things that we wish we could have a second chance. Many times I've considered myself a good man, and blessed beyond measure. I have also done many things I'm not proud of, and have asked for forgiveness. But I know we have to trust that each of us will try to do the right thing, whether we are in church, or in an entertainment establishment. We can't pass judgment on others since we do not know what is in their hearts. Only our Father has that information. We have been commanded to love one another. Period. No conditions." He held up his Bible, and said, "I cannot find in here where we are commanded to pass judgment." He paused, then said,

"Miss Langtry, Mr. Palladino, and Mr. Hoffman aim to give people a night they will remember the rest of their lives. They want them to hear music they have never had a chance to hear, for the sheer pleasure of seeing the smiles on their faces. To me, that is showing love to their fellow man."

With that said, Clay finished with some readings from the Bible, which he figured made his point more effectively than anything he had to say. Before excusing the congregation, he added one more point. "Some of you may have an interest in seeing Miss Langtry perform before she embarks on another tour next year. You will have that opportunity later in the month since they were such a rousing success last night. I will post the details of the dates of their next performances near the door." He ended the service with a prayer.

Morgan looked at Jack when they stood. "That was some sermon."

"I'd say Emma has made a lasting impression on our friend," Jack retorted.

Morgan nodded. "Yeah, I think she has." He glanced around at the people filing out. "I see a lot of head-nodding going on, but I wonder what the busy bees will be talking about tomorrow."

"I hope they take his words to heart," Rose said.

Emma didn't comment. She couldn't believe she'd just heard the man, who had barely spoken to her earlier in the day, give her such resounding praise in front of the whole church. Not only that, but when he glanced her way, she knew that something important had passed between them in that one look. Clay Hunt was definitely a puzzle.

Clay stood at the door of the church saying good-bye to the congregation when Granny approached. "That was a wonderful sermon." She shot Jack a glance to see if he was going to mention that he'd expected the pastor's sermon to be on the wages of sin.

Jack winked at her.

"Jack thought your sermon was going to be on the wages of sin tonight."

Clay smiled at Jack. "Sorry to disappoint. I'll get to that next week. *If* the congregation shows up next week."

"Oh, I wasn't disappointed. I thought it was a great sermon," Jack said.

"We all did," Addie added.

"I really appreciate all of you coming tonight. I know you've had a busy few days."

"It was too late for the children to attend, but be assured they will be here next week," Jack said.

"The children were worn-out from pestering Emma to sing for them," Addie said. "I'm afraid they asked her thousands of questions about the places she has been. I'm actually surprised she wasn't too tired to come."

Clay shifted his attention to Emma. "It was good of you to come." When he looked into her eyes, he felt . . . he didn't know what it was . . . but he was drawn to her. Like last night, he couldn't take his eyes off of her. She owned the stage. Despite the booming voice of the striking Carlo by her side, all eyes were fixed on Emma. Then tonight, each time he looked her way, he felt it was like she was the only person in church.

"I want to thank you for what you said," Emma said. "You've more than lived up to Granny's billing."

"Thank you." Clay was pleased that she'd enjoyed the sermon. He'd told the congregation what was in his heart; Emma did sing like an angel. But if anyone thought she was a meek, timid woman, they'd be in for a surprise. She carried herself as regally as a queen. Seeing her stand up to Frank last night gave him insight on the woman's character. She wasn't one to tolerate fools. When Frank tried to feed

her his well-rehearsed lies, she'd let him know she wasn't
falling for his story. She wasn't intimidated by Frank, and
she hadn't minced words as she told him exactly what she
thought of his lies. Clay admired that about her. "I see you
brought Sweetie. Do you think he liked the sermon?" The
dog leaned into his leg, and Clay scratched him behind
the ears.

"I think he likes you, with or without a sermon," Emma
said. Her dog seemed to like the pastor as much as he
did her.

"We are going to have a late dinner at the hotel. Would
you like to join us?" Morgan asked.

Clay's initial thought was to decline for the simple
reason he didn't understand his reaction each time he
looked at Emma. Was it attraction? Until he figured out
what he was feeling, he thought it best to steer clear of her.
Last night had been a night of contemplation for him.
Watching Morgan and Jack tease their wives, he realized
he wasn't over the loss of his wife. Until he'd put that chap-
ter of his life behind him, he couldn't see himself getting
involved with another woman. Not that Emma would be
interested in a small-town pastor when she had a real
prince infatuated with her. How could he compete with a
man like that?

"Join us, Clay. I won't let you sit here fretting over the
people that didn't come to services tonight," Granny said.

Clay didn't have the heart to deny Granny's request.
"I'd be delighted." Granny was right about one thing. He
was concerned about the opinions of the folks who didn't
come to church tonight. He'd worked hard to develop rela-
tionships with his parishioners, but that wasn't what was
occupying his mind tonight. Thoughts of Emma, Violet,
his son, and the ever-present Culpepper and Taggart had
dogged him all day.

Chapter Six

Entering the hotel restaurant, Morgan was escorting his party to a table when he noticed a woman he recognized walking through the dining room. He turned around to get Jack's attention, and inclined his head toward Leigh King. "Is that who I think it is?"

Jack peered around Morgan to look at the woman who had taken a seat at a table on the opposite side of the room. "Yep. Wonder what she's doing here."

"Who are you talking about?" Emma asked.

"That woman at the table by the window is Frank's girlfriend, the ex-girlfriend of the judge, Leigh King."

The women turned to look at the woman. "Isn't she too young to be the judge's girlfriend?" Emma asked.

"Why isn't she in Denver with Frank?" Granny asked.

"It would be my guess that Frank hid her out here at the hotel to keep her away from the judge. He couldn't take her to Denver and take a chance that the judge would find out," Morgan said.

"Does she know you two?" Emma asked.

"I don't think so, unless Frank pointed us out to her. We saw her in the restaurant in Denver, where there was a confrontation with the judge's daughter. The next time we saw her, she was unconscious in the middle of the street after the bank robbery."

"I'll be back in a minute. Go ahead and get seated." Jack turned toward the hotel registry.

All eyes were on Jack as he walked back to the table and took his seat. "She arrived Saturday, and the clerk said he didn't know how long she is staying. Frank was with her Saturday morning, and he hasn't been back."

"So Judge Stevens believes Frank has been looking for her, and all the while, he's been with her," Morgan said.

"She's a lovely woman, I can understand their attraction. But it doesn't say much for her judgment to get involved with Frank," Emma said.

"Frank's wife was a pretty woman too," Jack said. "And she ended up dead due to Frank's recklessness."

"It's hard to believe how these women fall for all of his lies," Morgan said.

"Frank was always a charmer when he wanted to be," Granny said.

"Do you think Frank thought you wouldn't recognize her?" Clay hadn't been able to get a good look at her, but he noticed her dark hair was the same color as his deceased wife's.

"Maybe. Maybe he didn't care one way or the other. It's a miracle she survived the shooting," Jack said.

"Miracles still happen," Granny said.

"But don't you think Frank would be worried that if you did recognize her you might tell the judge?" Rose asked.

"The judge probably wouldn't believe us. I can't say he's my biggest fan," Morgan said.

"Don't you think the judge would sever his relationship with Frank if he knew about his girlfriend?" Emma asked.

"If what Sheriff Trent said is true, Frank is closer to the judge's sister," Jack replied.

"Frank's probably been hiding her out at that gold mine the judge's sister owns in Black Hawk," Morgan said.

"Black Hawk is close enough so Frank can come and go to Denver in a day. I bet the judge's sister knows what Frank is up to with Mrs. King," Jack said.

Granny looked across the room at the young woman sitting alone. "I would doubt the judge's sister is privy to Frank's scheming. Her niece was Frank's wife, and I can't imagine she would be too happy with Frank if she knew he was involved with that woman. In a way, I feel sorry for her. She should have stayed with the judge, even if he is old enough to be her grandfather. Anything would be better than taking up with Frank."

"Maybe we should tell her," Emma said.

"She knows." Jack had seen women like Leigh King many times before. Women like her craved the excitement they thought they would find with a man like Frank.

Granny shook her head. "When she is an old woman, she'll be sorry for the choices she's made."

"If she stays with Frank, she may not live to see her old age," Morgan said. "I agreed with Sheriff Trent, she was involved with Frank in that bank robbery. You can't tell me that Frank and his wife just happened to be walking in front of the bank at the exact time that Mrs. King was leaving the bank." Morgan wasn't a man who believed in coincidences. At least, not such convenient coincidences when Frank was involved.

"You can't be serious, Morgan," Granny said. "You think a woman as pretty as she is would resort to bank robbery?"

"I'm very serious," Morgan said.

Jack agreed with Morgan. "Morgan's right. That little

scene in front of the bank was planned by Frank. Frank's wife and Mrs. King had already been in an argument in the restaurant. They caused quite a scene that was witnessed by a lot of people dining that night. When they ran into each other outside the bank, the bystanders said it was a real hullabaloo, and no one was paying attention to the bank being robbed. It was definitely staged."

Clay looked across the room, but he still couldn't see her face. "You called her Mrs. King. Had she been married before?"

"The sheriff said she was a widow," Jack said.

"If there was ever a soul who needs saving, I'd say it would be Mrs. King's if she's involved with Frank. She's so young; perhaps she didn't know what Frank was going to do." Just as Clay started to look away, Leigh King turned and looked his way. Clay felt as though he were looking back in time. He couldn't speak—he could barely breathe. At a distance, Leigh King looked exactly like his deceased wife.

"Don't you think young women can be deceitful?" Emma asked.

Clay didn't respond. His eyes were fixed on the woman sitting at the table alone.

"Well?" Emma said.

Clay realized Emma was speaking to him. "Pardon?"

Emma took a deep breath and said, "I asked if you thought a young woman could be deceitful."

"I guess I choose to believe such a beautiful woman has a heart to match." Clay tried to keep his eyes from drifting across the restaurant to the table by the window, but he had little success.

Emma noticed he couldn't take his eyes off of the young widow.

"I think I will stop at her table on our way out and ask

her to come to next Sunday's service if she is still in town." Clay wanted to see her up close. He had to see if she did resemble Violet, or if it was his imagination playing tricks on him.

Emma leaned over and playfully whispered in Clay's ear, "Are you certain you are interested in her soul, and not her beauty?"

Clay turned to look at Emma, but he didn't know how to respond. He couldn't tell her the reason he wanted to meet Mrs. King. He wasn't prepared to share that with anyone. "We shouldn't pass judgment."

Emma had only been teasing, but his tone told her that her attempt at humor had fallen flat. Emma turned to Addie and engaged her in conversation.

Morgan heard Clay's reply to Emma and glanced at Jack to gauge his response. Jack shrugged his shoulders. It was out of character for Clay to be so prickly.

As the group left the restaurant, Clay made a detour to Leigh King's table. After he introduced himself, she invited him to join her. She was getting ready to go back to her room, but she decided she'd rather converse with the handsome pastor instead of spending time alone in an empty room.

Emma watched them from the doorway with Rose and Addie right behind her.

Addie peeked around Emma's shoulder. "What do you think they are talking about?"

Emma arched her brow at Addie. "Whatever the pastor is saying, I'd say she's interested." Emma noted the way Leigh was leaning close to Clay, hanging on his every word.

"Wonder why he felt the need to speak to her tonight?" Rose asked.

Emma turned to look at Rose. "Why? Just look at her.

She is very beautiful, and I imagine more than one man in that room would like to meet her."

"I'm certain Clay thinks she is a lost sheep worth saving," Rose said.

"Now you sound like Granny," Emma retorted, but she was smiling. "Have you ever seen a sheep that looks like her?"

Rose and Addie laughed.

"Don't you think he's handsome, Emma?" Addie asked.

Emma couldn't deny the obvious. "Yes, I do, but he's a difficult man to get to know."

"I did notice he's been very quiet all day," Addie said.

Granny walked up behind the sisters. "The men have the buckboard in front of the hotel, and they are anxious to get home." She noticed the girls were watching Clay at the young woman's table. "Are you keeping an eye on Clay?"

"We wanted to see how he was going to get on with Frank's girlfriend," Emma said.

"I'm certain he'll have no problem," Granny said. "He can be a charmer when he wants to be."

"Couldn't prove it by me." Emma didn't think he'd been very charming throughout dinner. "Let's go."

"Shouldn't we wait to say good-bye to Clay?" Addie asked.

Emma turned to leave. "No, if he had an interest in saying good-bye to us, he would have." When Sweetie didn't immediately follow Emma, she looked at him and saw he also had his eyes on Clay. "Don't be a traitor, Sweetie."

"Where's Clay?" Morgan asked when the women walked to the buckboard.

"He's talking to Frank's girlfriend," Granny said.

Morgan and Jack assisted the women onto the buckboard. "I guess we shouldn't interrupt him if he is saving a soul. We need to be on our way. It's getting late."

* * *

Clay walked outside the hotel to see Morgan's buckboard was already at the other end of town. He felt guilty that he didn't say good-bye, but when he sat down with Mrs. King, he'd been so overwhelmed by the resemblance to his deceased wife that he could barely think straight. Violet had black hair and light blue eyes, just like Mrs. King. Though Mrs. King was a beautiful woman, he told himself she was not as lovely as Violet. No one had ever measured up to Violet in his mind. He couldn't imagine why Leigh was with that scoundrel Frank Langtry. Clay invited her to church next Sunday, and while she didn't commit one way or the other, she seemed pleased that he'd asked. He didn't mention that he'd been told she was traveling with Frank Langtry, and she didn't offer an explanation for being in town. She did mention she'd once lived in Colorado City with her husband, who had died not long after their marriage.

On his way back to his small home next to the church, Clay thought about three women. Seeing Mrs. King brought back so many sweet memories of Violet. When they married, it was the first time he'd felt like he knew his life's purpose. He wanted to build a life with Violet, provide for her and the children they would have. Losing her and Mark had nearly killed him. For years, he no longer cared if he lived or died. He'd lived for his family. He couldn't say he'd ever stopped grieving, but he'd stopped asking why his family was taken from him. He'd learned sometimes God was silent, and he had to wait to get answers to his many questions.

He walked into his quiet home, and the silence brought back other memories. He saw himself returning home to the fragrant aromas of dinner warming on the stove. The sound of his son's voice as he asked his mother question after question. Violet's soft and patient replies to their inquisitive son.

Clay set the pot on the stove to warm some leftover coffee. Emma's face flashed in his mind. She probably thought he was rude, and he couldn't disagree that he hadn't been friendly tonight. He didn't want to be attracted to her. He tried to push her image away; he wanted to think about Violet tonight. If he thought about Emma, he was being disloyal to the memory of his wife. Why should he find happiness again when his wife and child were dead forever? He didn't want to forget Violet's face, her voice, her sweet nature. If he married again and had children, those memories might fade. Seeing Leigh King tonight reminded him of all he'd lost. Had he imagined the similarities with his deceased wife, or was he just wishing it to be so?

He sat in a chair at the kitchen table and dropped his face in his hands, trying to get control of his errant thoughts. Emma was nothing like Violet. Emma was tall and imposing, with a personality more like a force of nature. There was nothing retiring about her. Quite the opposite. He couldn't imagine Violet ever standing up to a man like Frank the way Emma did last night. He'd often wondered if Violet had even considered shooting those men that fateful day. She was such a gentle soul that she didn't understand she needed to be prepared to face trouble if he wasn't there to protect her. Violet was the kind of person who would turn the other cheek. She'd never been exposed to killers like Culpepper and Taggart. No matter how much he tried to make her understand not all men could be trusted, it seemed beyond her comprehension such evil walked the earth. Clay felt he'd failed her in that.

Emma wasn't the kind of woman who would hesitate to

do what needed to be done. He could see her going toe to toe with men like Culpepper and Taggart. Why was he comparing his Violet to Emma? He shook his head at his own question. He couldn't survive another loss like he did four years ago. Maybe he was a coward, but he couldn't take a chance like that. Never again.

Chapter Seven

Emma was sitting at the kitchen table with Granny and Rose the next morning when she finally broached the subject that had been on her mind. "I want you two to tell me everything Frank has done."

Granny knew this particular conversation would take place as soon as Morgan left the breakfast table. "I'm sorry I had to send such bad news in my last letter, but we didn't want you to come home and find out about your brothers from someone else."

"Are you certain Frank killed Stevie?" Emma still could hardly fathom her eldest brother killed her youngest brother.

"I was there. The house was on fire, and Frank wouldn't let me go inside to see if Stevie was there. We don't know for sure if Frank killed Stevie, or if he died in the fire, but Stevie had to be incapacitated in some way not to leave the burning building," Rose said.

"Emma, you can't trust Frank, no matter what he says. If you see him when you are alone, get away from him. He's very dangerous, so never be alone with him," Granny warned.

Emma nodded. "I doubt I will even see him again. What do you think happened to make him this way?"

"I don't think Frank has been right in the head for many years, if he ever was," Granny said.

They sat in silence for a few minutes, each lost in their own memories of Frank.

"Emma, tell us about this prince who may be coming to America to court you," Rose said.

Emma looked at Rose, but her mind was on the letter she'd shoved in her reticule the day she arrived in Denver. "Oh, no! I haven't opened the letter."

"What letter?" Granny asked.

"The day I arrived a clerk gave me a letter. I shoved it in my reticule and forgot all about it." She jumped up from the table and ran to her bedroom.

When she came back downstairs she was holding the letter. She sat back down and looked at the envelope and immediately recognized the seal. "It's from Henri."

"Henri?" Rose repeated.

"Prince Henri d'Evereux." Emma opened the letter and started reading. She couldn't believe what she was reading. Henri was in America! He said he couldn't wait another year to see her again. He was in St. Louis, heading for Denver when he'd written this letter. He was coming to see her with the intention of courting her. Her eyes darted back to the date at the top of the letter. She mentally counted off the days. He could be in Denver any day now. She'd never expected he was so serious in his declaration of affection that he would actually follow her to Colorado. She couldn't deny he was handsome and charming, but he was a prince for heaven's sake. His world was light-years from hers, his background totally different from hers. She'd seen his lifestyle: servants seeing to his every need, guards surrounding him at all times, changing clothes ten times a day for whatever event was taking place. It all seemed so—unnecessary.

She'd dined with him several times before they'd left Europe, and the prince asked her to stay in France longer. But Andre had already arranged their tour schedule, and she didn't want to cancel any performances. If she had cancelled some of the performances, she wouldn't have stayed in Europe, she would have returned to Whispering Pines.

Then there was the fact that she wasn't ready to develop a serious relationship with anyone at this point in her life. It wasn't fame she sought. Most of the time she wished she wasn't recognized. Before all of the fanfare of her concert tour in Europe, few men had shown much of an interest in her. She'd always thought it was her height, or her off-putting direct manner that intimidated most men. But now, men seemed to be coming out of the woodwork to shower her with attention, and it made her uncomfortable. They didn't really know her on a personal level—they only knew her talent—and their sudden interest made her suspicious of their motives. Were they interested in her, or her fame? She had yet to figure out how she was to know the answer to that question. It was difficult for her to imagine that a prince wanted to court her, but at least she knew he was not interested in her fame.

She looked up from the letter to the questioning eyes of Rose and Granny. "He could be in Denver any day. He was in St. Louis when the letter was written."

"How exciting," Rose said. "Can you imagine a real prince coming here to see you?"

Emma shook her head. "I really don't know why he is wasting his time on me. I thought I made it clear to him I wasn't interested in marrying."

"Perhaps being a prince, he is not accustomed to a woman rejecting him," Granny replied.

"Are you not interested in marrying, or just not interested in marrying him?" Rose asked.

"I've never been in love, and while I like Henri, and naturally I'm flattered that he has an interest in courting me, I can't see what purpose it would serve." She explained her doubts about the sudden attention given that she was now considered famous. "Men weren't exactly beating down my door before my name became well-known."

"Maybe you didn't give them a chance. You are so self-sufficient that many men may be intimidated. I should think it would take more than an accomplished woman to intimidate a prince," Rose said.

"But I don't want to live in France," Emma said.

"Good," Rose said. She saw Granny glance her way, so she explained her feelings. "I'm sorry if that sounds selfish, but I want Emma to come home to live in Whispering Pines. I want her to have her babies here, so we can all be together and our children grow up together."

Emma laughed. "I may not marry and have babies, but it's been my plan to buy a ranch and live in Whispering Pines when the time is right. I have a nice nest egg now, and if I sing a few more years, I will have a secure future."

"Wouldn't you need a partner if you own a ranch?" Granny asked.

"I can hire a foreman," Emma said.

"I know Morgan would gladly help you," Rose said.

"I'm counting on it." Emma folded Henri's letter and stuck it in her pocket.

"Your prince is going to be disappointed to come all this way for naught," Granny said.

"I tried to make myself clear in Paris." Emma knew she had taken care not to do or say anything that might offer Henri encouragement. She specifically remembered telling him she planned to live in Whispering Pines when she stopped singing.

"There will be plenty of suitors in Whispering Pines when you are ready to settle down," Granny said.

Emma waggled her finger at Granny. "Don't go match-making. Anyway, we both know Rose and Addie already hooked the two most handsome men in Whispering Pines."

"They were fine catches, no doubt about it. But Clay might have given them a run for their money if given a chance." Granny remembered Morgan was jealous when he thought Clay had an interest in Rose. "Mark my words. You'll have men courting you if put out the right signals."

"I'm not interested in signals. I will sing for a while longer before I settle down."

A knock on the back door interrupted Granny's impending speech about Emma having children. Seeing her chance to put an end to Granny's schemes, Emma jumped up to answer the door.

"Good morning," Clay said when the door swung open and he saw Emma standing there.

Emma didn't know who she expected on their front porch so early in the morning, but it certainly wasn't the good pastor. "Good morning." Emma figured he wasn't there to see her, so she stepped aside and invited him into the kitchen. Her traitorous dog came running to him as though he were welcoming a long-lost friend.

Clay greeted Sweetie with an ear rub. "How's the big guy doing this morning?"

Granny was already out of her chair and grabbing a cup for coffee. "Clay, what brings you out here so early?"

"I came to apologize for getting sidetracked last night, and not saying good-bye to all of you. I didn't want you to add rudeness to my list of faults." Clay hung his coat and hat on the hook inside the door.

"Nonsense. No need for you to apologize about anything. Please sit down," Rose said. "Can we offer you some breakfast?"

Clay smiled. "I don't smell flapjacks, so I guess not."

Rose and Granny laughed, but Emma didn't understand the joke.

Granny glanced at Emma, and explained, "The last time Clay had breakfast with us Morgan challenged him to a flapjack-eating contest."

"Now, Granny, in all fairness, I didn't know it was a contest," Clay said.

"Morgan knew. That was all that mattered." Granny placed the cup of coffee in front of him. "He thought you were interested in Rose, and he wasn't about to let you get the better of him."

"Oh, Granny, Morgan thought no such thing," Rose said.

Clay and Granny chuckled at Rose's innocence. Rose had been completely unaware of what was happening that morning.

"Morgan was simply hungry that morning. If I recall correctly, he'd already been up for hours working on the ranch," Rose added.

Granny patted Rose on the shoulder before she sat back down. "You ask him about it sometime."

"How did the meeting go with Mrs. King?" Emma asked coolly.

On his ride to the ranch, Clay told himself he was coming to express his apology for being rude last night. He didn't come all this way to see Emma, yet he couldn't keep his eyes off of her. "I think it went well. She was delighted I invited her to church, and said if she is still in town, she will certainly join us."

Emma gave him a dubious look. "Did she mention if my outlaw brother would be joining her?" Emma knew her tone was sharp, but she intended to let him know she was still angry with him. Morgan had gone out of his way to take them back to church last night even though everyone was tired. They all agreed they wanted to show support for Clay. To Emma's way of thinking, he didn't seem to appreciate their effort. That was what angered her, not that he left them to talk to a beautiful young woman.

Clay could tell by Emma's tone that she wasn't pleased with him. He'd already seen for himself that she didn't hold back when she had something on her mind. "No, ma'am. She didn't mention Frank, nor did I."

"What was she like?" Granny asked. "Do you think she is the kind of woman who would plan a robbery with Frank?"

"No, Granny, I don't. She was a delightful young woman, extremely well-spoken and mannerly. Though she had been married for a short period of time, I believe she is quite naïve."

Emma almost snorted. She figured he was politely criticizing her for speaking her mind. Well, the devil with him. "Men are easily fooled by a pretty face. She left the judge when Frank came along. I wouldn't call that naïve."

Rose and Granny were surprised by Emma's harsh words, but they both remained quiet.

Clay ground his teeth together. He didn't want to say something to offend Granny's granddaughter. "I don't intend to pass judgment. I've always found it important to look at one's heart."

"So you could see her heart in such a short period of time?" Emma asked sweetly.

Clay took a sip of his coffee while he thought of a diplomatic response. "I think I could." Clay did think Leigh was a sweet, young woman. He thought Frank probably deceived her about his past, and being a trusting soul, she believed him.

"Do you think she didn't know what she was doing traveling alone with a man who wasn't her husband?" Emma continued. She wasn't buying Leigh King's innocent act for a minute.

Clay held his palms in the air. "I just asked her to join us at church. That's all. We didn't discuss her personal life." He didn't understand why Emma was grilling him. He'd come here to apologize, so he gulped back his coffee and stood. "I just wanted to say I didn't intend to be rude last night."

Emma bit her tongue to keep from saying he may not have intended to be rude, but he was rude.

"Don't worry about it, Clay. We didn't give it a second thought." Granny shot Emma a warning look, one of those looks she used to give her when she was a child, to let her know she'd overstepped her bounds. "It was nice of you to ask Mrs. King to church. If I see her again before Sunday, I will tell her she's welcome to sit with us."

Emma remained quiet. Granny had a way of making her point.

"Well, I must be on my way." Clay nodded to Rose and Granny before he left the table. "I'll see you Sunday."

"Emma will see you out." Granny fixed her eyes on Emma and inclined her head to let her know she should get out of her seat and see Clay to the door.

Emma jumped up and nearly ran to the door. She

reached for Clay's coat from the hook and threw it at him. She couldn't believe Granny thought she would be interested in *him*. It was obvious he was looking for a younger, more attractive woman—exactly like Leigh King. As soon as he got a look at Mrs. King last night in the restaurant, he'd stared at her through the entire meal. While Clay was buttoning his coat, Emma stood there tapping her toe, trying to hurry him along.

Last button fastened, Clay reached for his hat at the same time Emma snagged it from the hook. His hand covered hers and he yanked it back as though she'd stuck him with a hot poker. "Sorry."

Emma shoved his hat into his stomach, smashing it in the process. "No problem." She opened the door and nearly shoved him onto the porch. "Have a nice ride back to town." She tried to sound pleasant for Granny's benefit since she knew she was listening. All the while she was thinking, *I hope you freeze*. She slammed the door behind him.

Outside in the cold air, Clay took a deep breath, wondering what had just happened.

He'd intended to make amends this morning for his behavior last night. Morgan had invited him to dinner and he'd failed to say thank you. So much for good intentions. That woman—Emma—he'd thought about her all night. Why he was fool enough to do that, he didn't know. He walked down the stairs, stopped—and looked back at the closed door—shook his head, and turned to his horse. He reached for the reins wrapped around the post—but stopped. He turned back around and marched to the door. Frustrating woman. He rapped on the door with his fist.

Within seconds Emma opened the door again and glared at him. "Did you forget something?"

He hesitated. Why had he knocked on that door again? He was an idiot if he thought this woman had an interest in him. He cleared his throat. "Yes, I did."

"What? I gave you your hat and coat," she said impatiently.

He cleared his throat again. Maybe he was catching a cold. "Yes."

Silently Emma waited.

Hearing her toe tapping again, he took his hat off, bidding for more time to think through what he was about to say. "I thought—I'd invite you to dinner tomorrow night in town."

Emma's mouth dropped open, and no quick retort came to mind.

Clay almost smiled. Her toe tapping came to an abrupt halt. He doubted this formidable woman had been rendered speechless in her entire life. He didn't wait for a response. "I'll pick you up at five o'clock."

Sweetie nosed his way around Emma and jumped on Clay, and Clay rubbed his ears. "Bye, Sweetie." He turned around, walked down the stairs, reached for his reins, leapt in the saddle, and rode away. Never once did he look back, but he was confident she was still standing on the porch watching him.

Chapter Eight

By the time Clay arrived home he'd almost talked himself into turning around and heading back out to Morgan's ranch. He wanted to cancel the date he'd just made. What in the world had possessed him to do something so completely out of character? He hadn't invited a woman to dinner in years. Morgan and Jack both told him it was time for him to get on with living, but he shouldn't have listened to them. Why he'd decided to invite Emma, of all women, was a mystery to him. It wasn't as though she had given him any indication she was attracted to him. As a matter of fact, it seemed to him she went out of her way to be cool to him. He certainly didn't want to be attracted to her. On the other hand, he didn't want one of Granny's granddaughters to dislike him. He hadn't intended to ask her out; all he wanted to do was apologize for being rude last night. He didn't know what happened. One moment, he was thankful he got out of there with his skin intact—she seemed determined to flay him for some reason—and the next minute he was inviting her to dinner. She'd gotten under his skin, and he didn't understand why he didn't simply ignore her.

Tired of thinking about what to do, he made some

coffee, walked into the small parlor, and sat down. The woman gave him a headache. She wouldn't allow him to apologize, and she accused him of being rude when she was the one being rude. He finished his coffee, leaned back, and closed his eyes. He had to call on some of his parishioners this afternoon, but he felt as if his head were about to explode. He told himself he would relax for a few minutes and leave as soon as his head stopped throbbing.

"Violet! Violet!" Clay yelled through the white mist, but she wouldn't answer him. He repeated her name over and over, hoping she would hear him. In an instant the mist cleared, and he saw her walking toward him with a bouquet of wildflowers in her hand.

"Sit with me," she said, making her way to the blanket he'd placed on the ground. But she stopped and turned to her son behind her.

A moment later, Violet reached for Mark's hand, and together they started walking away from him. Violet turned back to him and smiled. "We will wait for you." He watched, feeling helpless as they disappeared. Why didn't she ask him to go with them?

"Wait!" He watched the spot where they had vanished for a long time, hoping they would return. Growing frustrated that he could no longer see them, he started to turn away, but he saw a flicker of movement. She was back! No, it wasn't Violet. The woman was tall, nothing like the delicate, petite woman he loved. It was Emma Langtry. He didn't want her here, not in this special place where he had asked Violet to marry him. It was their place, and Emma had no business intruding. "Why are you here?"

She gazed at him with her large blue eyes, but she didn't reply.

He wavered between telling her to go away, and a

longing he didn't understand. He felt angry with himself for wanting her to come closer. An instant passed, and Emma also disappeared.

He was sitting on the ground holding his dead wife and son in a field ablaze with colorful wildflowers. He wanted to be with them. He'd done everything he could to get himself killed. Each time he'd faced one of the killers who had murdered his wife and son, he'd pray that they'd kill him when he challenged them to a gunfight. But he was the one who always walked away. Was he left on this earth to endure the pain for some reason he didn't understand?

The dream changed yet again. He was standing in the middle of the street in Deadwood. He was facing down one of the men who had been on his ranch that day. He barely recognized himself. Four years of hate and seeking retribution had taken its toll. He'd become accustomed to surviving on little sleep, and rarely having a decent meal. He looked like a madman with his scruffy beard, long hair, and death in his eyes. He felt a weariness so deep in his bones that he wasn't certain he was human any longer. The man he once was no longer existed. Some said he was little better than the men he'd hunted down. They were right. He said something to the man he was going to kill. It didn't matter that he couldn't hear what he was saying, he knew the look in his own eyes. Like the other men he'd killed, he expected the man to say the same words. He wasn't the one who'd pulled the trigger that day, he wasn't the one who killed his wife and little boy. Clay didn't care. The man needed to die just like the other men who had been on his ranch that day. His hunt would end when he found the remaining two men who killed Violet and Mark. But until that day came, he wasn't going to leave any of the men breathing air that his wife and son could no longer breathe. Clay whipped his pistol out and shot the man dead before the man's pistol left his holster.

* * *

Clay awoke with a start. He knew he'd been dreaming of Violet and Mark. But then he remembered Emma was in this dream. She wasn't part of his past, and he felt the flame of resentment. He wouldn't allow her to interfere with his memories of his family. If the dreams ended, he might never see his wife and son again. And that was something he didn't know if he could live with. He'd loved his life on his ranch with his wife and son. He'd been happy then. They were the reason for his very existence; the motivation to get out of bed in the morning and work sixteen-hour days on the ranch. He could only relive those days in his dreams, but he couldn't let them go.

He felt like a dog chasing its tail. He loved seeing them, but the pain of waking always overwhelmed him. And he was reminded of the price he'd paid with his soul for his revenge. God forgive him. He bowed his head and prayed for forgiveness, the same prayer he'd said so many times before. Logic told him he'd been forgiven the first time he'd asked, but each time he remembered the men he'd killed, he felt the need to ask again.

He closed his eyes and thought of the day he'd asked Violet to marry him. It was a beautiful summer day, and he had placed the quilt by the lake—the special place where he'd planned for days to ask for her hand in marriage. He hadn't known Violet long—she'd only moved to Kansas a few months before—but he knew he loved her. He thought he fell in love from the moment he met her. She was everything a man could want, or need in a wife. Violet was as beautiful as her name, and she was the most gentle woman he'd ever known. She was young and naïve, but he looked forward to introducing her to the pleasures of married life.

He knew they'd face hardships—everyone did—but he envisioned a long and happy life together.

He leaned over and took her chin in his hand, urging her face closer to his. He was so close, all he had to do was lean in just a little bit and his lips would be covering hers. He did. The kiss was meant to be chaste, but when his lips met hers, he forgot all about his good intentions. The kiss was sensual, and he was overcome with longings he'd been able to control until that moment. He'd tempted fate, and his self-control was nearly lost. Before he considered the consequences of what he was doing, he wrapped his arms around her and pulled her on top of him as he stretched out on his back.

Violet immediately pulled away and scooted off his body. "Clay, what on earth are you doing? You know that isn't proper."

Clay ran a hand over his face, and squeezed the bridge of his nose between his thumb and forefinger. No, he hadn't been proper; he'd lost his head. "I can't take it anymore, Violet, you have to marry me."

Violet laced him with a look that he'd not seen before. For someone so gentle, he thought he was getting a glimpse of Violet annoyed for the first time. Yet the inflection in her voice didn't change. "What do you mean, you can't take it anymore? Am I so terrible to *take?*"

Clay straightened and looked her in the eye. "No, honey, I don't mean it that way. I mean I want to marry you. I would right this minute if you will have me." When she remained quiet, he said, "You know we've been seeing each other for a few months now. Don't you want to marry me?"

She smiled up at him sweetly. "How many children do you want?"

Clay didn't know if she was laying a trap for him, but

either way, he thought he was man enough for the job. "We can have one a year if you want."

Violet laughed. "Well, maybe not that many." She looked thoughtful for a moment, then asked, "What if we have daughters instead of sons?"

He leaned in and nuzzled her neck. "That's fine with me, as long as they look like you."

She turned her head to him so he would kiss her again. "Are you positive you want to marry me?"

Clay pulled away; this time he was the one with questions. He'd thought from the day they met that they would marry, but she may have changed her mind. "Yes, I'm positive. Do you want to marry me?"

"Yes, I do."

"Then what are we waiting for? The sooner we marry, the sooner we can—" He kissed her again to get his point across.

"Father will be back later today. You can speak to him then."

"Let's marry this Saturday." Clay didn't think he had the restraint to stay away from her much longer.

She smiled. "Saturday would be perfect."

"Why were you so rude to Clay this morning?" Rose asked when she was alone with Emma, cooking dinner.

"Rude? Me?" Emma asked innocently. "He was the one who was rude. Not even saying good-bye to Morgan last night after he was kind enough to include him in our dinner party."

"But he came here specifically to apologize," Rose reminded her.

Emma shrugged. "The point is, he should have been more mannerly last night."

Rose frowned at her. "No, that is not the point. You were rude and you know it."

Emma didn't want to discuss Clay Hunt. Yes, she had been rude, and she didn't know why. She'd asked herself the same question a thousand times today. She'd also asked herself why she hadn't refused his dinner invitation. He might be the last man she wanted to dine with. "Do you want me to peel the potatoes for dinner?"

"That would be very helpful," Rose replied. She knew her sister was thinking over her question. She'd always been evasive when she didn't want to talk about something.

"You were terrible to him," Rose said.

Emma made a face at her sister, and then threw her hands in the air. "I was terrible, wasn't I? Why do you think he was so interested in talking to Frank's girlfriend? Don't you think that was odd? Did you notice how he kept staring at her all through dinner? Now *that* was rude. He ignored all of us."

Rose thought about Clay's actions last night. She had noticed that he seemed particularly interested in Leigh King. "I think he felt sorry for her. He was on that stagecoach with me, and he saw firsthand how Frank acted. He probably just wants to save her from Frank."

Emma was skeptical. "I think it's more than that. I think he's interested in her."

Rose didn't get her meaning. "He's the pastor of the town and he takes an interest in the people here."

"I mean I think he's interested in her, not as a pastor, but as a man."

"You aren't serious," Rose said.

"Very serious. Being a pastor doesn't mean he can't be smitten with a woman. He's not married, is he?"

Rose thought Emma was acting like she was a wronged woman. "Are you jealous?"

"Jealous? Why should I be jealous? I don't even know the man." Emma told herself it wasn't jealousy, she simply didn't approve of rude behavior.

"Maybe you want to know him better," Rose suggested.

"I most certainly do not. What do you really know about him?"

"I met him on the stagecoach from Boston. We rode all the way together, and he was a perfect gentleman. Morgan and Jack both like and respect him. What more do I need to know?" Rose asked.

"Where did he preach before he came here? Why did he come to a small town like Whispering Pines to preach? If he is so good, why isn't he preaching in a larger town like Boston?"

Rose looked at her sister. "Why do I need to know all of those things to know that he is a good person? Besides, Granny wrote to churches to see if they could recommend someone, and she was given Clay's name. I don't think we could have found a more worthy man."

"People are often not what they seem," Emma countered.

Rose smiled. "Then why didn't you tell him not to bother picking you up tomorrow night if you are so concerned about his character?"

Now that was a question Emma couldn't answer. "When he arrives, I may tell him I changed my mind."

Granny walked into the room, and she'd overheard the last part of their conversation. "No, you won't. If you do not want to go to dinner with Clay, you can take yourself into town early enough to tell him before he makes that ride out here in a buggy. I won't have you being unkind to anyone, especially Clay."

Rose and Emma exchanged a look of surprise.

"Granny, I was teasing. I wouldn't really do him that way," Emma said.

Granny seemed appeased, and smiled at her eldest granddaughter. "I'm glad. I would hate to think you've changed that much. I understand you've always been quick to give your opinions, but Clay is a good man. No, he hasn't been a perfect man his whole life, but he's suffered because of his choices. He's also had a lot of sadness."

"What kind of sadness?" Emma asked.

"That's not for me to say. If he wants you to know, he'll tell you. Of course, he might be a bit more inclined to tell you things if you treat him a little nicer."

Emma hadn't made up her mind if she wanted to know anything about Clay. What was the purpose? He'd obviously set his sights on Mrs. King.

"You might also remember how he stood up for you in church. I can tell you some of the members were mighty angry at him for going to Denver," Granny reminded her.

"I don't understand why he came to the performance if he knew he was going against their wishes," Emma said.

"He had the gumption not to back down," Granny said. "You heard what he told them. He was supporting a member of the church family, and that a pastor would do the greatest good where sin abounds."

Chapter Nine

After midnight, Dutch Malloy led the gang through the meandering trails in Purgatory Canyon. At his instruction, they dressed in dark clothing, and rode quietly through the canyon floor. He'd learned the hard way that sounds carried a long way in this canyon. Lawmen, just like outlaws, usually made the same mistake of giving away their location by doing something stupid. Dutch planned to take the men to Frank's hideout, a place that had proven to be safe for them between rustles. Frank always said he'd never seen anyone near the place.

Dutch figured since Frank was the only one in the gang without a bounty on his head, they'd never see him again. And that fact rubbed Dutch the wrong way. Frank had the good fortune to marry a judge's daughter, but that didn't make it right that he wasn't on a wanted poster like the rest of them. Dutch had never had Frank's luck, but he hoped that was about to change. The best way he could get back at Frank Langtry was to find Culpepper and Taggart and steal back their money. If what they had heard was true, Culpepper and Taggart had been holed up in Purgatory Canyon since they'd robbed them. He figured that was good news since they couldn't exactly spend money in

Purgatory Canyon. If they were able to get the money back, Dutch planned to make certain Frank found out. Harper wasn't a wanted man, and when he rode back to Denver, he could let Frank know about the money. Dutch knew he could count on Frank to show up if he knew they had stolen the money back from Culpepper and Taggart. This time, Dutch planned to settle the score with Frank.

Almost two hours had passed before they found the small cabin. Dutch rode to the lean-to they'd constructed the last time they were there to shelter their animals.

"I'd say this is a good hideout. I'm surprised you found it in the first place," Harper said.

"Frank found it a long time ago," Dutch said. "I figure tomorrow we'll go down to the area where we will have a bird's-eye view of who is coming and going in the canyon. Frank said there are more cabins, so maybe we'll get lucky and spot some smoke. If Culpepper and Taggart are in here, you can bet they have a fire in this weather."

"I already smelled smoke before we entered the canyon," Harper said.

Dutch didn't doubt Harper's word; he'd never met a more experienced tracker.

"Don't that mean they can spot the fire from our cabin?" Corbin asked.

"Frank told me that's why he liked this spot. The fire couldn't be seen from the other cabins in the canyon. Let's just hope they don't have Harper's nose. If that old Sioux hasn't died, he'll know where Culpepper and Taggart are hiding out. I brought some whiskey for him in case he doesn't feel like talking."

"Do you know his hideout?" Harper asked.

"Yeah, Frank showed me. It's a ways from here. We'll have to wait until morning. I don't think I can find it in the dark," Dutch replied.

Before dawn, Deke and Corbin left the cabin and made their way up on a top ledge to see if they could spot smoke, while Dutch and Harper went in search of Indian Pete. They were within ten feet of the old man's cabin, when they heard the distinct sound of a hammer being cocked back behind them.

"What do you want?" Indian Pete asked.

Dutch turned slowly to face the older man with his hands in the air. "We want to talk. You remember me? I was with Frank Langtry last time I was here."

"I remember Langtry." Indian Pete spat on the ground as if saying Frank's name left a bad taste in his mouth.

"We ain't with Frank now. We're looking for some men that we think are hiding out in here. Killers by the name of Culpepper and Taggart."

Indian Pete gave Dutch a blank stare, and Dutch made a move to reach inside his coat pocket for the whiskey bottle he'd brought along. "I brought whiskey." At Pete's nod, Dutch pulled the bottle from his pocket.

"Why are you looking for these two men?"

"Like I said, they are killers and they robbed us. We want what they took from us."

The old man turned his eyes on Harper. "I've not seen you here before."

"I've not been here," Harper said simply.

"What did these men take?"

Dutch didn't hesitate to tell the truth. "Money, guns, and all of our supplies. Killed one of our men." Dutch removed the cap from the whiskey bottle and passed it to the old man.

Uncocking his rifle, Indian Pete held it with one hand as he accepted the bottle. "Those men are here." He pointed to a rock, indicating the men should sit. After he took a drink, he handed the bottle back to Dutch. Dutch took a swig and gave it to Harper.

"Do you know where?" Dutch asked.

Indian Pete nodded. "I know."

"If you point the way, I'll leave you with some money," Dutch said.

"I'm an old man. I need supplies for winter. I don't leave this canyon anymore."

Dutch looked at the old Indian's sun-weathered face, thinking he looked more like his saddle than man. He was so thin, a stiff wind could blow him over the canyon walls. Dutch couldn't imagine what it would be like to survive in this canyon for years. Frank had spent a lot of time in this canyon, and Dutch wondered if that was what was wrong with him. Half the time, he thought Frank was plumb loco. Indian Pete had been captive to the rocks for so many years, it was surprising he wasn't part of the landscape by now. "I'll leave you all of our supplies, and whatever Culpepper and Taggart have with them, you can keep."

Those terms agreed with the old man. "I'll lead you to the cabin."

"Do they know you are in this canyon?" Harper asked.

"No. They've never seen me. But they are not at their cabin."

"What do you mean?" Dutch said.

"They rode out this morning, but they are coming back."

"How do you know?" Harper asked.

"They left their supplies and two pack horses," the old Sioux said.

"Show us the way," Dutch said.

Dutch whistled for Deke and Corbin to follow them as the old man led them halfway around the canyon on foot. Dutch had to hand it to the old man; he was as surefooted as a mule, and he knew how to fade into the rock. Dutch thought the old Sioux was more like a ghost than man. He wondered how Frank ever saw him in the first place. The tiny shack where Culpepper and Taggart were hiding out was well concealed by the inhospitable landscape. Dutch didn't think they would have ever found the place without the old Indian's help.

Harper walked to the back of the shack and found the horses. Deke took a position in the rocks above the cabin to watch the entryway to the canyon. If the killers returned while they were searching the shack, Deke could signal from his location. Dutch, Corbin, and the old man walked inside. Just as Indian Pete said, Culpepper and Taggart had left a lot of supplies behind.

"Wonder where they went?" Corbin asked.

"They've left before, but they come back the next day," Indian Pete said.

"If we take their supplies, do you think they will find you?" Dutch asked the old man.

"They will never find me." The old Sioux had hidden out in these rocks too many years to be careless.

Harper stuck his head inside the door. "Dutch, come to the back of the cabin. I think I found what you are looking for."

Reaching the back of the cabin, Harper led them to a rocky ledge where someone had gone to some trouble to cover the opening beneath the ledge with some brush. Harper had shoved the dead brush aside, and Dutch kneeled down on one knee and looked under the ledge. He couldn't believe his eyes. Saddlebags, guns, rifles, everything Culpepper and Taggart had stolen from them that night in the shack outside of Whispering Pines was under the ledge. He looked up at Harper and shook his head. "How'd you see this?"

Harper grinned. "It was the dead brush stuffed into the opening. It didn't look natural."

"This is everything they stole from us that night." Dutch started pulling out their belongings. When he realized the saddlebags were full, he tore into one. "Well, I'll be. I ain't never been this lucky in my entire worthless life. I thought Frank Langtry had all of the luck, not me. No, sir, not me." He pulled a fistful of money from the saddlebag. "As Frank always said, I think Providence just smiled on me."

"Don't count it now. Let's take everything and get the heck out of here," Harper said.

"You're right. We need to walk out of here fast." The men threw the saddlebags on their shoulders while Indian Pete loaded the supplies from the cabin in a knapsack.

On the way to their cabin, the old man turned to take a different trail, and Dutch said, "You sure they don't know the location of your cabin?"

"They will not find me," Pete replied.

"We're going to ride out of here. We'll leave our supplies in the cabin; they are yours for your help. I have a few more bottles of whiskey, too." Dutch wanted to be long gone before Culpepper and Taggart came back.

The old man nodded and disappeared into the brush.

The men wasted no time saddling their horses as soon as they got back to their cabin. "When we get out of this canyon, we'll ride until we find a safe place for the night, and we'll split the money then," Dutch said.

They rode out of Purgatory as if Satan were nipping at their heels. They didn't slow until they'd ridden for two hours, and only stopped so the horses could rest. They continued on at a more casual pace, pausing every hour to give the horses a breather, until it was too dark to go on. They'd ridden north thinking that would be the only direction they might not run into Culpepper and Taggart.

Harper dismounted and looked back over the land they'd just covered. "I swear I think someone is dogging us."

Dutch turned to look. "I didn't see anything amiss."

Harper shrugged. "Maybe too many years of watching my back." He tossed his saddlebags on the ground, then lifted his stirrup to loosen his girth, but hesitated. The hairs on his neck told him he wasn't imagining things. He dropped the stirrup back down. "I think I'll just go have a look before we settle in for the night."

"We'll wait before we start a fire," Dutch said.

"Just to be on the safe side, ride west for a spell. I'll catch up to you," Harper said.

"Sounds good."

Dutch, Deke, and Corbin rode west for two hours before they stopped to wait for Harper to show. They were freezing, but they didn't want to start a fire and give away their location. Dutch knew Harper would find them. Finally they heard a horse coming through the trees, but in case it wasn't Harper, they hid behind some boulders with guns at the ready.

"It's me, boys," Harper said.

Dutch walked from the brush. "What'd you find?"

"We're being followed, but it's not Culpepper and Taggart. Two lawmen, and one I recognize from Denver. Sheriff Trent."

"That probably means U.S. Marshal Holt is riding with him," Deke said.

"They could be looking for Culpepper and Taggart," Corbin said.

"Yeah, but they could be looking for us, too," Dutch said. "How long you reckon we have before they catch up to us?"

"They stopped and built a fire. But that could mean they were trying to throw us off, or they decided to get after us again at first light." Harper had a bad feeling that these two lawmen were not planning on resting long.

"What's your best guess, Harper?" If there ever was a man Dutch respected more than Harper for his trail savvy, he hadn't met him yet.

Harper rubbed his whiskers. "I think they are trying to throw us off. They'll be on our tail after the horses rest for a spell."

Dutch looked at the men. "Do you want to split up, or stay together?"

"I say we stay together," Deke said.

"Me, too," Corbin added.

"Let's split this money up real quick." Dutch didn't say it aloud, but he was thinking if the shooting started, then one or two of them might live to spend the money.

They pulled out all of the money, and Dutch started dividing it in four stacks.

"I don't feel right about taking a fourth of the cut. I didn't do much for it," Harper said.

"That was our deal, and if not for you, we wouldn't have found it anyway. You didn't have to show me that hiding spot, Harper. I would have never thought that brush was out of place. You could have kept it all to yourself." Dutch thought Harper more than earned his money by being so perceptive. He glanced at Deke and Corbin, and they were both nodding their heads in agreement.

"I appreciate it, Dutch. And if you boys don't mind, I'm going to go ahead and head back to Denver so I can leave this money with my sister."

"You think it's safe for you to ride to Denver?" Dutch asked.

"I'll take the scenic route." Harper debated whether to

tell Dutch the reason he wanted to get the money to his sister, but he thought it was only fair. "Dutch, I didn't want to say earlier, but I saw the doctor in Denver, and he says I don't have much time left."

Dutch was taken by surprise. "What do you mean?"

"I got cancer. I want to make sure my sister gets this money before I go toes up," Harper said.

Dutch put his hand on Harper's shoulder. He became emotional thinking about never seeing his friend again. "You should have said something sooner."

"I was going to Mexico knowing it could be one of the last jobs where I could make some good money. You've given me a way to leave my sister something so she won't have to worry about raising those kids by herself."

"If—well, if anything happens to you, I'll look in on her if I ain't dead, or in the hoosegow," Dutch said.

Dutch's promise meant a lot to Harper, and his voice cracked with emotion when he responded. "I appreciate that, Dutch."

The two men shook hands, and Dutch finished counting the money. "It looks like they spent some, but we each get almost nine thousand dollars."

Deke and Corbin smiled, but Harper's features were grim. "I don't want to spoil your fun, but you boys be careful. With that bounty on your head, all sorts of killers will be looking to make a buck. Maybe you should consider hiding the money somewhere, and take your chances by turning yourselves in. No one has to know you have the money, and if you tell them you didn't shoot anyone, that it was Frank, maybe they'll go easy on you."

Dutch knew Harper had a point. They might do some time in the territorial prison, but if they didn't turn themselves in, they stood a good chance of being killed for the bounty. "Harper's right. We might do better with the law."

Deke took the money Dutch handed him. "I ain't going to prison."

Dutch handed Corbin his money. "What about you, Corbin? There's no poster on you. I think it'd be wise for you to take off alone."

"I hate leaving you boys," Corbin said.

Harper glanced at Dutch, and said, "I don't want you boys getting killed. Life is short enough when the law ain't chasing you."

Dutch gave Harper his cut, and then stood there staring at his share of the money for several seconds. The other men were waiting to hear what he had to say. He released a deep breath, and extended his money to Harper. "Take this to your sister. Tell her I may be in jail for a spell, but when I get out, I'll come for it. If she needs it before I'm out, tell her I understand. When I get out of jail she can count on me to take care of her the rest of her life, and her kids. If she'll have me. You can rest easy, Harper."

Harper choked up and could hardly speak. "I think she'll like that idea just fine." He knew his sister had always had a soft spot for Dutch, but Harper always told her not to hold out hope. Dutch had always been a wild one, and Harper wasn't certain he'd ever settle down and go straight.

"I'll be good to her, Harper. You've got my word on that."

Harper took the money, unbuttoned his coat, and stuffed the cash inside his shirt. If the lawmen caught up with him, he figured he would show them what was in his saddlebags if asked. The way he saw it, the law had no reason to be looking for him.

Deke and Corbin looked at each other. They'd never ridden without Dutch.

"You leaving us here?" Corbin asked.

"I'll ride toward the lawmen. That'll give them some time trying to figure out what to do with me." Dutch fixed his eyes on Deke. "Deke, you could always give your money to Harper. Both of us could go to jail, and they'd never have to know we have the money. We'll tell them we were robbed by Culpepper and Taggart, and that Frank was in on it from the get-go. When we get out of jail, we'll have a nice little nest egg." He turned his eyes on Corbin. "Corbin, you need to go with Harper."

Deke took his money out of his saddlebag and handed it to Harper. "Dutch trusts you, so I reckon I will too. Heck, I ain't never spent more than a night or two in jail, but I guess it makes more sense than always looking over my shoulder waiting for someone to collect a bounty."

Corbin finally made a decision. "Harper, you mind if I tag along with you?"

"Not at all. We'll be in Denver by the time Deke and Dutch get there." Harper put a hand on Dutch's shoulder. "You two keep your story straight. Culpepper and Taggart robbed you of the money, nothing else. Tell them where those two are hiding and offer to help them. That might go a long way with the judge. Your money will be waiting with my sister if I'm gone. You can trust her."

"If those two lawmen have been following us, they'll know there were four of us," Dutch said. "I'll tell them two friends just happened on us and rode a while with us."

Harper shook their hands. "Give them my name; they'll know me. Tell them I'm headed to Denver, and I'll say Corbin has been with me for a while. I hope I see you boys again."

Chapter Ten

Clay Hunt was right on time to pick Emma up the following night. He couldn't say he wasn't nervous, because he was. The last time he had been this tense thinking about a date was when he was a young man and he'd asked a girl to his first dance. Good manners had been the only thing that kept him from breaking the engagement with Emma.

When Morgan opened the door, he thought Clay looked like he was on the verge of running like a scared rabbit. "Clay, come on in." Morgan pointed to the parlor. "Can I get you some coffee?"

"No, thanks." Once he became a pastor, he no longer imbibed in spirits, but if anything made him inclined to reconsider that decision, it would be facing Miss Emma Langtry tonight.

"So you're taking Emma to dinner," Morgan said, grinning. He could tell Clay was nervous and he was enjoying every minute of it.

"That's the plan." Clay paced the room instead of sitting.

"That Emma is quite a character," Morgan said.

Clay looked at him, waiting for him to expound on that

statement. When Morgan didn't say more, he said, "What do you mean?"

Morgan chuckled. "I mean any man who would make a wrong move on her would have his head handed to him on a platter. That's one woman who can take care of herself."

Recalling how Emma had stood up to Frank, Clay couldn't disagree with that statement. So why was he standing here ready to stick his neck out waiting for that platter like a Christmas turkey? He had no reasonable answer to that question. He stopped pacing and glanced Morgan's way. "I asked her to dinner so Granny would know I support her granddaughter."

Morgan gave him a long look. "Really? I think after your sermon, everyone in Whispering Pines is aware you support Emma Langtry."

Clay nodded, and started pacing again. Then he abruptly stopped and turned toward Morgan. "I want her to feel welcome."

"Uh-huh."

Three more steps—stop. "It's important for the congregation to know they can count on their pastor."

"Uh-huh."

Three steps—stop. He glanced at Morgan again, primed to say more, but he couldn't think of one more thing to say.

"Are you ready?"

At her question, Clay's eyes slid to the doorway. There stood Emma wearing a beautiful red dress, much finer than any woman in Whispering Pines normally wore. Clay felt as though his feet had taken root to the floorboards. Heaven help him, she would no doubt attract a lot of attention in that dress. The color was definitely not going to blend into the background. He thought she looked beautiful, but as a pastor, he didn't want to be forced to confront men who might gawk at her.

Seeing Clay wasn't saying anything, Morgan said, "That's some dress." He glanced back at Clay and almost burst out laughing at the expression on his face. In case the pastor hadn't figured it out yet, he was definitely smitten with Emma. "Don't you think she looks beautiful, Clay?"

Emma gave Morgan a look that said he was going to pay for that comment the next time she saw him.

Clay managed to nod as he cleared his throat. "May I help you with your cloak?"

Emma handed her fur-trimmed cloak to him. "Thank you." Emma could tell he didn't care for her dress. He was trying to cover her up as fast as he could. She'd chosen this particular dress specifically to make him uncomfortable. That's what he got for acting so smug when he'd caught her off guard and asked her to dinner. It was obvious he'd only asked her out because of Granny. He'd mentioned several times how kind Granny had been to him after he'd arrived in Whispering Pines. No doubt he would have preferred she wore something a bit more sedate and boring. If he thought she would dress to please him, then he didn't know Emma Langtry. Granny made it clear she would be upset if she cancelled the date, but that didn't mean she couldn't make him regret asking.

"It's starting to snow, so I brought along extra blankets." He was making idle conversation just to take his mind off of her dress. When he draped Emma's cloak over her shoulders, he noticed how good she smelled.

"When can we expect you two kids home?" Morgan said.

"Obviously after dinner," Emma retorted with more than a hint of sarcasm in her voice.

Morgan opened the front door for them, and saw the snow was picking up speed. "It could get bad out there before you two make it home."

"Would you prefer to make it another night?" Emma

asked, thinking that he had to be having second thoughts about this date after seeing her red dress.

Clay felt he'd lost his mind asking her to dinner in the first place, and it was tempting to say they should postpone. But he'd come this far, so he was determined to see things through. "If it is too bad after dinner, you can always stay at the hotel for the night."

Hearing he didn't want to cancel made her feel like smiling, and she didn't know why. She wanted to cancel the date, didn't she? She looked at Morgan and said, "Don't worry if we are not back at a reasonable hour. You'll know I decided to stay at the hotel." She petted Sweetie good-bye. "You stay here tonight."

"I'll look after Sweetie," Morgan said. "You two kids have fun."

Emma laced him with a look that would have made a lesser man tuck tail and hide.

Even wrapped in two blankets, Emma was shivering on the way to town, but she didn't dare sit too close to Clay to find warmth. If they happened on someone, the gossips would have his reputation ruined before sunrise. While she didn't mind raising a few eyebrows with her red dress, she didn't want to cause real harm with his church members. Still, she thought it was unfair that he seemed impervious to the cold while her teeth were chattering.

Clay tried to think of small talk on the way to town, but he was out of practice courting a woman. Most of his conversation was asking her if she was cold. It seemed like an inane question since he could see her shivering. He briefly thought about putting his arm around her and pulling her close. As far away as she was sitting on the seat, he didn't think that would be a good move unless he wanted to lose an arm. Even though there was some space between them, he could still smell her perfume. She smelled delicious. His wife didn't wear perfume. No—he'd promised himself he wouldn't think about Violet tonight.

Finally arriving at the hotel, Clay quickly ushered Emma into the restaurant. He chose a table near the blazing fireplace, and moved it even closer to the fire. "You should be warm soon. I'll take the horse to the livery and be right back."

He hurried to the livery and then ran back to the hotel. There were a few diners entering the restaurant, but it looked as though the crowd would be thin tonight.

She'd watched him as he walked back into the restaurant. He was tall, and while she wouldn't consider him thin, he wasn't overly muscular. Something about the way he moved, the way he noted everyone around him, told her he was a man keenly aware of his surroundings. And that made her think there was more to this man than she knew.

After the waitress brought the coffee Emma ordered while waiting on Clay, she looked at him and asked, "Why did you invite me to dinner?"

"Shouldn't I have asked?" While Clay was not accustomed to such a straightforward woman, he liked her candor. In fact, he admired her for asking what she wanted to know without resorting to feminine wiles.

"I know some of the church members didn't approve of you seeing my performance. I would think I'm the last person you would want to be seen with."

"Maybe I wanted to get to know you," he replied, surprising himself with his revelation.

She stared directly into his warm amber eyes. He was a confident man, and a man who wouldn't hesitate to be truthful. "Do you?"

There it was, Clay thought. Time for truth. But what was the truth? She was the one who intruded on his dream with his wife. He didn't understand it, but somehow he knew it was important. He hadn't taken the time to think through what he was willing to reveal tonight. Someday maybe he'd need to tell her everything, but he didn't think the time was right. "Yes."

"Why?"

Clay picked up the cup of coffee the waitress delivered at some point. He took a sip, stalling for time while he thought about how to respond. "I'm not sure why. Do you need to know right now?"

Emma considered his question. Granny had always told her she was too impatient. "I don't suppose I need to know this minute."

Clay leaned a bit closer to her, placed his hand over hers, and lowered his voice. "Why did you accept my invitation?"

For the first time in her life, Emma knew what it felt like to blush. When his warm hand touched hers, she felt a shiver all the way down her spine. "Do you need to know this very minute?"

Clay grinned at her. "I don't suppose I need to know this minute."

Emma was lost in his mind-boggling smile. Why did Rose always have to be right? He was so devastatingly handsome, he took her breath away. She couldn't stop looking at his mouth. What would it feel like to be kissed by him? Oddly enough, she wondered if he had reservations about kissing a woman since he was a pastor.

She'd never asked Granny if her grandfather had taken her breath away. Now that she thought about it, she didn't need to ask. She remembered the way her grandparents looked at each other. It was a look that said theirs was a deep, loving union, with a shared intimacy that can only happen when two souls are destined to be together. Was Clay a man who could look at a woman like that? Had he looked at a woman like that in his past? Had he been in love?

Though they chitchatted throughout dinner, neither one was at ease. A nervous tension filled the air, yet, they didn't want the dinner to end. It was Emma who mentioned it was time to leave due to the late hour. "I think they are ready to close. Perhaps we should start home."

Clay looked around the room, and was surprised to see they were the only two people remaining. "Yes, I think we should."

Reaching the lobby, they saw it was snowing harder than before they'd arrived. "I guess this means I will have to stay the night," Emma said.

Clay agreed, and they walked to the desk where Emma registered. The clerk handed her the key, but Clay took it from him. "I'll walk you to your room."

Emma waited until they were far enough away from the clerk so he couldn't hear their conversation. "That may not be a good idea." She gave a slight incline of her head toward the clerk. "Someone may get the wrong impression. You know the damage wagging tongues can do."

Clay nodded. He walked back to the clerk. "Jimmy, I'll be back down in a minute, so would you have the restaurant slice me a piece of that apple pie to take home with me? And would you have someone take some warm water to Miss Langtry's room, and anything else she might need? She didn't plan on spending the night in town, but the weather has forced her to do so."

"Yes, sir," Jimmy replied.

Clay reached for Emma's elbow and escorted her up the staircase. Reaching her room, Clay opened the door and

stuck his head inside to make certain it was empty. He
turned to her and placed the key in her hand. "Keep your
door locked. The hotel is safe, but you don't want anyone
walking into the wrong room by mistake."

"Thank you for a lovely dinner." She'd been tense during
dinner, and that in itself was a unique experience for her.
She'd dined with a prince and hadn't been nervous. The attraction she was feeling was uncharted territory for her.

Clay leaned over slightly, and Emma thought he was
going to kiss her. He looked into her eyes and the anticipa-
tion mounted. Emma could almost feel his lips on hers, but
instead of kissing her on the lips, he took her hand in his
and brought her fingers to his lips. His lips lingered on the
back of her hand for seconds longer than anyone watching
would deem appropriate. "Thank you for accompanying
me to dinner, Miss Langtry."

If she'd dropped into a puddle at his feet at that moment,
she wouldn't have been surprised. He completely overwhelmed her senses. Granny had mentioned how charming
he could be. "Good night."

"I will see you in the morning. Perhaps we can have
breakfast before I take you home."

"Seven?" Emma managed to ask.

"Yes, ma'am. If you need anything, have someone come
and get me."

Emma had a restless night. She hadn't been able to get
the charming Clay Hunt out of her head. She could tell he
was nervous at dinner, just as she was. It made sense
they would both be tentative around each other. After all,
they were the most unlikely pair, and she'd certainly never
expected to be so attracted to him.

She got up early to dress for breakfast. The clerk was

nice enough to bring her some items for her toilette last night, but unfortunately she was wearing the same dress. She scolded herself for not packing a bag last night. Few people were in the restaurant last night, but her red dress was certain to attract a lot of attention in the light of day. She prayed the snow would prevent people from venturing outside to breakfast at the hotel.

Her excitement at seeing Clay this morning was building as she left her room and headed to the restaurant. When she reached the doorway leading to the restaurant, her excitement quickly disappeared. She spotted Clay seated at a table with a woman. Even though the woman's back was to her, she recognized Leigh King. Emma felt her temper rising. She wasn't going to interrupt their conversation, so she decided she would go back upstairs to retrieve her cloak and walk to the livery. She wondered why he'd invited her to breakfast as he obviously had other plans. Why didn't he just invite Mrs. King to dinner last night too?

Clay saw Emma just as she turned from the door. "Emma. Wait." Within seconds, he was by her side. "Didn't you see me?"

"I see you are busy," Emma responded.

Remembering Emma's reaction the last time he'd stopped to talk to Leigh, he wanted to avoid any misunderstanding. "She happened by my table, and I invited her to join us."

"Us?" Emma stopped abruptly and Clay nearly ran into her. She started to point out that he was sitting there alone when the pretty widow happened by, but she forced herself to be civil. "I'm really not hungry. I'm going to the livery." Emma didn't consider herself a particularly attractive woman, and certainly next to Leigh King she knew she couldn't compare. She briefly considered Clay might be

using her to make Mrs. King jealous. Maybe he wanted her
to think he was much in demand by the opposite sex. She
grudgingly admitted that would be out of character for
him. She regretted not cancelling their dinner, no matter
what Granny said. Well, no matter. She was going home,
and it wouldn't be necessary for her to be in his company
again.

"Why are you going to the livery?" Clay asked.

"For a buckboard to go home." She turned from him
and started to walk away. "Good morning."

He reached for her arm and pulled her to a halt. "I
brought you to town, and I'm taking you home."

She glanced toward the restaurant, and saw the woman
waiting for him. "Once again, I think you have a prior
engagement. She is waiting for you. I am not."

Realizing she was angry with him, Clay released her
arm. He didn't know what to say, so he remained silent as
he watched her walk away.

After she retrieved her cloak from her room, she returned to the desk to settle her bill.

"Pastor Hunt took care of the bill last evening," the
clerk told her.

"You can give Pastor Hunt his money back. I will pay
for my room."

"He thought you didn't bring money with you," the
clerk explained.

Emma figured Clay had said as much to the clerk to
keep him from gossiping. "Well, I did bring my money,
and here you go." She pulled money from her reticule and
placed it on the counter. After she settled with the clerk,
Emma didn't spare a glance into the restaurant. She headed
for the door of the hotel, but she thought she heard her
brother's voice coming from inside the restaurant. She
turned around, walked back to the doorway of the restaurant

and peeked inside. Sure enough, there was Frank leaning over the table shouting at Clay.

"You stay away from her!"

"Frank, this is the pastor," Leigh said. "Why are you so angry?"

"Shut up, Leigh," Frank said.

"But, Frank . . ." Leigh stopped when Frank turned his icy eyes on her.

Clay stood, and being several inches taller than Frank, he hoped Frank would think he was threatening enough without a pistol. "Frank, why don't you calm down and have a seat?"

"I'm telling you to stay away from her. If you're man enough, we can settle this in the street right now."

Emma decided she'd heard enough. Frank had just called Clay out, and she couldn't let this continue. She hurried to the table and said to Clay, "There you are. I've been waiting to leave. Are you ready?"

Frank glared at Emma. "The pastor is busy right now."

Clay didn't know why Emma was intervening when she'd just made it perfectly clear she didn't want to be near him. He reached for her elbow and pulled her to his side, and away from Frank. "Frank, I told you I don't carry a weapon. I have no reason to have a gunfight with you."

"I'll lend you a gun. Come on, Preacher, you don't want to look like the coward you are in front of the ladies." Frank's eyes darted from Leigh to Emma. "I guess you must fancy yourself as some kind of ladies' man."

"It's not like that, Frank," Leigh said. "He invited me to church services. He was making me feel welcome here. I'm lonely when you're not here."

Frank ignored Leigh and glared at Clay. "What's it going to be, Preacher?"

"As I said, I have no reason to fight you, Frank. Mrs. King

is telling you the truth. I invited her to our services, nothing more." Clay watched Frank's every move. He didn't trust him for a second, but he wasn't going to be goaded into a gunfight.

"It's like I thought, you're a coward," Frank said.

"Frank, I don't care one way or the other what you think of me. And Mrs. King is invited to our services anytime she wants to come." Seeing how angry Frank was, he feared for Leigh's safety. He turned his eyes on her. "You don't have to go with him."

Leigh's gaze darted from Frank to Clay. She found it exciting that Frank was so jealous. The preacher was a handsome man, and she liked him. More than liked him. She wouldn't mind taking up with him when Frank wasn't around. She certainly didn't want Frank to kill him. "Let's go to my room, Frank."

Frank grinned, but he wasn't looking at Leigh. "How can I turn down an offer like that, Preacher Man?" He gaze slid to Emma. "Looks like you found yourself a real brave man." He reached for Leigh's hand and pulled her through the restaurant.

Emma cast a glance Clay's way, but he was watching Frank and Leigh walk upstairs to her room. Emma walked away without another word.

Clay followed her out to the sidewalk. "Emma, I'll get the buckboard."

He was talking to her back, because Emma didn't slow down; she continued to march down the sidewalk. "That's where I'm going right now. No need to trouble yourself."

Clay caught up with her in a couple of strides. "I am not going to let you go home in this weather alone. I don't know why you are so angry with me. And I didn't need you to come to my defense against your brother."

Emma stopped and faced him. "In case you haven't

heard, my brother is dangerous. I believe I heard you say you didn't carry a gun."

"That doesn't mean I can't handle the likes of Frank Langtry."

Emma arched her brow at him. "Do tell. How do you stop a bullet?"

Clay clutched her elbow in his firm grip and urged her toward the livery. He had no intention of standing on the sidewalk having this discussion for all to hear. "Frank is mostly bluster."

"Of course. That explains why everyone is afraid of him. You know what Frank did to Rose, and that he is most likely responsible for the death of our younger brother. How do you think you can protect yourself from him?"

"I'm not a woman he can intimidate."

She had to agree with him there. Yet she didn't see how he would defend himself if Frank wanted to shoot him.

Chapter Eleven

The ride to the ranch was a dismal affair. Emma wasn't talking, and Clay didn't know what to say. He'd told Emma the truth; Leigh King did walk by his table, and he'd planned to introduce her to Emma when he'd invited her to sit with him. It was obvious now that it wasn't the wisest decision he'd ever made. It troubled him that the steps he'd taken to get to know Emma better had been sidetracked. But he couldn't ignore the fact that he wanted to help Leigh if he could. He preferred to believe he wasn't drawn to her because of her resemblance to Violet. Like Violet, Leigh was young and sweet, and vulnerable to the evils of the world. Clay felt it was his responsibility to help Leigh realize that she was making a mistake to waste her life on a man like Frank Langtry.

They were just a few miles from town when Clay heard a horse coming, riding up fast behind them. He pulled the buckboard to a halt, and turned around, expecting it to be Frank.

It wasn't Frank, but the young man from the telegraph office. He reined in beside the buckboard and handed Emma a telegram. "I thought I saw you leaving the livery. I knew I could catch you."

"Thank you." Emma reached into her reticule to find some coins for the young man, but Clay beat her to it. After he tossed a coin to the messenger, the young man turned around and rode away.

"You don't have to pay my way," Emma told him.

"I know, Emma. I didn't know if you had money with you last night, so I paid for the room. If you think I don't recognize you are a successful woman, you are incorrect in your thinking." He hadn't been able to sleep last night for thinking about Emma. His interest in her made no sense. She was a successful woman, making more money than he would ever make as a pastor. What could he possibly have to offer her? And why was he thinking about her when he wasn't ready to be in a relationship?

Emma read the telegram and shoved it into her reticule.

"I hope it's not bad news." He wondered if she'd received word from that prince who was coming to America to court her.

"No bad news. Carlo says we have another performance on Saturday in Denver."

"I'd like to see another performance. Would you allow me to take you to Denver?" Clay waited for a reply, but she said nothing. It'd been so long since he tried to figure a woman out that he thought he'd forgotten how. Maybe he should just ask why she was so upset with him. "Do you want to tell me why you are so angry with me?"

His question got her attention. She whipped her head around to face him. "The best I recall, the other night when you were trying to woo Mrs. King, you were rude enough not to even say good night to Morgan. He'd gone out of his way to come back to town for the service even after he'd worked hard all afternoon after we got home from Denver. He was kind enough to invite you to dinner, and you didn't bother to even say good-bye to him. You were too busy talking with Mrs. King. Just like this morning. I came downstairs and found you with Mrs. King *again*. Perhaps you invited the wrong woman to breakfast."

"Why should I not invite a woman to sit when she passes by my table? If you had joined us, I planned to introduce you. I think you would like her. And I was not trying to woo her."

"That is what it looks like to everyone else." Emma knew she sounded petty, but at the moment she didn't care.

"I came to apologize to Morgan—to all of you. Why won't you accept my apology? I didn't intend to be rude."

"Was your apology sincere when you did the same thing today?" Emma countered.

"My apology was sincere. I did not do the same thing today. I wasn't ignoring you, and I certainly intended to introduce you if you'd given me the chance."

Emma felt like she was on the verge of tears. "I have one question for you. Why didn't you just invite Mrs. King to dinner instead of me? You seemed to have a keen interest in her."

Clay didn't really answer her question. Instead he told her how he felt responsible for all people in need.

Several miles before they reached the ranch, Clay finally quit trying to explain his motives. He was as frustrated as Emma. If he thought the weather was frigid, it had nothing on Emma's attitude. She didn't seem to believe a word he said, and in all honesty, he knew he wasn't being totally truthful. He wondered if God considered it a lie if details were omitted.

Pulling the buckboard to a halt in front of the house, Clay hadn't even set the break before Emma jumped to the ground and ran into the house without a word of good-bye.

Morgan was walking out the door at the same time, and she flew past him like a blur. He saw Clay sitting there looking at the door as if he wasn't quite sure what had just taken place. "Have a nice evening?" Morgan asked.

"Fine."

"Come on in and warm up. There's fresh coffee on the stove." Even though Rose thought he was blind to Granny's matchmaking schemes, Morgan knew something was up. And he recognized a case of frostbite when he saw it, and Clay looked like it would take more than a pot of coffee to unthaw.

Once they were in the kitchen, Morgan pulled a chair out for Clay. "Want some breakfast?"

"I sort of had some of my breakfast. Coffee's fine." He had managed to eat a few biscuits while he was waiting on Emma for breakfast, before Mrs. King joined him.

Morgan poured two cups of coffee and sat down at the table with Clay. Clay told him about his encounter with Frank.

"Wonder how long he'll be in town," Morgan said, knowing Rose would be a nervous wreck if Frank was anywhere near the ranch.

"It's anyone's guess, but Leigh seems intent on staying with him." Clay finally told him about his morning, and what had transpired that caused Emma to be in a huff. "I came by to apologize for my rude behavior yesterday, but she wouldn't let it go. Then I made the mistake of asking her to dinner."

"Was it a mistake?" Morgan asked.

"Yeah, a big one. We left on good terms last night, but when she saw Leigh at my table this morning, she was ready to take me behind the woodshed. Strangest thing was, when Frank called me out, she actually came to my defense. She acted as though I couldn't handle myself."

"Sounds like a Langtry woman. Why do you think it was a mistake to ask her out?"

"She was so upset with me over Leigh. No matter what I said, she wouldn't listen."

Morgan took a drink of his coffee and watched his friend. Something was on his mind, but he didn't know if he was ready to talk about it. But he saw how Clay had watched Leigh King that first night he saw her. "Do you want to tell me what draws you to Leigh King?"

Clay looked at him, and sighed deeply. "It's that obvious?"

"Afraid so." Morgan wasn't going to lie to him; everyone noticed he couldn't keep his eyes off the woman.

"She looks exactly like Violet. When I first saw her, I almost thought my deceased wife was sitting across the room."

Morgan heard the misery in Clay's voice. "I'm sorry, Clay. I had no idea."

Clay had a far-away look in his eyes, and Morgan knew he was thinking about his family. "I still dream about them, you know."

"It's understandable." Morgan didn't know what to say to ease his friend's mind. "Did you tell Emma?"

"No. I didn't want to talk about that on a first date. If you can call it a date. It was the first time I had dinner alone with a woman—well, since my wife."

"Don't you think it's time . . ." Morgan hesitated to finish his sentence. He didn't want to sound callous, but it had been over four years since the death of Clay's family. He thought his friend deserved some happiness. "Time to get on with your life and find some peace again."

"That's what I told myself when I was thinking of asking Emma to dinner. But once I was in the restaurant enjoying myself, I almost felt guilty. I'm sitting there having a nice dinner and my family is dead."

"Clay, you have nothing to feel guilty about. I know this sounds harsh, but life is for the living. Your wife would want you to be happy. Just as you would want her to be happy if it had been the other way around. It doesn't mean that you will ever forget them." Morgan remembered the night when he'd thought Rose was dead. He didn't know how he would have been able to find a way to go on, but he wanted to think at some point he would have decided to live again and not just exist.

"I've told myself that. That night we went to hear Emma sing, for the first time in four years I thought it was time for me to give it a try. Then Leigh King walked in that restaurant, and it all seemed like a cruel joke. I felt like Violet was telling me I wasn't allowed to move on."

"Does she really look that much like your wife, or do you think it's possible that you want to see a resemblance?"

"There's some differences, but at a distance it was hard to tell."

"Clay, I can't pretend to know what you went through. Maybe it would help if you talked about your wife and son, instead of keeping everything bottled inside. Why don't you tell Emma?"

"I doubt she'll talk to me again. You saw how she ran through that door. She didn't even speak the last few miles home." He told Morgan about asking to take her to Denver for her next performance.

"She didn't answer one way or the other?"

"No, not a word. I'd say my chances with her are slim at this point." Clay was disappointed by the way things had turned out, but he'd told himself he didn't have much to offer Emma anyway.

"If you still want to have a chance, there may be a way to work something out," Morgan said.

Later that day, Emma asked Granny and Rose if they felt like walking to Addie's for a visit. As they walked through the pine tree range on the boundary of the ranch,

Emma said, "Do you remember all of the hours we spent in here when we were young?"

Rose smiled. "Of course, I cherish all of those memories. We'll be collecting pine cones soon for our wreaths. Remember when we would make them for Morgan and then make Granny take them to him because we were too afraid of him?"

"I remember. I also remember Addie and I thought we always heard people laughing when we were in the pines, but you always heard singing. It's so quiet in here today." Emma looked up at the trees. "I guess there's not enough wind today."

Granny and Rose looked up at the same time. "That's unusual," Granny said. "I've never heard it so quiet in here."

Rose shivered, thinking of the day she ran through the trees to the farmhouse. It was the day Frank had kidnapped her. "The day of the fire at the farmhouse, I ran through here and I thought I heard someone telling me to turn back."

"Was anyone in here?" Emma asked.

"I didn't see anyone." Rose shrugged. "I'm certain it was my imagination, but it was quiet that day, just like now."

"You used to say when you came in here with Frank you heard whispers," Emma said.

Rose nodded. "It was eerie, and Frank always said he couldn't hear anything, but I know he did."

"It doesn't seem like Frank ever told us the truth about anything," Emma said.

"Enough talk about Frank," Granny said, thinking Emma was discussing everything this morning except her dinner with Clay. "You haven't said much about your dinner with Clay. How did that go?"

"It was fine." All day Emma had mentally rehashed their

dinner, and their disastrous morning. She'd told herself she hadn't overreacted at seeing Clay with that woman. He tried to make their encounter seem innocent, but Emma had a feeling there was something else going on.

Granny and Rose exchanged a look. They knew Clay was downstairs this morning with Morgan while Emma was in her room.

"Clay was in the kitchen talking to Morgan this morning," Rose said.

"Yes, I know." Emma had heard their deep voices carrying through the house, but she wasn't about to go downstairs to find out why Clay was there.

"Are you planning on going out with him again?" Rose asked.

"No. I don't think we have much in common." Emma thought it best to face the fact that Clay was only being nice to her because of Granny. He certainly wasn't as interested in her as he was the beautiful widow.

"You didn't happen to see Mrs. King in town, did you?" Granny had a feeling Emma liked Clay more than she was admitting.

Emma knew she wasn't going to avoid this conversation with Granny. Granny was like a dog with a bone when she wanted to know something. "As a matter of fact, I did. Clay and I were going to meet for breakfast, but when I came downstairs he was sitting with Mrs. King."

Now they were getting at the heart of the matter, Granny thought. "Did you meet her? What is she like?"

"No, I didn't meet her."

"How did you avoid meeting her if she was sitting with Clay?" Rose asked.

"I walked away." Emma didn't tell them that Clay came after her. "When I came back downstairs with my cloak, Frank was in the dining room, threatening Clay."

"What?" Rose exclaimed.

Emma explained what had taken place between Clay and Frank. "Frank was all bluff. He walked away with Mrs. King, and that was that."

"Do you think that young woman is afraid of Frank?" Granny asked.

"I most certainly do not. I think that woman is looking out for her own best interest. She left the judge for Frank. If she thinks Clay would be a better man to meet her needs, then she will latch on to him." Emma didn't care that she wasn't being very Christian in her thoughts, but it was what she truly felt.

"What do you girls think about going into town tomorrow to do some Christmas shopping?" Granny asked.

Emma and Rose glanced at each other, each wondering why Granny changed the subject.

Thankful to be conversing on any subject other than the good pastor, Emma said, "I think that sounds lovely."

"Yes, I've been wanting to go into town before the weather gets too bad," Rose said.

"Good, and while we are there, we are going to invite Mrs. King to lunch," Granny said.

"You can't be serious, Granny," Emma said.

Granny smiled. "Oh, I'm very serious. You think Clay has an interest in this woman that is more than platonic. If that is true, I think we should find out what type of person she is. I see no reason why we shouldn't meet her."

Emma could think of a hundred reasons. "Why should we interfere at all?"

"I don't see it as interfering. Perhaps this young woman needs some female guidance. If she's all alone in the world, she may not have a guiding hand to help her avoid the pitfalls of falling into the wrong hands. Why should we judge someone without knowing her circumstances?"

Granny always knew how to make one feel small, Emma thought. The truth was, she had prejudged Mrs. King. It always angered her when people judged her by the places she performed. "I guess you're right, Granny. She probably is all alone in this world and just doing the best she can. But what if Frank is still in town with her? He didn't want her talking to Clay, and I can't imagine he would be thrilled to have her talking with his family."

"Granny, I don't think that is a good idea. We don't want to anger Frank," Rose said. "All I want him to do is leave town. As long as he's here, I worry about Morgan."

"Morgan can take care of himself. You need to show more faith in your husband. And I, for one, am tired of living my life worrying about what Frank will or will not like. We've spent too many hours on Frank as it is. Enough is enough. Why should we stand by and allow him to ruin another woman's life?"

"But you know the marshal thinks she was in on the robbery," Rose said.

"I guess it's time we found out one way or the other," Granny replied.

Chapter Twelve

As long as Frank Langtry was around Whispering Pines, Morgan didn't want him anywhere near Rose. When the women said they planned to go to town to do some Christmas shopping, Morgan told them he would take them.

"As long as Sweetie is with us, Frank won't bother us," Emma said, trying to alleviate Morgan's concern.

"I trust Sweetie is a good protector, but he's no match for a gun." He glanced at the giant dog. "You know, Emma, you should call him Rufus. It has to be demoralizing for him to be called Sweetie. No one would think he's fierce with that name."

The thought of someone shooting Sweetie made a shiver run down Emma's spine. She promptly felt for the pistol inside her cape pocket that Carlo insisted she carry. She would never allow anyone to threaten Sweetie, even if that meant she had to shoot a person. "He likes Sweetie. Anyway, he has a way of making his point whether he's called Sweetie or Rufus."

"True enough." Morgan recalled how Sweetie responded to Frank. The dog seemed to know whom to trust. "Why don't you ladies tell me again why you want to have lunch with Leigh King? You know we all think she was involved in that robbery."

"We've discussed that, Morgan, and we want to find out if it's the truth," Granny said.

Morgan chuckled. "Do you think she's going to admit to playing a role?"

Granny swatted his arm. "Of course not. But don't you think I've lived enough years to tell when someone is lying to me or not?"

Morgan figured Granny had a point. "I think you can, Granny." He glanced at Emma. "What do you think, Emma? You think she was involved?"

"I was inclined to think that, but Granny told me I wasn't giving the woman a chance. I will follow Granny's lead and withhold judgment until we've talked to her."

Morgan pulled in front of the hotel right before noon and helped the ladies from the buckboard. "I'll walk in with you to see if Frank is here."

Once inside the hotel, Granny walked to the doorway of the restaurant and peeked inside. "She's not in there, Morgan."

Morgan walked to the desk and asked the clerk if Mrs. King was still registered. The clerk told him she was in her room, but she usually came downstairs for lunch at noon. The clerk also told Morgan that Frank Langtry left earlier, but he didn't know if he'd left town. Morgan walked back to the ladies and related the information from the clerk.

"Perfect. Now that Frank is gone, we will have ample opportunity to dine in peace," Granny said.

Morgan leaned over and kissed his wife. "I'll be in Jack's office, and I'll keep an eye out for Frank in case he returns."

The ladies walked into the restaurant, chose a seat in the center of the room so they could see Leigh if she came in.

"Granny, do you want me to go to her room and just ask if she would like to dine with us?" Emma always preferred to take the most expedient route.

"Be patient. I'm certain she'll come downstairs. Who wants to stay cooped up in a hotel room all day?"

Rose looked up and saw Mrs. King in the doorway. "There she is."

Granny put her hand on Emma's arm. "Go ask her to join us before she takes a seat."

Emma didn't argue; she walked over to Leigh and said, "I'm Emma Langtry. My grandmother, sister, and I would like to know if you would care to join us for lunch."

Leigh was definitely taken by surprise. "Frank told me yesterday that you are the famous opera singer."

Emma forced a smile. "Would you care to join us?"

Leigh looked around the room as though she thought Frank might jump out from behind the curtains. "I'm not certain Frank would approve. I don't mean to be rude, but he doesn't seem to care much for his family."

"I think you can understand why the family has had a falling-out with Frank," Emma said in her usual forthright manner.

"I'm learning a lot about Frank," Leigh said.

"Where is he now?" Emma asked.

"He said he didn't finish his business in Denver, and he was going back there for a few days. He promised he would be back soon so we can go home before Christmas."

Emma took that opportunity to find out more information. "And where is home?"

"Black Hawk—Frank works at the gold mine there."

"Since you are here alone, why not dine with us?"

Emma turned and led the way to their table without giving Leigh an opportunity to refuse.

After the introductions to Granny and Rose, Leigh said, "Well, I guess it can't hurt to have lunch with you since Frank isn't here." She started to sit by Emma, but one look at the giant dog by her side made her select a seat with one empty chair between them.

"When will Frank be back?" Granny asked.

"He said in a few days," Leigh replied.

Once they ordered their meal, Granny made it a point to talk about various topics until their food was delivered to the table. She was determined to find out why this lovely young woman was with Frank in the first place.

"Tell me, how did you come to know Frank?" Granny asked.

Leigh explained that she was introduced to Frank by Judge Stevens. "The judge and I were acquainted when I lived in Colorado City."

"Do you mind me asking why you don't go with Frank to Denver?" Emma asked.

"Frank doesn't want the judge to know where I am." Leigh glanced down at her plate, and seemed to hesitate before continuing. "Actually, the judge became quite fond of me. I'm afraid I considered him more of a father figure, but he became obsessed with me."

Rose and Emma glanced at each other. They knew she wasn't telling the truth.

Granny finally thought it was best to be direct. "Do you know of Frank's past, my dear?"

"The judge dismissed all charges against Frank. He was innocent or the judge wouldn't have done that," Leigh said.

"I can assure you that my brother was not innocent," Rose said.

"Frank told me he wasn't guilty."

"I don't mean to be an intrusive old woman, but you seem like such a lovely young woman, and I can't understand why you would trust your future to Frank. Frank is my grandson, but he has not led the kind of life that would be advantageous for a young woman," Granny said.

"Frank loves me and I love him," Leigh said.

Seeing she was having no impact warning her about Frank, Granny changed tactics. "I understand you were shot during the robbery in Denver."

"Yes, ma'am, and Frank helped me through my recovery," Leigh replied.

"How did you get shot?" Emma asked.

Leigh hesitated. "I was coming from the bank when I saw Frank and I stopped to talk to him. The robbery happened right at that moment."

"I understand Frank's wife was killed at the same time. That must have been terrible for you," Granny said.

"Yes, it was terrible." Leigh pulled her handkerchief from her reticule and held it to her eyes.

Clay walked into the restaurant and his eyes immediately zeroed in on Emma. He didn't know if she would chop his head off, but he decided he would stop and say hello to her. Just a few feet from the table, he noticed the other woman at the table along with Rose and Granny. He almost turned around when he saw Leigh, but Sweetie spotted him and ran to greet him. Once everyone at the table turned to see him, he had to stop and say hello.

"Clay, how nice to see you. Why don't you join us?" Granny asked.

He removed his hat and acknowledged the women with a nod, his eyes lingering on Emma longer than the others. "I don't want to intrude on your conversation."

Emma tried not to look at him, but she couldn't help herself. She really wanted to know if he was looking at Leigh King. When she glanced up at him, he was looking directly at her.

"You aren't intruding. Please sit with us," Granny insisted.

The only empty seat was between Emma and Leigh. He had a feeling he was going to regret this decision, but he pulled the chair out and sat down.

"Mrs. King was telling us how she came to be shot in that bank robbery," Granny said.

"It's a blessing that you survived a bullet wound," Clay said politely. He didn't want to say anything that would keep him in the doghouse with Emma.

"I'm very fortunate. I was just saying how Frank helped me during my recovery," Leigh said.

Clay bristled each time Leigh said something complimentary about Frank. Maybe someone needed to tell her the truth. "Did Frank tell you how we met?"

"No, he didn't. I know he was upset yesterday when he saw us together, but he thought . . . well, he thought something he shouldn't have." She wanted Clay to think that Frank thought she was interested in him. She'd made it no secret that she liked handsome men, and the pastor was definitely attractive. And she did want Frank to know she found Clay attractive. "How did you meet him?"

"Rose and I were traveling from Boston on the same stagecoach. We stopped on the trail and were about to witness Frank's hanging, but Rose asked Morgan to take Frank to jail instead of hanging him. There was an accident and Rose was injured, and Frank rode away without any concern over the welfare of his sister." Clay didn't soften his words. It was time Leigh understood the kind of man she was taking for a companion.

Leigh stared at him for a moment before her eyes

skittered over Frank's family. "Frank has told me he's done some things he's not proud of, but I know he loves me."

Everyone was silent for a moment, and Clay turned to Emma, and said, "Did you tell your family I'm taking you to Denver next week for your performance?"

Emma hadn't told him he could take her to Denver. But considering how direct he was with Mrs. King, she found her attitude softening toward him. "No, it completely slipped my mind."

"You have another performance?" Granny said.

"Yes, but we will be performing again on the Saturday before Christmas, so it's not necessary for you to attend this one. It will be the same performance as our last one."

"Christmas will be here before we know it, and we have a lot to do before then," Rose said.

"I would love to see your performance," Leigh said.

Emma thought if Clay invited her along she would find a different way to Denver. Without a doubt, Leigh King was not being truthful. The woman was well aware that Frank was an outlaw. Not only that, but Emma felt Mrs. King was definitely involved in that robbery. Everyone else might believe her fake tears, but Emma wasn't buying them. She couldn't wait to hear what Granny had to say. Even though Granny was inclined to want to believe the best in everyone, she also had a knack for sensing deceit.

Clay remained silent, so Emma said, "You should have Frank take you to Denver."

"I will see what he says," Leigh replied.

"Clay, will we have a late sermon next Sunday since you are taking Emma to Denver?" Granny asked.

"I haven't asked Emma, but if she doesn't mind, we will be coming back that night." Clay glanced at Emma and waited for a response.

"That would be fine with me. I appreciate your offer,

but I will need to leave early Saturday so we have time to rehearse."

"I don't mind. I'm delighted to see another performance," Clay responded.

"It may not be as appealing as the first time you heard it."

Clay smiled at her. "I assure you, if it is half as good as your last performance, it is worth hearing again. I will gladly be your escort for the later performance, too." He thought he deserved a medal since he'd made it clear to everyone at the table he wanted to escort Emma to Denver. Even Emma couldn't say he was trying to woo Mrs. King.

Emma didn't know what to make of his solicitous behavior. When he sat down, she'd expected him to give his undivided attention to Mrs. King, but it was quite the opposite. "That may not be convenient for you. I will need to go to Denver a few days before that performance. We haven't rehearsed the songs and we will need some time to practice."

"I will be happy to take you to Denver, return home, and come back for the performance." Clay's intention was to prove to Emma that he wasn't interested in Mrs. King for any other purpose than helping her escape Frank's clutches.

Lunch ended and everyone said their good-byes. Granny, Emma, and Rose left to do some shopping and Clay left the hotel with them.

When they reached the mercantile, Granny said, "Morgan is at the sheriff's office visiting with Jack."

"Then I will say good-bye to you ladies here and visit with the men." Clay tipped his hat, and winked at Emma.

As soon as Clay was far enough away to keep from overhearing, Emma said, "Well, Granny, what do you think of Mrs. King?"

Granny stopped just outside the mercantile and turned to her granddaughters. "Sadly, I think she was involved with that bank robbery, just as Morgan and Jack said. It pains me to say something like that about such a lovely young woman, but there it is."

"I thought the same thing," Rose added. "She didn't really shed one tear, even though she did try to convince us otherwise."

"I noticed the same thing. She's definitely in on it with Frank," Emma agreed. "And I doubt she will be going to Denver. Frank doesn't want her there."

"The real question is, why does he keep going back to Denver?" Granny asked.

Once the women left the mercantile, Emma needed to go to the telegraph office to send a telegram to Carlo informing him of the time she would be arriving on Saturday for their rehearsal. They were walking down the sidewalk when Emma saw Clay across the street walking with Leigh King. They were going in the direction of the church, and Mrs. King had her arm looped though Clay's.

In Emma's estimation, they looked very absorbed in their conversation. "I guess he couldn't stay away from her long."

Not having seen Clay, Rose and Granny gave Emma a perplexed look. Emma pointed across the street. "It looks like they are having a serious conversation."

"Now don't jump to conclusions. She may have sought him out. Maybe she needs to discuss something and would feel more at ease if she discussed it in the church," Granny said.

Emma rolled her eyes.

Chapter Thirteen

The night before Emma was expected in Denver for her next performance, she was in the kitchen helping Rose and Granny with dinner. As she was carrying food to the table, she noticed an additional table setting. "Are we having company for dinner?"

"I guess I forgot to mention that Morgan asked Clay for dinner. Morgan knew he was taking you to Denver tomorrow, so he invited him to spend the night. That way, you two can leave as early as you need," Rose said.

"Yes, you did forget to mention that to me," Emma said. She'd been so excited Clay was going to take her to Denver, right up to the moment when she stepped out of the mercantile and saw him escorting Mrs. King to the church. "I had planned on asking someone else to take me tomorrow."

"At lunch you allowed Clay to think he was taking you," Granny said. "It would be ill-mannered of you to offend him by asking someone else."

"Why would you want to ask someone else?" Rose asked.

"I think he has better things to do than to ride me back and forth to Denver." Such as escort Leigh King around town, she thought. Maybe she should suggest he take Mrs. King to Denver since she wanted to see the performance.

"If he had better things to do, he wouldn't have offered," Granny replied.

Hearing a knock on the front door, their conversation ended.

"Emma, would you get the door?" Rose asked.

Emma tightened her lips at the suggestion. "I know what you two are trying to do, but it is not going to work. The pastor and I have about as much in common as I would have with a rattler."

Granny laughed. "That sharp tongue of yours has often reminded me of a rattler."

Emma couldn't help but smile as she left the kitchen. Before she reached the door, it opened, and Morgan and Clay walked in together.

"Look who I found on the porch," Morgan said.

Clay removed his hat and smiled at Emma. "Hello."

"Hello," Emma replied unenthusiastically.

Hearing Clay's voice, Sweetie scampered from the kitchen and ran to Clay.

Clay gave Sweetie his usual ear rub, thinking at least Sweetie was glad to see him, if not Emma.

"Is dinner ready?" Morgan asked.

"Yes," Emma said.

"Good, I'm starving." Morgan walked ahead toward the kitchen, leaving Emma with Clay.

"How was the shopping trip?" Clay asked.

"Good." She wanted to ask him if he'd spent his day with Mrs. King.

"Did you buy me a Christmas gift?" It surprised Clay how he enjoyed baiting her. He hadn't teased a woman in a long time.

"I did not," Emma said.

"Don't you plan on giving me a present?" Clay saw the blush rising up her neck. Emma wasn't as indifferent being teased by a man as she wanted everyone to believe.

Emma didn't know what to make of his flirtatious manner. "I hadn't given it a thought."

Clay leaned in to her ear and whispered, "I like home-made cookies."

Emma couldn't walk to the kitchen fast enough. It was a new experience having a man fluster her. She'd always managed to have a witty comeback, but her mind went totally blank when Clay teased her. "If you want dinner, you'll follow me to the kitchen."

Clay chuckled. "Yes, ma'am."

After dinner, Clay offered to wash dishes. "Maybe I can talk Emma into drying."

"Thank you, Clay, but you are our guest," Rose said.

"I want to help." He glanced at Morgan, silently telling him to get Rose out of the kitchen.

Morgan got the message. "I appreciate that, Clay. I can spend some more time with my wife tonight."

Emma noticed no one asked what she preferred. When everyone left the room, Clay stood and gathered the dishes.

"I should have asked if you prefer to wash or dry." He'd often helped his wife in the kitchen. No, he wasn't going to think about Violet tonight.

"I can do both," Emma said. "You can go on in the parlor and relax."

Her words landed like a bucket of cold water on his thoughts. "I know you can do both, but I want to help."

"Have it your way. You can wash." She thought men hated washing dishes.

Clay considered her indifferent mood tonight. She had been very friendly at lunch the last time he saw her, but tonight she hadn't strung together more than a few words

each time he said something to her. She was a hard one
to figure out. He rolled up his sleeves and pumped water
into the sink. "Why don't you tell me about some of your
travels?"

Emma placed the dishes she was carrying on the counter.
"I doubt that would interest you very much."

Clay put one long arm on the counter next to her and
leaned around to look into her eyes, and said, "It interests me."

Emma felt as though she couldn't catch her breath. Her
gaze traveled from his eyes to his mouth. He was grinning
at her. A flirty, lopsided grin. Almost as if he knew she was
thinking he was the most attractive man she'd ever laid eyes
on. "Why?"

"Why what?" he asked.

"Why does it interest you?"

He moved an inch closer. "You interest me."

She blinked. "Why?"

"Why what?"

"Why do I possibly interest you?"

Clay's grin grew wider. "Do you always ask so many
questions?"

"Only when things don't make sense," she replied.

She was truly a perplexing woman. "What doesn't make
sense?"

"Why you seem to have an interest in me. That is, until
Mrs. King always happens along. Are you the kind of man
who simply enjoys flirting with women?"

"Why, Emma, do you think I'm flirting with you?"

What did he think he was doing leaning down so close
to her face that she could see the gold flecks in his beautiful eyes? "Aren't you?" If he wasn't a pastor, she might be
inclined to pull his face to hers and give him a kiss he

wouldn't soon forget. That would probably shock him all the way back to his pulpit.

"I guess I am. But I don't flirt with Mrs. King."

"You two certainly seem to have a lot to say to each other," Emma said.

"You were sitting right beside me at lunch. You heard every word I said," he said.

"We saw you after we left the mercantile. You were walking down the sidewalk with Mrs. King, arm in arm. You seemed very engrossed in your conversation. So much so that you certainly didn't notice us."

So that was what had a bee in her bonnet tonight. "I didn't seek her out. She was going to the church and saw me on the sidewalk going the same way."

Emma thought he smoothly evaded what they were talking about. "It seems you two are destined to be together."

"I don't know what you mean by destined to be together. She said she had some things to discuss, so we walked to the church together. Nothing more."

Again, he didn't say what they discussed. "Frank doesn't want her around you, so why are you provoking him?" She thought she knew the answer to that question. He was attracted to the woman, plain and simple.

Clay moved away, leaned his hip against the counter, and folded his arms over his chest. "Why don't you tell me why I should be concerned about what Frank thinks?"

She looked at him as though he'd lost his mind. "For one reason, he called you out. For another reason, he's not above shooting you in the back. You seem to forget he's dangerous."

"I haven't forgotten anything. I was on that stagecoach with your sister when Frank threatened her life. But I can't live my life worried about what Frank might do. That young woman is in need of help, and it is my duty to help her if possible. I am the pastor of this town. I won't place my responsibilities aside because I worry that Frank won't like what I say or do."

"Do you intend to get in a shoot-out with him?" Emma demanded.

"Of course not. That goes against everything I believe now." Clay had faced those demons when he was searching for Culpepper and Taggart. He wasn't that man any longer. At least, that's what he kept telling himself.

The man was beyond frustrating. "How do you plan to defend yourself against him? If he hears you are spending time with his woman, you can bet he will come after you. Your Bible won't stop his bullet."

He searched her eyes. "Is it Frank you're worried about, or is it something else?"

"I know my brother. But I also know Mrs. King and Frank were involved in that robbery together."

"How do you know that?"

Emma threw her hands in the air. She wasn't going to change his mind. He didn't want to believe what was in front of his face. "For heaven's sake, the woman cries fake tears. You can bet she's up to her pretty little neck in that robbery."

"I think Frank was involved, but I don't believe she was." Clay replayed in his mind everything Leigh had told him. She'd discussed that day at the bank when Frank's wife got shot. Leigh seemed truly distraught over the whole ordeal. He thought she was indeed a young woman in need of some guidance.

"Then tell me why she doesn't go to Denver with Frank."

"You know she doesn't want to face the judge. She felt safe with Frank, and that was why she left with him." Clay had revealed more than he'd intended.

Emma walked to the table and collected more dishes.

"You can believe her if you choose, but you are the only one who does."

When she reached the sink again, Clay leaned over and placed a chaste kiss on her cheek. He pulled back and almost laughed at the surprise in her eyes. "I haven't kissed her, if that is what you were wondering."

She opened her mouth to make a snappy retort, but nothing came out. It took a few seconds, but she finally found her tongue. "I most certainly was not wondering that."

Clay winked at her. "I think you were."

Emma picked up the wet dishcloth and threw it at him. It slapped him right on the nose.

The cloth slid down his nose and into his hands. "Thank you. I was looking for that."

"You can dry, too." With that said, Emma marched from the room, up the stairs, and slammed her bedroom door shut.

Clay stood there looking at the empty room for several seconds, wondering what in the heck just happened. All he did was give her a little kiss. Did she think pastors didn't kiss?

Sweetie walked across the room and leaned against his leg.

"You have a very confusing mistress, Sweetie," Clay told him.

Morgan walked into the room. "What was that all about?"

"I have no idea. One minute, things were going along pretty well, or at least I thought so. The next minute, she threw this at me." Clay stuck the dishcloth out for Morgan to see.

"Did you say something that made her mad?"

"No, I gave her a little peck on the cheek. Then she threw the wet cloth at my nose."

"And you weren't discussing anything?" Morgan was skeptical. Rose had already told him why Emma was in a snit.

"We did discuss Mrs. King. Emma thinks she is involved in Frank's schemes. I told her I thought she was wrong."

"Clay, I hate to tell you, but Emma is right. Mrs. King is not the innocent woman you want to believe. The sheriff thinks she had taken up with Frank even before his wife was killed."

Clay was genuinely surprised. "Even if that is so, she has come to me for advice, and I can't turn her away. Emma seems to think Frank will shoot me in the back."

"You go against him, he'll have no problem doing just that."

"I can't worry about that. I have a responsibility to people who seek help."

"What happens if he catches you somewhere and you aren't carrying a gun? He'll shoot you no matter what."

"Then I guess he shoots me." Clay wasn't indifferent, but he'd made his mind up years ago not to carry a gun. Neither Frank Langtry, nor men of his ilk, were going to change him now.

"What if Frank threatens someone you care about? What then?" Morgan had always wondered what Clay would do if he was forced to defend another person.

Clay didn't hesitate in his response. "I wouldn't let him hurt anyone."

"Clay, we are supposed to defend ourselves against men like Frank."

"You may be right, Morgan. I've taken more than one life in a fight before. But even if it's considered a fair fight, it takes its toll on your soul. Sometimes death is not the worst thing that can happen to a man. A man can die a little at a time if he's not walking the right path. If I've learned one thing in this life, I know there are things that haunt a man that's a whole lot worse than dying."

Morgan picked up a cloth. "I guess I'll dry."

Emma stomped around her room for several minutes. Of all the nerve. How could he just lean over and give her a little kiss like that? What was wrong with him? She hadn't encouraged him, she hadn't wanted him to kiss her. She walked to her bureau and started pulling the pins from her hair. When she looked in the mirror, her hands stilled. Her cheeks were rosy, and her eyes held a sparkle she had never seen before. For the first time in her life, she thought she actually looked pretty. She lifted her hands to cup her warm cheeks. Maybe Clay saw the same thing when he looked at her. Was that why he'd kissed her? Who was she kidding? She'd wanted to know what it would feel like to be really kissed by him, and not on the cheek. Men had kissed her, and with much more amorous intent than Clay's tender peck. Still, the way his lips brushed her skin seemed much more intimate than any kiss on the lips she'd ever received. He'd said he hadn't kissed Leigh King. She didn't want to admit that she had thought that was a possibility.

Was it possible he was really attracted to her and not Mrs. King? Either way, it would prove disastrous for his career. She didn't think most people would accept their beloved pastor courting a woman who sang in saloons. They would probably be more inclined to accept Leigh King. She glanced in the mirror at her reflection. *Stop being fanciful*. Clay was an extremely handsome man, and he'd just been flirting with her, the way some men were inclined to do. Men! She'd seen men like him before, the kind that liked to know they could attract women. When the woman hinted she had an interest in him, they'd run for the hills. A spark of inspiration came to her mind. She would call his bluff. The good pastor was going to get what he deserved for toying with her.

Clay was lying in bed in the guest room at Morgan's house. He didn't know what possessed him to plant that little peck on Emma's cheek. At that moment, she'd looked so delectable, he couldn't resist. Emma was a beautiful woman, even if she was giving him the devil over Leigh King every time he turned around. He thought they were all wrong about Mrs. King. Certainly no woman as lovely as she was could be capable of being as deceitful as everyone painted her. He knew she was living in sin with Frank, but who was he to judge? That wasn't his job. His job, as he saw it, was to lead people to God's house, to listen to their troubles, and offer hope. Too many people set themselves up to judge others. He'd often reminded his congregation that God didn't select perfect people to be his disciples. If that had been the case, and God only wanted perfect people, Clay knew he would never be in the position he was in today. He'd made more mistakes than Leigh King could ever make. If ever there was a reason to believe in second chances, all he had to do was look at himself.

He realized he hadn't asked Emma what time she wanted to leave in the morning, so he jumped out of bed, pulled on his pants, and quietly walked down the hall to her bedroom door.

Hearing the knock, Emma pulled on her robe before she opened the door. She expected to find Rose or Granny on the other side, certainly not Clay. "Yes?"

The first thing Clay noticed was the white nightgown buttoned to her throat, and she had a white silky robe covering that. Her long auburn hair was loosely cascading over her shoulders. He didn't think he'd ever seen a more beautiful sight. "I didn't ask what time you wanted to leave in the morning."

"I'd like to leave right after breakfast, if that is convenient for you," she said sweetly. Oh, yes, did she ever want to be alone with him tomorrow. She would have him running back to Whispering Pines quicker than one could say johnnycakes, with his tail between his legs.

"That would be perfect." Clay lingered a minute. He couldn't think of anything else to say, but he didn't want to walk away.

"Is there something else you wanted?" Emma said.

He stared at her a minute longer and said, "Good night."

Chapter Fourteen

On the way to Denver, Emma snuggled up to Clay's side. She was so close, she could smell the soap he'd used that morning. Much to her surprise, if she was making him uncomfortable, he was hiding it well. She'd hatched her plan last night to give him a taste of his own medicine. At the moment, her plan didn't seem to be working all that well. He was congenial in his conversation, and quite considerate of her comfort in the cold. When it started snowing, he stopped the buckboard to retrieve another blanket to cover her. She couldn't have asked for a more attentive traveling companion. She'd even gone so far as rest her head on his shoulder, but she was getting no reaction from him.

Clay didn't know what Emma was up to, but there had been a drastic change from the way she'd treated him last night. Maybe that peck on the cheek softened her up a bit. He sort of liked the new Emma sitting close to him, and listening attentively to his every word. She hadn't once brought up the subject of Leigh King, and for that, he was thankful. That was a subject they would have to agree to disagree about.

All night he'd thought about how pretty she looked in

her white nightclothes, with her hair draped over her shoulder. He'd never expected her to be in such a congenial mood this morning. Maybe he was making some headway after all. After talking to Morgan, he felt a whole lot better about his future. He had to concede Morgan was right when he'd said Violet would want him to find happiness again. His wife had a great capacity for love, and he knew deep in his heart she'd want him to have another family. Problem was, he didn't know if he could ever handle another tragedy like the one he'd faced years ago. But he told himself he had to practice what he preached, and live by faith. Whatever happened in this life, he knew his faith would see him through. Life was unpredictable, and folks needed to find happiness where they could. He told himself to slow down and stop getting ahead of himself. He knew what he was feeling toward Emma, yet he had no earthly idea if she would ever have an interest in him. He knew he flustered her when he'd kissed her cheek last night.

Normally he thought he knew when a woman was interested in developing some kind of relationship, but Emma was hard to read. Just because she was snuggled up to him right now didn't mean that she wouldn't be giving him the devil in an hour. Granny said she was headstrong, and she hadn't been exaggerating. Emma definitely had a mind of her own, and she wasn't afraid to speak it. He liked knowing a woman could stand up for herself, and not allow a man to walk all over her. He respected that. Before he got too far ahead of himself, he needed to find out what she wanted in life.

"Emma, do you plan on singing for a long time?"

That was the first question he'd asked her about her future. "I plan to sing for a few more years, unless . . ."

She couldn't find a way to say she wished she could find a husband like her sisters and settle down on a small ranch.

Clay glanced her way. "Unless what?"

"I plan on buying some land near the farm, maybe even a few acres from Morgan. I'd like to have a ranch. I've saved money, and I thought I might be able to buy some land next year. I'd have to hire a foreman, of course, but I want to be near my family."

Of all the things she might have said to him, it surprised him that she wanted a ranch. That was a tall order for a single woman. When he thought about it, if a woman could run a ranch on her own, it would take a woman like Emma. "Do you think you are ready for that now?"

"Yes, I do." She wondered where he was going with this line of questioning. "Why do you ask?"

"I own a ranch in Kansas."

She didn't know he'd lived in Kansas. "Is that your home?"

"It was. I left there four years ago. I have a man who keeps it going for me."

"Do you plan to go back there?" The thought that he would leave Whispering Pines one day saddened her.

Clay couldn't say he hadn't thought about going home. His wife and son were buried there. Jonas was getting up in years, and he wouldn't be able to take care of the place forever. Once he'd arrived in Whispering Pines, he hadn't given a lot of thought about going back to Kansas. He thought of Whispering Pines as his home now, and he had good friends here. "I hadn't planned on going back."

She heard a slight change in his voice as if some sad memories had surfaced. "Do you plan on staying in Whispering Pines?"

"As long as the folks will have me. I like it here."

Emma wondered if he worried about being seen with

her. If some of the congregation got wind of this outing they may try to ostracize him for not toeing the line. "If taking me to Denver is going to cause you problems . . ."

Clay didn't allow her to finish her thought. "Hold it right there. I've talked to the folks who had objected the most about me going to Denver to see your performance. It seems like word about my sermon got out, and they are the ones who should be remorseful. I am not living my life worried about being judged by others."

Granny told her he had backbone. "So they aren't holding it against you?"

"If they are, they'll get over it."

"I know Granny would never want you to leave Whispering Pines."

Turning to look at her, Clay said, "Emma, do you ever want a family?"

Emma laughed. "To do that, one must marry first."

Clay nodded. "That would be the wisest course."

She realized he was waiting for a real response. "Maybe . . . someday . . . I don't know."

"What about this prince fellow who is supposed to come to see you? Is he a possibility?"

"Henri? No, I wouldn't want to live in France."

Clay noted she didn't exactly say she wasn't interested in the French prince. "Would he live here?"

"Of course not. He's a prince."

"Can't they give up their titles or something?"

"I never asked. I can't imagine a man giving up his title in his own country to live somewhere else."

Clay thought many men would do a lot of things for the woman they loved. But then, he'd never been a prince, and titles meant nothing to him. "I imagine it has happened at some point in history."

Emma didn't respond; she looked up and saw they were

already in Denver. Time had passed so quickly, and now she was regretting they didn't have more time to spend together.

Clay pulled the buckboard in front of the Grand Crystal Hall, and assisted Emma to the ground. "I think I will do some of my Christmas shopping, and I'll be back for tonight's performance."

"I will arrange for you to sit in the same place as before." Emma stared into his eyes. She didn't want him to leave, but she couldn't ask him to stay. "I'll see you then."

Snowflakes started swirling around them, causing Clay to look at the sky. "We'd best be prepared for a cold ride home."

Emma had been nice and toasty sitting so close to him on the ride to Denver that she hadn't give a thought to the cold. "I just hope the snow holds off until after we are home."

Clay tipped his hat. "See you later." He jumped back into the buckboard and was just pulling away when he heard a man calling Emma's name. He glanced up to see a very well-dressed gentleman, accompanied by two burly men, headed in her direction. There was no doubt in Clay's mind this was the very man they had been discussing. Prince Henri d'Evereux. Without thinking, he pulled the buckboard to a halt in the middle of the street to watch the reunion between Emma and the prince.

Emma turned to see Henri walking toward her. "Henri!"

Henri bowed politely, reached for her hand, and brushed his lips over her glove. "Emma, I'm delighted to finally see you again."

"I must say I was quite surprised when I received your letter. I never expected you to come to America." Emma hadn't even given a thought to what she would say to Henri when he arrived. Her mind had been occupied with thoughts of Clay Hunt.

Henri arched his brow. "Surprised? Did you think I would allow such a jewel to flee from me? As you could not spend more time in Europe, I decided I would spend time in your fabulous country. I am intrigued by this vast land. Shall we go in for some lunch and I will tell you of my travels?"

"I'm sorry, Henri, but I was just going in to practice with Carlo and Andre. I just arrived from Whispering Pines a moment ago."

"Carlo told me you were visiting your home. We could have a late dinner after your performance."

"I will be returning to Whispering Pines after dinner. Our town pastor graciously drove me today and he will be at the performance tonight, waiting to take me home."

"I will accompany you home. There is a hotel in Whispering Pines, no?"

"Yes, of course, we have a hotel. But I'm afraid our small town is not nearly as grand as Denver. I'm certain you will find it quite boring."

"As long as you are there, it couldn't possibly be boring." Henri took her elbow in his hand and escorted her into the Grand Crystal Hall.

Clay flicked the reins and headed to the livery. So that was the prince. Clay felt he'd made a mistake not escorting Emma into the hall. His manners wooing a female were rusty. If he wanted to develop a relationship with Emma, he was going to need to improve in that area. The prince was an impressive-looking man, tall and elegant, in dress and manner. He wondered if the prince was the kind of man who would leave his home country if he found a woman he loved. The answer was obvious. The man didn't come all of this way just to hear Emma sing. The man had to be in love. How could a small-town pastor compete with that? Did he want to compete for Emma? Maybe before committing himself one way or the other with that answer, he'd see how the wind was blowing. He had a hard time believing a woman would reject a prince who'd traveled halfway around the world for her.

Once Clay had taken the buckboard to the livery, he walked around town planning to do some shopping for Christmas. He'd spent some time in the local mercantile, and when he walked outside, a man passing by stopped in front of him.

"Clay, is that you?" Harper Ellis asked.

Clay stuck out his hand. "It sure is. How are you doing, Harper?" He asked the question, but his eyes told him Harper wasn't doing well. He was much thinner than Clay remembered, his complexion was gray and his eyes were sunken.

"I'm good. I'm in Denver for a nice long visit with my sister."

"I hope she is well," Clay said.

"She is, and her children are growing like little beanstalks." Harper wondered if he'd heard about Culpepper and Taggart. "I guess you never ran down those killers, Culpepper and Taggart."

Clay shook his head. "I'm a pastor now in Whispering Pines. I had to let all of that go."

"Jonas wrote me and told me you'd changed. Maybe you should know I ran into some friends of mine a few weeks ago, and they are in the Denver jail right this very minute waiting for the judge. They told me that Culpepper and Taggart robbed them, killed one of their men, and stole the money from the bank robbery here in Denver. Sheriff

Trent and Marshal Holt were on their trail, but they didn't find them."

"Are you talking about the men who rode with Frank Langtry? They are the ones in the Denver jail?"

Harper nodded. "One and the same. They aren't bad men, they just got mixed up with Frank Langtry. They turned themselves over to the marshal and the sheriff. Frank Langtry was involved with that robbery, and they are going to testify against him."

The one question that was on the tip of Clay's tongue suddenly felt bitter. He wanted to ask if Leigh King was involved, but he equivocated. Would it make a difference to him if she was involved? Either way, she was a young woman who needed assistance. The question remained unasked. "I don't know if Judge Stevens will believe anything bad about Frank. I hear he's partial to him."

"He might be partial to Frank, but there's two men willing to testify in court that Frank planned that bank robbery."

As the men were saying good-bye, Clay asked again, "Are you sure you're doing okay?"

Harper leaned in and said, "Doc says I got cancer. He don't give me long, so I'm spending the time with my sister and her kids, trying to make their life easier while I'm here."

Clay put his hand on Harper's shoulder. "Doctors don't have the final say in the matter."

"I was never one to go to church, if that's what you are suggesting." Harper thought he knew the direction Clay was headed.

"This isn't about going to church, this is about faith, Harper."

"Are you saying the doctor doesn't know what he's talking about?"

"Not at all. I'm just saying doctors don't have all the answers. Maybe you should just think about it."

Harper was silent for a moment. "Maybe you're right."

After Clay left Harper, he walked to the jail to speak to Sheriff Trent. The sheriff confirmed Frank's gang was occupying his jail, and the men were waiting on the judge's return to hear what they had to say.

"Why are they going to testify against Frank?" Clay asked.

"They said they didn't shoot anyone, and they aren't willing to take the blame for Frank. They also told me Culpepper and Taggart stole that money."

"You believe them?"

"I do. They had their fill of Frank Langtry, and it rubs them the wrong way that he's the one walking around without a bounty on his head."

"Are you planning on arresting Frank?" Clay asked.

"We'll have to wait on the judge to get back. His sister said he should be back in a few days. Marshal Holt is still out there trying to track down Culpepper and Taggart. He has a feeling they could be close."

"I hope he finds them before they find him."

Clay arrived a few minutes early for Emma's performance, and he stopped to greet some of familiar faces he saw in the crowd. To his surprise, there were several of the folks in attendance who had been adamant he not attend her performance in the first place. He acknowledged them warmly, and reassured them they were about to see a performance they would never forget. When he reached the balcony, he was surprised to see the prince along with his two bodyguards sitting in the same box.

The prince stood and bowed slightly when he saw Clay approach. "Emma said we would be sharing the box with you, Mr. Hunt. I'm Henri d'Evereux."

Clay noticed the prince introduced himself by his given name without his title, and he introduced his bodyguards. Clay wasn't schooled in proper etiquette when meeting a prince, but he figured he was like any other man, so he extended his hand. "Nice to meet you." He then shook hands with the bodyguards. "Please call me Clay."

As they waited for the performance to start, the prince discussed the many times he'd been honored to hear Emma's performance in France. It didn't take long before Clay knew for certain that the prince had come to America to court Emma. By the many questions the prince asked, Clay felt like he was being sized up as competition. Considering he hadn't decided where he wanted his relationship with Emma to go, he kept his responses brief. The more they talked, Clay discovered he really liked the man, and thought Emma should be flattered that the prince was pursuing her. He imagined most women would consider him an excellent prospect for a husband. But Clay told himself the prince wasn't the man for Emma. However, he wasn't willing to concede he might consider himself the right man.

After the final curtain call, Emma saw both Clay and Henri near the door waiting for her. She regretted that Henri traveled all this way if his purpose was to court her, but she'd made every attempt to be clear about her intentions to stay in Whispering Pines. She dreaded to tell him she intended to ride back to Whispering Pines with Clay.

"Clay, would you care to join us for dinner?" Henri asked.

Clay was surprised by his question. He glanced Emma's way, thinking she'd made a change in plans and hadn't had a chance to tell him. "Thanks for the offer, but before the performance it had already started to snow, so I asked the restaurant to prepare something we can take with us."

Emma walked to the door and looked out. "It's really coming down. I think we should leave now."

"Let's go to the hotel and I will retrieve my luggage. I will take you to Whispering Pines," Henri said.

"Henri, I think I should ride with Clay. He is accustomed to this weather. Perhaps you should stay in Denver if you are insistent on attending the next performance." Emma didn't want him to come to Whispering Pines tonight.

"I insist on taking you home, and I will stay there so I can see you tomorrow," Henri said.

Clay didn't like the idea of Henri escorting Emma home. He told himself he was concerned because Henri didn't know the territory. "Sorry, Henri, but we have a saying in this country: 'The man that brings the girl to the dance takes her home.'"

Henri stared at him, trying to understand what he was saying. "We aren't at a dance. I'm traveling to Emma's home tonight, and I will take her with me."

"Nope. I'm sorry, but that's not going to happen," Clay said. No way was he going to entrust Emma's safety to a tenderfoot.

Henri looked at Emma. "Emma, tell this gentleman that I'm taking you home."

"I'm sorry, Henri, but Clay is right. He should take me home. He was kind enough to go out of his way to escort me to town, and we planned on returning together. The weather out here can get nasty very quickly, and Clay would know what to do. You should wait to come to Whispering Pines when it is not snowing. This is not a country to ignore bad weather." Emma hated to pray for a foot of snow, but right now, that was what she was doing.

Clay was half-aggravated that she was telling Henri the only reason she wanted to ride back to Whispering Pines with him was due to the inclement conditions. Before he made a fool of himself, he thought there was no better time to find out what she really wanted. If she wanted this prince, then he thought it was time to fish or cut bait. "If you want to ride with Henri, I can follow you to make sure everyone gets there safe and sound."

Emma's eyes snapped to Clay's. What was he doing? She was trying to keep Henri in Denver, and Clay was all but giving him the opportunity to go to Whispering Pines. "I think that would be foolish. Henri can come to Whispering Pines when the conditions improve."

Henri's gaze bounced from Emma to Clay. "Why don't we all stay in Denver tonight, and see what the weather presents tomorrow?"

"I can't stay. I promised my family I would return tonight. Not only that, but I didn't plan on staying overnight, so I didn't pack a valise." Emma was tired of all of this talking. She'd learned from Granny how to take control of a situation, and now was the perfect time to employ her skills. She took a deep breath, raised her chin as though she was preparing to command an army, and said, "Now, enough of this nonsense. Henri, if the weather improves, feel free to visit Whispering Pines whenever you choose. My family would love to meet you. If the weather doesn't improve, I will see you at my next performance." She turned her attention on Clay. "Are you ready to depart?"

Clay's features were impassive when he nodded his answer, but on the inside, he was smiling. Although Henri was not pleased with her decision, he said good-bye and walked out the door.

Before they made it out the door, Emma heard her brother's voice. She turned around to see Frank walking toward them. Clinging to his arm was an elegantly dressed older woman.

"Emma, I'd like you to meet a big fan of yours. This is Judge Stevens's sister, Mrs. Ruth Stevens Winthrop."

Emma politely smiled at the striking woman as she noted the sparkling diamond brooch adorning her dress. So this was the woman with the massive mansion on the hill who owned a gold mine. "Pleasure."

"I thoroughly enjoyed your performance, my dear," Ruth said. "It's not often we get to hear such talent in Denver. But we are endeavoring to make this a city where gifted people like you will want to perform. What do you think of this venue?"

"It's lovely, and I'm certain you will attract many artists." Emma didn't really know what to say to the woman, and she wanted to get away from Frank before he and Clay had words again.

"I do hope you will speak highly of our establishment," Ruth replied.

Emma thought the woman had developed a tactful way to make certain people understood her influence in the community. "May I introduce Clay Hunt?"

Ruth raked her eyes over Clay and smiled. "Mr. Hunt, do you also live in Whispering Pines?"

"Yes, ma'am, I do."

"He's the pastor in Whispering Pines," Frank offered.

Ruth seemed surprised at that piece of news. "I must admit I've never seen many pastors as young as you."

Emma caught the look that passed over Frank's face. She wondered if that was the real reason he didn't want Leigh King around Clay, because women found him attractive. "Our family feels very fortunate to have him in Whispering Pines."

Clay glanced Emma's way, thinking she'd never been so liberal with her praise. He thought she might be trying to circumvent any problems with Frank. He had a feeling Frank might be inclined to mind his manners around his wealthy benefactor.

"Perhaps you would do us a kindness and hold a service in Denver one Sunday. I'm certain our pastor would be thankful for a reprieve," Ruth said.

Emma had to hand it to the woman; she wasn't hiding her interest in Clay. She had no doubt this woman was accustomed to having her way.

"Whispering Pines keeps me pretty busy," Clay said.

Frank glared at Clay. "He stays busy with the women in Whispering Pines."

Ruth bristled at Frank's impolite comment. "I'm certain the pastor's duty extends to men as well." She smiled at Clay again, and added, "Please think over my request. I would consider it a personal favor to hear some new material from the pulpit."

"I'll give it due consideration," Clay promised politely.

"Frank, why didn't you bring Mrs. King to the performance? She mentioned she would like to come," Emma said sweetly.

The comment wiped the smirk off of Frank's face, and for the first time in Emma's memory, Frank had no response.

When Clay and Emma walked away, Emma glanced back at Frank and Ruth. Frank was whispering something in Ruth's ear. Ruth pulled back a fraction from Frank and smiled up at him. Emma watched as Frank leaned over and brushed a kiss over Ruth's lips. It was so fleeting that Emma didn't think anyone not watching intently would have noticed. She had a feeling there was more to that relationship than anyone knew.

Chapter Fifteen

Emma and Clay had been traveling for nearly an hour when the wind picked up and snowflakes were swirling in every direction, making it difficult to see more than a foot in front of them. Clay feared it wasn't going to improve. "Maybe we should turn back and stay in Denver."

"I'm not going back to Denver. If you want to go back, then I will drive the buckboard myself," Emma said. "I told Granny we would be home tonight. Even if we turned back and sent a telegram, they wouldn't get it until morning. She would be worried sick about us."

Clay was having second thoughts about traveling in these uncertain conditions, but he wanted to please Emma. He certainly didn't want Granny to worry.

It wasn't long before they were facing near-blizzard conditions, and they could no longer see the trail. He pulled the buckboard to a halt. "Emma, this is dangerous. I can't see the trail."

Emma turned around to view the trail behind them that had instantly disappeared. "We can't see going back to Denver, either. Do you know where we are?"

"Not exactly, but I think we might be near a cabin I've seen off the trail." He jumped down from the buckboard.

"Where are you going?" Emma was afraid he was going to say they would walk the rest of the way to Whispering Pines.

"I'm going to look around to see if I can find some shelter. There are two abandoned homes along this trail. I think there's an old shack about thirty yards in that direction." He pointed to the area, and added, "It may not be much, but it will keep us warm tonight." He pulled his rifle from the back of the buckboard and handed it to her. "If you don't see me in fifteen minutes, fire off a round." He started to walk away, but he turned back and said, "Do you know how to do that?"

"Yes. But I want to go with you. I don't like the thought of sitting here alone worrying that you might get lost." Unable to see anything but swirling snow, she had no sense of direction.

Clay knew if he walked a foot away, he wouldn't be able to see her. He didn't like the thought of leaving her alone either, so he walked to the horse, released him from the buggy and took him by the reins. He helped Emma from the buckboard and onto the horse's back. After he retrieved the blankets and the basket of food he'd ordered from the restaurant, they slowly trekked through the dense brush. After several minutes, Clay became concerned that he was way off course, and if they didn't find shelter soon, it could go from bad to worse.

He slowly moved forward and within minutes, he thought he saw a structure. "I think I see it."

"I don't see anything," Emma replied.

They walked a few more feet, and Clay said, "Do you see it now?"

Emma was thrilled to see the dilapidated structure in front of them. "Yes."

After tying the horse to the rail at the front of the shack,

Clay walked up the steps to the front door. When he opened the door, he struck a match to look inside. Surprisingly, the place looked like it had been recently swept out. There were some chairs and an old table arranged in front of the fireplace, and there wasn't a cobweb in sight. That could mean one of two things: someone may have been passing through and used it for the night, or men like Frank Langtry's gang knew about the place and stopped here frequently. He quickly decided it didn't matter; they couldn't stay outside in the cold to look for another place. They'd have to take their chances that no one else would be out on a night like tonight. He hurried back to Emma and helped her from the horse.

After ushering Emma inside, Clay lit an oil lamp on the mantle before inspecting the fireplace. "It's been cleaned recently, and there are logs already placed for a fire. At least we'll be warm tonight." In no time he had a fire going before he went outside to see if he could find a sheltered spot for the horse.

While Clay was outside, Emma looked around the small one-room shack. Someone had cleaned the place recently, and she wondered if they planned on returning soon. The small room was warming up quickly, so Emma removed her cloak and started unpacking the food in the basket. It surprised her that Clay had been so considerate to ask the restaurant to pack a meal for them. She speculated about his plans if the weather hadn't taken a turn for the worse. It was too cold for a picnic, but they could have stopped and started a fire off the trail. She envisioned the two of them cuddled close together by a fire sharing a meal. It made for a rather romantic scene in her mind. She chided herself for having such starry-eyed notions. Clay had probably ordered the food because he was hungry, plain and simple. Since the meal consisted of fried chicken and biscuits, he could have eaten as he drove the buckboard.

Clay was carrying more logs, along with a saddlebag and his rifle, when he walked through the door. "I found an old lean-to behind the house. The horse will be fine tonight." He placed the logs beside the fireplace, removed his coat, and placed it over his rifle on the table. "It feels good in here."

"The chicken smells delicious. Thank you for thinking of having a dinner prepared to take with us."

"I had planned on taking you to a small ranch that's for sale not too far from Morgan's. I thought about selling my ranch in Kansas and buying that piece of property. That is, if I can get Jonas to come out here and work." Actually, he'd only been thinking seriously of buying the place in the last few days. He'd seen it before, but he couldn't say he would have considered such a move until now.

"Jonas?"

"Yes, Jonas Meeker. He runs my ranch in Kansas." Clay reached inside his saddlebags and pulled out a coffeepot and some beans, along with two cups. "I brought this along in case we had that picnic."

Emma smiled. "A good hot cup of coffee sounds heavenly."

"I'll have it ready in no time." Clay opened his canteen and poured water into the coffeepot.

"Why did you want me to see that ranch?" Emma was thrilled to hear him say he had made plans tonight if the weather had cooperated.

Clay's hands stilled. He hadn't expected that question, and he hadn't thought through the reason he wanted her to see the ranch. "You mentioned living in Whispering Pines when you stopped singing. I guess I just thought you might like to see the place."

"That was very thoughtful of you."

Once the coffee was boiling, Clay poured two cups and they sat at the table and ate some chicken.

"What did you think of Mrs. Winthrop?" Emma asked.

"She seemed like a nice woman," Clay said.

"Wonder what she sees in Frank."

Clay shook his head. He had to admit he'd wondered the same thing. "Maybe she needs companionship."

Emma eyed Clay. While she admired him for trying to see the good in everyone, she hoped he didn't have a blind side when it came to people who shouldn't be trusted. "I think she has another purpose for Frank. I just can't figure out what it is."

Clay wanted to broach the subject of Leigh King, but he wanted to do it in a way that didn't ruin their pleasant night. But he was determined to talk to Emma tonight while they were alone about what was important to him. He may not have another chance. "Emma, the prince all but confessed he intended to ask you to marry him."

"He's definitely taken me by surprise. I didn't really think he was going to come to America. I guess he's accustomed to having his way."

Clay took a sip of his coffee, but his eyes remained on her face. He thought she looked beautiful in the firelight. He hadn't really asked her if she was interested in marrying the prince, and she gave no indication as to her thoughts about him showing up in Denver. "He thinks very highly of you."

Emma wanted to ask him what he thought about her.

Now was the time to find out what she wanted, Clay thought. Was he ready to tell her what he was feeling? He took a deep breath, and said, "I want to talk to you about Leigh King."

"What?" Of all the things Emma wanted to talk about at the moment, Leigh King was at the bottom of the list.

Clay held up his hand and said, "Just hear me out. I know you think I have an interest in Mrs. King, but that's not exactly the way it is. I wanted to explain why I seemed— taken with her."

"You're not only taken with her, you can't seem to stay away from her," Emma said testily.

"She looks exactly like my deceased wife," he said quickly before she wouldn't give him a chance to explain. He slowly expelled a deep breath, and he felt a portion of the burden he'd been carrying was finally released from his heart.

His statement took a moment to register in Emma's brain, and when it did, she said, "You were married?"

Clay nodded. "We lived on our ranch in Kansas. Violet was my wife, whom I loved dearly, and we had a son."

Emma realized he'd said *deceased* wife. "Where is your son?"

Clay explained what happened to his wife and son that day on his ranch. It seemed like yesterday he'd heard those shots in the air, yet the pain he'd carried had lasted an eternity. He stood and started pacing as he described the life he'd had with his wife and son.

Emma could see he was lost in his memories of the woman he loved more than life. She didn't utter a sound, but she couldn't stop the tears as his story unfolded.

He held nothing back from her, including how he'd hunted down the men who had killed his family. By the time he stopped talking, Emma felt as though her heart was torn in half.

"I'm so sorry." Emma wiped her tears away. Whatever she said seemed so inadequate. "I didn't know you had been through so much."

"When I became a pastor, the one thing I learned is we all have pain in our lives. Some of us learn to live with it, some of us let it eat us alive. I did the former too long, until I came to my senses."

"I'm glad you let go of your vendetta," Emma whispered.

"The two men who killed my wife and son are the same two men the marshal is looking for," Clay said. "I can't in all honesty say I didn't want to go with the marshal to track them down when he told me he was going to Purgatory Canyon. Even if I had joined him, I know I wouldn't have killed them. I just wanted to see them for myself. I want justice for my family."

"Of course you do. That's understandable," Emma said.

Clay sat back down next to her. "Emma, I loved Violet, and I guess I never thought I would feel that way again. I'm not certain I even wanted to feel that way again, mostly out of fear of losing another person I loved."

"That's understandable too." Emma understood what he was saying, though she didn't want to hear that he would never love again, particularly now that she realized her feelings for him were deeper than she wanted to admit. Tonight when they were talking with Henri, Emma knew she'd already lost her heart to Clay. "I can understand now why you were naturally attracted to Mrs. King when you first saw her."

"I was curious about her. She looked so much like Violet that I think I wanted to be around her to remember my wife. I was afraid I was forgetting what Violet looked like. I didn't want to forget. I don't want to ever forget them."

"You will never forget them." Emma reached over and tenderly stroked his cheek. "They will always be in your heart."

Clay reached for her hand. The fact that she understood his feelings tugged at that place in his soul, the place he thought he locked away forever. He pressed his lips to her palm.

It was such an intimate gesture, Emma's heart started to thump loudly, and her gaze remained fixed on his lips. She wanted to feel his lips on hers, and just as that thought flitted through her mind, Clay gently placed her hand back on the table.

Thoughts of Violet came rushing over him. He wasn't ready to let her go. Not just yet.

Part of him wanted to kiss Emma so badly, he could actually taste her. But he needed to get control of the past. "Emma, what I was trying to say a moment ago was, I've never given another thought to having a family again . . ." He wanted to add *until I met you,* but he didn't. Instead he said, "I've not let go of the past." Thinking about Violet and Mark made him question if he really did want to move on with his life. He couldn't let them go.

Emma's heart almost leapt with joy when she thought he was going to proclaim some deeper feelings for her. But he didn't. He professed nothing other than his complete devotion to his deceased wife. It wasn't that she didn't understand—she did—but that didn't lessen the hurt when he'd admitted his fidelity to Violet. Four years was a long time to mourn.

Both of her sisters had told her that they thought they had fallen in love the first time they saw their husbands when they returned to Whispering Pines. Emma had never considered the possibility of love at first sight, but now she wasn't so sure. Was she in love with him? Is that why her heart felt like it was splintering into tiny pieces at this very moment?

She glanced at his large, strong hands on the table, and she felt like bringing his palm to her lips. Instead, she placed her hand over his and gave him a gentle squeeze, hoping she could offer some comfort even though her heart was breaking. "One day it will get easier."

Though she didn't say the words, she thought as long as Leigh King was around, Clay wouldn't be able to resist the beautiful widow. She was the constant reminder of all that he'd lost. All that he had loved.

Chapter Sixteen

Hearing a knock on the bedroom door, Morgan pulled his pants on, and hurried to see what was going on. Granny was standing there with a frantic look on her face. "What is it, Granny? Are you ill?"

"I'm worried about Emma and Clay. They should have been home hours ago. The snow hasn't stopped and poor Sweetie is pacing the floor. I think he knows something is wrong."

Morgan ran his hand over his face. "What time is it?"

"It's one o'clock."

"Let me get my shirt." Once Morgan threw some water on his face and donned his shirt, Rose had pulled on her robe, and they all made their way to the kitchen.

"I'll make us some coffee," Rose said.

Morgan walked to the window and looked outside. Several inches of snow had accumulated since they had retired for the night. "Don't you think Clay decided it would be better to stay in Denver?"

"He might have, but I know Emma, and she was determined to come home. She didn't say as much, but I think she was worried the prince might be in Denver," Granny replied.

"Doesn't she want to see him?" Morgan asked.

Granny pulled cups from the shelves and placed them on the table. "She didn't mind seeing him, but she's in love with Clay."

"Granny, Emma didn't say that," Rose said.

"She didn't have to say the words. I've never seen Emma get so aggravated with a man like she does Clay. It was all but written on her forehead every time his name came up in conversation. She told us she had no intention of marrying the prince."

"She did get very angry with Clay over Mrs. King," Rose agreed. Rose remembered feeling the same way about Morgan when another woman would show the least amount of interest in him.

Morgan laughed. "If it makes you two feel better, I think Clay is in love with her too. He was all lathered up when he thought she wasn't going to let him take her to Denver yesterday."

Granny clapped her hands together. "I just knew it! I bet we will have a Christmas wedding."

"Now, Granny, don't get your hopes up. It may not turn out that way," Rose warned.

"You know as well as I do, for all of Emma's independence, she would love to be married and have children." Granny knew Emma was a strong, self-determined woman, but she also knew her granddaughter had a lot of love to give a man.

Rose reached over and squeezed her husband's hand. "Do you think Clay will ask her to marry him?"

"I wouldn't be surprised." Morgan had a feeling that was exactly the reason Clay wanted to take her to Denver, though he didn't say as much. Morgan hadn't told anyone when he was ready to ask Rose to marry. It may have seemed like a hasty decision, but it'd been on his mind day and night once he saw her. He thought it was a funny thing how men reacted before they realized they were in love. In his case, he kept trying to avoid his feelings. Rose would get under his skin, make him so angry he felt like he could chew through nails. But once he faced the fact that no one could get under his skin like Rose, he had to face what was really going on. He was in love, and he couldn't wait to make her his wife. He had a feeling Clay was going to come to the same conclusion about Emma, if he could put the past behind him.

"Do you think they had trouble trying to get home?" Granny asked.

Morgan agreed with Granny that Emma and Clay probably left Denver. "As soon as it gets light, I'll go to town and send a telegram to Sheriff Trent in Denver. He'll find out if they decided to stay the night and let me know."

"Good," Granny said. "I'm sorry I woke you."

"Don't be." Morgan glanced at Sweetie, who was sitting by the back door looking so sad that it broke his heart. He didn't want Granny or Sweetie worrying. Morgan stood and reached for his coat by the back door. "I'll go get Jack, and we'll take Sweetie and ride the trail to Denver. I know if they are stopped somewhere on the road, Sweetie will find them."

Sweetie jumped up and started wagging his tail.

Clay had arranged a comfortable spot on the floor near the fireplace so they could stay warm. Emma didn't complain; she enjoyed being in Clay's company no matter the circumstances. When she fell asleep, Clay watched her for a long time. Emma was nothing like Violet, but he felt a deep connection with her. He wondered what it would be like to be married to her and build a new life filled with fresh hopes and dreams.

He knew if he did move on with his life, he would want children. They could never replace his son, but he would love them just as much. Not wanting to fall sleep, Clay shut his eyes and thought about his past.

The door opened slowly, with the barrel of a pistol barely visible pushing it wider. Clay was so deep in thought that he didn't hear the door opening, but when he felt the cold air, he knew it was too late. The barrel of the gun came into view. He wasn't a careless man, but tonight his mind had been preoccupied with the woman beside him, and the woman in his past. His rifle was still on the table under his coat. Leaping to his feet, he started to make a move for the rifle, but two men charged through the door before he'd taken the first step.

"I swear, Win, we find the strangest people in cabins every time we come this way," Joe Culpepper said.

Win grinned. "Don't we, though?"

Emma was startled awake at the sound of men's voices. She sat straight and glared at the two men. "Who are you?"

Win Taggart laughed. "Honey, we're the men of your dreams."

Emma shuddered. She glanced at Clay, and saw the way he was intently watching these two men. Emma stood, and with the same confident presence she employed on stage, said in a haughty tone, "Who are you and what do you want?"

"Why, you're a feisty thing." Culpepper turned his eyes on Clay. "Your woman always do the talking for you?"

"What do you want?" Clay asked, not taking the bait.

"What do you have?" Win asked. He looked Clay over and saw he wasn't wearing a holster. "Where's your pistol?"

"I don't wear one."

Culpepper walked to the table and Clay held his breath, hoping he didn't see the rifle. He flipped open the lid on the basket. He stuck his hand inside and pulled out a piece of chicken. "Hey, Win, we have some chicken here."

Win kept his gun pointed at Clay as he walked over to the table and grabbed a piece of chicken. "What are you two doing in our cabin?"

"This cabin has been abandoned for years," Clay said.

"Maybe. But we've been here for a few days, so I figured it's ours now," Culpepper said. He waved his gun at Clay. "And you didn't answer my question."

"We were headed to Whispering Pines and got caught in the storm. I guess if you've been out in it, you know it's blowing pretty hard out there," Clay said.

"Where you coming from?" Win asked.

"Denver." Clay looked at Emma, silently hoping he telegraphed for her not to reveal too much to this pair of killers. He'd recognized them once they called each other by name.

Culpepper stared hard at Emma. "I've seen you somewhere before."

Clay held his breath, but Emma said, "I doubt that."

"I know I've seen your face before." Culpepper motioned with the barrel of his gun at Clay. "Is this your husband?"

Emma glanced at Clay, and seeing his almost imperceptible nod, she said, "Yes. Now why don't you tell us who you are and what you want."

"Excuse our manners." Culpepper removed his hat and bowed. "I'm Joe Culpepper and this here's"—he pointed to Taggart—"Win Taggart. We're looking for some hombres who stole something from us."

Emma tried to remain calm. These were the two men she and Clay had been discussing earlier. Now she understood the look on Clay's face as he was staring at the two men who had killed his family. She admired him even more for maintaining his composure.

"Maybe you've heard of us," Taggart said.

"Should we have heard of you?" Clay said.

"Most people have," Culpepper said.

Both men sat at the table and helped themselves to the rest of the chicken while pointing their guns on Clay and Emma.

Clay leaned his hip against the table near his coat, trying to appear as casual as possible looking down the barrel of a gun. "Are you headed to Denver?"

"Yep, we sure are. We need to see some men about some money." Culpepper looked at Taggart and said, "Win, why don't you go on out there and unsaddle our horses and bring in the whiskey. I'll watch these two."

Win stood and headed to the door. "Don't eat all that chicken, I'm still hungry."

"We got some food in our saddlebags," Culpepper responded.

"It ain't as good as that chicken."

Win left the cabin, and Culpepper turned his attention on Clay. "Why ain't you wearing a gun?"

"I'm a pastor," Clay replied. Let him go on thinking he didn't have a weapon.

Culpepper let out a hearty laugh. "Is that a fact?"

"It's a fact. I'm the pastor in Whispering Pines."

Chewing with his mouth open, Culpepper said, "And

that's the reason you go around out here in this country without a pistol?"

"That's right."

"Don't you think that's pretty stupid considering the kind of men who could ride up at any time? You never know who might stop in your cabin." Culpepper laughed at his own joke.

"It's happened before," Clay said.

Emma stood and picked up her cape that had been covering her. She knew if they were going to have a chance to get out of this situation it had to be while Culpepper and Taggart were separated.

Culpepper followed her movement with the barrel of his pistol. "What do you think you are doing?"

Clay was at one end of the table, so Emma stepped closer to the opposite end. A quick glance at Clay said he was watching her, and she saw his eyes slide to the rifle on the table. Culpepper's eyes were on her. "I'm cold." With great flare, and knowing Culpepper was intently watching her, Emma swirled her cape, causing the material to fan out wide, brushing the killer's gun hand. Distracted by the movement of the cape, Culpepper didn't notice Emma had pulled her pistol from the inside pocket. She had Carlo to thank for that move; she'd seen him do the same thing numerous times. Carlo always told her the hand was quicker than the eye.

At the same time, Clay grabbed his rifle and pushed the muzzle against Culpepper's temple. "Drop the pistol."

Culpepper turned his head toward Clay, but held on to his gun. "Preacher Man, you ain't gonna shoot me."

Clay had already made up his mind he would pull the trigger to protect Emma. He'd seen what these two killers were capable of doing, and he wasn't going to give them another chance to kill. He stared into Culpepper's eyes to let him know he shouldn't take that gamble.

Emma cocked her pistol and moved closer to Culpepper. "He might not, but I assure you, I won't hesitate."

Culpepper dropped his pistol on the table. "If this don't beat all. I ain't never been snookered by a preacher and his wife before."

Clay couldn't help but smile at Emma's courageous move. She was some woman. "There's a knife in my saddlebag. Tear strips from that blanket and tie him up."

Emma picked up Culpepper's pistol and handed it to Clay. She put her own pistol back inside the pocket in her cape. She hurried to do as Clay instructed. Once she tied Culpepper's hands behind his back, she bound his feet to the chair.

Clay set his rifle aside and covered Culpepper's mouth with his bandana. He didn't want him calling out to Taggart. Clay opened Culpepper's coat to search him for other weapons. He didn't find anything but three playing cards in his pocket. All were the ace of spades with bullet holes through the center. "I guess you won't be using these tonight." Clay threw the cards on the table, then reached into his shirt pocket and threw a card on top of the three.

Culpepper glanced down at the card Clay threw on the table. He looked up at Clay, and the question he couldn't ask was in his eyes.

"You left this on my wife and son four years ago in Kansas."

Emma thought she saw true fear in Culpepper's eyes.

Clay stared hard at the man who'd killed his family. "I trailed you for a long time. I always wondered how I'd feel when I came face-to-face with the men who had killed a woman and young boy. I never understood how anyone could be so evil that they would kill for no reason. Kill people who couldn't hurt them. I'm not able to forgive you, but I'm not going to kill you. Your judgment day will come, and you will get what you deserve."

Within minutes, they heard Taggart stomping his feet on the porch. Clay cocked Culpepper's pistol and stood behind the door. Emma stood to the other side with her pistol pointed at the door.

Taggart came inside carrying saddlebags, but his gun was in his holster.

"Drop your holster to the floor," Clay instructed.

Seeing Culpepper tied up, Taggart saw there was nothing he could do.

"Slowly, with your left hand," Clay warned.

Taggart complied and let his holster drop to the floor.

Clay motioned with the barrel of the pistol. "Now sit in that chair."

Emma repeated the process of tying Taggart's hands and feet. After she was satisfied he was secure, she fished through the provisions in the saddlebag. She pulled out some coffee beans for Clay to see. "I'll melt some snow and make us some more coffee."

"Sounds good."

Emma walked outside and filled the coffeepot with snow. Trying to calm her nerves, she took a deep breath of cold air. She'd stayed calm during the ordeal, but that didn't mean her insides weren't churning. When she walked back inside, Clay was by the door waiting for her, the pistol still in his hand.

"Where did you get the pistol?" Clay asked.

"Carlo insisted I have a pocket sewn inside my cape so I could have a pistol if I ever needed one. With Sweetie beside me, I've never needed it."

Clay didn't like the thought of Emma being in situations where she had to protect herself. "You're an amazing woman, Emma."

She leaned close to him and whispered, "I'm sorry you have to face these two."

"I never knew what I would do when I saw them. I never wanted to take another life, but I didn't know if I could let them live. Now I know."

In her opinion, not only was he a man of courage, but one of great integrity.

Chapter Seventeen

The foot of snow made it difficult for Morgan and Jack to match Sweetie's urgent pace. Once they'd stopped in Whispering Pines to send a telegram to Sheriff Trent, they didn't have long to wait for his reply. Clay and Emma had left Denver last night. Though more snow was falling, Morgan and Jack jumped back in their saddles and headed toward Denver with Sweetie leading the way.

When Sweetie would get too far ahead of the men, he'd stop and wait for them. Morgan had a feeling the dog was asking why they weren't moving fast enough to suit him. They were almost at the halfway point between Whispering Pines and Denver when Sweetie left the trail. So far, the men had seen no indication that Clay had made it this far, so when Sweetie diverted through the brush, Morgan whistled for him.

The dog came running from the trees, and Morgan said, "That's not the way to Denver, Sweetie."

Sweetie stood in front of the horses, forcing the men to stop. The dog stared at them, then turned his head to the left as if he wanted them to follow him off the trail.

"What do you make of that?" Jack asked.

"I don't know, but Emma tells me he's the smartest dog she's ever seen. You know how animals are. He probably knows something we don't. I say we follow him." Morgan turned his horse in the direction of the trees.

"That's what I thought you were going to say." Jack urged his horse to follow Morgan's.

Sweetie loped ahead, and once they were several yards off the main trail, Sweetie came to a stop.

Morgan pointed to an old rundown shack that would have been easily missed if not for Sweetie. "That's some dog."

"I'd forgotten that shack was there," Jack said.

They dismounted and slowly approached the cabin. Morgan nudged Jack's arm and pointed to the ground. Though partially covered by the newly falling snow, they could see some tracks indicating horses and a buckboard had come this way. If the buckboard was Clay and Emma's, then two men on horseback had to be with them.

Morgan drew his gun and slowly opened the cabin door, but Sweetie bounded through the opening. Seeing the room was empty, Morgan and Jack followed Sweetie inside to have a look around. Morgan walked to the fireplace and placed his hand over the dying embers. "Whoever was here hasn't been gone long."

Jack picked up the playing cards from the table. "Morgan, you'd better look at this."

Morgan walked to the table and saw what Jack was holding. "Culpepper and Taggart."

"Yep." Jack stuffed the cards into his pocket.

Sweetie was sniffing the air almost as if he was sniffing a tasty steak. Following the dog's lead, Morgan breathed deeply. "I smell Emma's perfume."

"Are you sure that's not Sweetie you're smelling. That dog smells better than most women," Jack said.

"He hasn't had a bath since he's been at the house. It's Emma. She's been here." Morgan was confident Emma had been in this room.

Sweetie walked around the room sniffing and whining before he walked out the door. Morgan and Jack followed him outside.

"We have tracks to follow now," Morgan said, mounting his horse.

They rode behind the cabin and started following the tracks. Sweetie was leading the way when he stopped suddenly and cocked his ear to an area on the far side of the cabin.

Morgan and Jack caught his movement and stopped. When Sweetie growled low, the men pulled their pistols.

Marshal Holt came riding through the brush with his pistol drawn. Seeing Jack and Morgan, the marshal holstered his pistol. "What are you two doing out here?"

"We're looking for Clay and Emma. They were coming back from Denver last night and we think they were here," Morgan said.

The marshal inclined his head toward Sweetie. "Didn't she have him with her?"

"No, she left him with me last night. What are you doing out here?" Morgan asked.

"Following Culpepper and Taggart."

Jack and Morgan exchanged a glance, and Jack said, "I think you are a few hours too late." Jack pulled the cards from his coat pocket and handed them to the marshal. "These were on the table in that cabin. We're following a buckboard along with two horses."

The marshal didn't like the sound of that. If Culpepper

and Taggart happened on Clay and Emma, he was surprised they hadn't already been shot. "Let's be on our way."

Within minutes they realized the buckboard and horses were headed to Denver. The men were forced to pick up speed when Sweetie switched into another gear, kicking up snow as he ran.

"There's the buckboard ahead," Jack said. "Looks like there are two riders behind the buckboard."

"Sweetie!" Morgan yelled, in an effort to stop the dog. He didn't want those killers to shoot Emma's dog.

Sweetie didn't slow down as he leapt on the back of the buckboard and made his way to Emma on the seat.

"Sweetie! What are you doing here?" Emma wrapped her arms around her dog as he crawled onto her lap.

Clay pulled the buckboard to a halt and reached for his rifle. When Morgan, Jack, and the marshal rode up, he took a deep breath. "I'm glad to see you." He pointed to Culpepper and Taggart tied to their horses. "We were taking them to Denver."

Marshal Holt could hardly believe his eyes. Two of the most famous killers he'd been tracking for what seemed like years were tethered to their horses with strips from a blanket, and bandanas tied around their mouths. "How did you manage to capture these two?"

"You can thank Emma for her quick thinking," Clay said. He told them how Emma captured Culpepper's attention when she donned her cape.

"Smart move, Emma," Morgan said.

Marshal Holt rode to Culpepper and pulled the bandana from his mouth. "Where's the money you stole from Langtry's gang from that bank robbery?"

"I don't know what you're talking about," Culpepper said.

Holt pulled a playing card from his pocket. "Here's your

calling card that was left on the man you killed. Two other men said you took the money."

Culpepper's eyes slid to Taggart. "Sounds like you got a tall tale, Marshal. Anyone can leave a card on a dead body."

"True enough, but I got two men sitting in jail waiting to testify they saw you two kill that man and steal the money."

"In jail you say?" Culpepper smiled. "You got two jail-birds giving you a tale to save their own hides. It's their word against ours," Culpepper said.

Before the marshal covered Culpepper's mouth, Clay said, "Why did you kill my wife and son that day?"

"We never killed no woman and kid," Culpepper replied.

Clay wasn't surprised Culpepper wouldn't answer the question. "Where did you sell my horses you stole?" Clay had never forgotten about Moonrise. He'd asked the same question of the men he'd killed from Culpepper's gang. They'd said Culpepper and Taggart had the horses with them.

"We didn't steal no horses," Culpepper said.

The marshal glanced Clay's way as he covered Culpepper's mouth with the bandana. "They won't confess, Clay. I still have a list of other charges as long as my arm that'll keep them in the territorial prison for the rest of their days." He untied their horses from the buckboard. "You two can go on to Whispering Pines; I'll take them in."

Jack looked up at the sky. "It looks like the sun is coming out, so I'll ride with you to Denver."

"I'll ride along, too," Morgan said. "Clay and Sweetie can see Emma home safely."

* * *

Frank Langtry was escorting Ruth to the hotel for lunch when Marshal Holt, Morgan, and Jack rode into town with Culpepper and Taggart. Frank could hardly believe Holt had finally caught up with the pair. Culpepper spotted Frank on the sidewalk and glared at him.

"Who are those men?" Ruth asked.

"Joe Culpepper and Win Taggart. They're killers."

"They look absolutely vicious. Do you know that one staring at you?"

"Yeah, I met them once. That's Culpepper doing the staring. He killed a friend of mine." Frank decided after lunch he'd go to the jail and talk to Dutch to find out what was going on. He'd heard talk that his gang would testify against him, so it seemed prudent for him to find a way to break them out of jail.

Sheriff Trent escorted Culpepper and Taggart to the cell next to Frank's gang, and instructed his deputy to hang close to hear what conversation took place between them.

The deputy left the adjoining door cracked a bit and pulled a chair to the opening. The prisoners couldn't see him, but he could hear them, and it didn't take long for Culpepper to confront them.

"I know you were in Purgatory Canyon and stole that money."

"What money?" Dutch Malloy asked.

"You know what money I'm talking about. You found it behind that cabin," Culpepper responded.

"What makes you think we were even in Purgatory Canyon?" Dutch asked.

Culpepper gripped the bars separating them. "I know it

was you. When Win and I get out of this place, you'd better hope you're locked away so we can't get to you."

Dutch laughed. "You're scaring me to death."

"If you know what's good for you, you'd better be scared."

After Frank walked Ruth home, he headed toward the jail. He saw Sheriff Trent, Marshal Holt, Morgan, and Jack walking out of the jail, heading in the direction of the hotel. He needed a way to get the deputy out of the jail so he could talk to Dutch and Deke without an audience. When he passed a kid on the street, he thought of a plan. Pulling the young man aside, he gave him some coins along with his instructions. "Don't forget, tell the deputy that two men are getting ready to have a gun fight at the other end of town." Frank wanted to get the deputy as far from the jail as possible.

Frank waited for the deputy to hurry from the jail before he walked in. He quickly headed through the doors leading to the cells.

Dutch was the only one who noticed when Frank walked through the door. "What are you doing here, Frank?"

Before Frank spoke, he glanced at the other men in the cells. Culpepper and Taggart were in the adjacent cell. "I wanted to talk to you about getting you out of here," Frank said.

Dutch laughed. "What makes you think we want out of here?"

"Why would you want to stay in here?"

"I guess you could say we are tired of running. You're the only one who ain't living like an animal, barely scraping by. I hear tell you have all the money you want. While we have a bounty on our heads, you're eating fine steaks and courting that rich woman around town."

"I was coming to Las Vegas with some money," Frank said.

Dutch glared at him. "Frank, you're nothing but a liar. Always have been. This time, you are going to see how it feels to be on the other end of things. When we testify against you, it's going to help us out with the judge."

This time, Frank was the one who laughed. "You think the judge, my father-in-law, is going to take your word over mine?"

Though Dutch didn't want to admit it, Frank planted a seed of doubt in his mind. The judge could give them a harsh sentence, and it'd be a long time before they saw daylight again, if ever. "I wouldn't be surprised if the marshal doesn't find your girlfriend and get her to testify against you," Dutch said, hoping to give Frank something to think about.

"Langtry, the judge may not believe them, but I bet when I tell him we took the bank money off of you and your men, he might be inclined to believe me," Culpepper said.

Frank and Dutch turned to see Culpepper standing near the bars from the other cell.

Frank narrowed his eyes at Culpepper. Culpepper had gotten the best of him once, and Frank was determined it would never happen again. "That just confirms you're not only a killer, but a thief. I don't think the judge will believe you any more than he will Dutch. If you think you are going to pin anything on me, you'd best think again. Not only am I in tight with the judge, but his sister is a wealthy woman who is bound and determined to defend me."

"We might ask for a new judge," Culpepper said.

Frank ignored him and turned back to Dutch. "Where's Corbin?"

"Don't know. He rode off on his own a while back." Dutch wasn't about to tell Frank anything. Corbin was terrified of Frank, and it was best if he steered clear of him.

"How did you get our money, Langtry?" Culpepper asked.

"What money? What are you talking about?" Frank asked.

"The money we stole from you. How did you know where we hid it in Purgatory Canyon?" Culpepper replied.

Frank glanced at Dutch. "What's he talking about?"

Dutch threw his arms in the air. "He says someone stole the money they took from us."

"I haven't been to Purgatory Canyon," Frank said. "Dutch?"

"Nope, we never made it there. We stayed in Las Vegas. We were riding back this way when the marshal caught up with us."

Suddenly Frank became very interested in talking to Culpepper. "How much of that money did you have left?"

"Enough to last a long time."

Frank didn't expect a straight answer. "Where'd you hide it in the canyon?"

"The back of one of the cabins," Culpepper said. "Who else knows that canyon as good as you?"

"I know it better than anyone, but I haven't been there." Frank turned and walked out the door. He figured if Culpepper and Taggart rode straight to the canyon after they robbed them, they had to have a good sum of money left. That riled Frank. He told himself he had a good thing going with Ruth, but it was going to take time to get what he wanted. Ruth would make certain he'd have more money than he'd ever needed, but Dutch said they were going to testify against him, so he was going to have to make a move. He wasn't worried about Judge Stevens protecting him, but what if their case did go before another judge. Could he bank on Judge Stevens to keep him out of prison? There was always the possibility that the judge would find Leigh King. What then?

Forty thousand dollars. That much money in his hands at one time called to him. He thought Culpepper was telling the truth about someone stealing the money. It could have been Dutch and Deke. Maybe. But none of them knew the canyon like he did. There was only one person who kept track of who came and went in that canyon. Indian Pete. If he didn't steal the money, Frank would bet he knew who was in that canyon that did.

Chapter Eighteen

It had been a long, nerve-wracking twenty-four hours, and Emma and Clay were both quiet on the trip home. Clay was disappointed with himself that he couldn't seem to find a way to let go of the past. He told himself even if he could, he still had doubts that a woman like Emma would marry him when she could marry a prince.

Emma broke the silence when she asked why Clay asked Culpepper about horses.

Clay told her about Moonrise, and how much he loved that horse. He'd looked for Moonrise in every town he rode through for four years. "I always thought I would find her one day."

They were only a mile from Whispering Pines when Clay heard horses behind him. He pulled to a halt and picked up his rifle.

Emma turned around and recognizing the riders, she said, "It's Henri and his guards."

The prince did say he would come to Whispering Pines today, and Clay had to give him credit. He'd wasted no time leaving Denver this morning. Clay thought if he had a real chance with Emma, he would do whatever he could to win her hand. He nearly dropped the reins when he realized what he was thinking. He wanted Emma, and that thought made his heart feel whole again. He had to find a way to tuck the past away so he could live again. Logically he knew there was nothing he could have done that day when his wife and son were killed. He'd been out on the range just like every other day. Still, he'd blamed himself, and for all of the years that followed that day, he hadn't allowed himself to think about finding happiness again.

He glanced at Emma and saw she was watching Henri, but he couldn't tell by her expression what she was thinking. She didn't look happy to see him, but then, she didn't look unhappy. It would be a tall order to compete with a prince, but if Emma offered a single word of encouragement, he'd do whatever it took to win her heart.

"You almost beat us home," Emma said when Henri reined in at the buckboard.

Henri looked surprised. "You mean you are just now arriving?"

"Yes, the snowstorm forced us to stop," Emma replied.

"I saw no place to lodge on our ride," Henri said.

"It was an abandoned cabin we happened upon." Emma wasn't going to lie to him, but she saw the disapproving look on his face. "We had no choice. We couldn't see where we were going, and if we'd stayed out in the snow we would have frozen to death."

"Of course." Henri looked at Clay and said, "Thank you for seeing to Emma's welfare. As you can tell, she is very special to me."

Clay understood Henri's feelings. "As she is to me."

Emma was surprised by Clay's admission. "Henri, you can follow us to the hotel."

They reached the hotel, and when Henri invited Emma to dine with him, she said. "Henri, why don't you come to the ranch for dinner? I'm very tired and I don't think I will feel like coming back to town. It was a long night, and I can tell you all about it over dinner. There's plenty of room at the ranch, and if it snows you can plan to spend the night."

As much as Clay thought he shouldn't object to Emma offering the prince lodging in the event of bad weather, he didn't like the idea of him staying under the same roof with her. Not that he expected anything inappropriate would take place. He'd been alone with her in the cabin, and it was perfectly innocent. The memory of him kissing her palm flashed through his mind. He wasn't sure why he had made such a bold move, but he was glad he did.

"I do not want to be a burden to your family," Henri said.

Good, Clay thought, Henri was a gentleman.

"You will not be a burden," Emma said. "We'd love to have you join us."

Clay thought Emma seemed very eager to have Henri come for dinner. She must be more interested than she'd admitted. He was a prince, he reminded himself. That kind of attention would turn any woman's head.

Henri pulled his horse close to the buckboard and reached for Emma's hand. He brushed a kiss over her gloved hand. "In that case, I will be delighted to accept your invitation."

Uncharitably Clay wanted to click the horses and run Henri over. The only reason he didn't was because he was the pastor, but if Henri had kissed her palm the way he did, he might have forgotten that minor point.

"We'll expect you by seven," Emma said.

As Clay was preparing to pull away, one of his parishioners, Bob Reed, rode next to the buckboard. "Pastor, there were a few of us waiting for you at the church this morning."

Clay opened his mouth to speak, but nothing came out. With everything that had transpired that morning, he'd totally forgotten it was Sunday. "Bob, I'm sorry. Emma and I were caught in the snowstorm last night coming home from Denver. We were forced to stay in one of the abandoned cabins along the trail."

Bob's expression went from sociable to judgmental in a split second. "What were you doing in Denver?"

"Emma had a performance there last night." Clay didn't feel more of an explanation was in order.

"Are you telling me that you and this"—Bob flung a hand in Emma's direction as he continued—"woman . . . spent an entire night alone together?"

Clay dropped the reins in his lap. "Now, Bob, don't make it sound like it was a situation that could have been avoided."

Bob gave a loud harrumph. "It could have been avoided if you didn't patronize a place like that saloon in Denver in the first place. Here we are waiting on our pastor for our Sunday sermon while you're holed up with some . . ."

Clay landed him with a look that said he was treading on thin ice. "Watch yourself, Bob. This is not the time or place to have this discussion."

Bob sneered at Emma. "We'll see about this. I will be talking to the other folks about this situation today. I don't know what kind of pastor would take up with the likes of a woman who sings in a saloon. You may not be the right man for our church." Bob turned his horse and rode away.

"Oh, Clay, I'm sorry," Emma said.

"Why is that man upset? I do not understand," Henri said.

Clay didn't understand it either. Of course, he knew nothing inappropriate happened. But if he looked at the situation from Bob's perspective, it was reasonable to question why a logical-thinking pastor managed to get himself in such a quandary. "Folks out here take a dim view of a man and a woman spending the night alone in a cabin if they are not married."

"But it could not be helped, no?"

"No, we had no alternative. There was a blizzard and we couldn't see the trail. It was too dangerous to travel," Clay replied.

"You know this will be the gossip for a week or more," Emma said.

"Don't let it worry you." Clay didn't like the way Bob had looked at Emma. He was going to ride to Bob's place and have a talk with him as soon as he left Morgan's ranch.

Granny invited Clay to have lunch before he rode back to town. As he was leaving, Morgan rode in and Clay met him in the stable. "Did you have any problems?"

"Not a bit. Culpepper and Taggart were as meek as little lambs," Morgan replied. "Clay, I'm real sorry you had to run into those two killers. I know it couldn't have been easy for you."

"Morgan, to tell you the truth, it was almost a blessing to know I didn't want to kill them."

Morgan saw the relief in his eyes. "Good. You're a good man, Clay. You've nothing to worry about on that score." Morgan removed his saddle and hoisted it on a rail. "Anything of import happen between you and Emma?"

Clay shook his head. "I thought I would express my feelings for her, but I couldn't seem to let go of Violet. Then the strangest thing happened."

"What's that?"

Clay told him about Henri being in town and Emma inviting him to dinner tonight. "When she was talking to Henri, I knew he wasn't the right man for her. I decided then and there that I would give Henri a run for his money."

"I think that means you need to come to dinner tonight," Morgan said.

"Emma told Henri if the weather turns, he can spend the night. You may have a full house."

"There's enough room. You don't want him here alone with her, do you?" Morgan thought if there was another man vying for Rose's attention, he'd definitely spend the night.

"No, I don't. But do you think she would turn down a proposal from a prince?"

"Granny is convinced she wants to stay in Whispering Pines, so I'd say the odds are stacked in your favor."

Clay looked skeptical. "Look at the kind of life she could have married to Henri."

"It doesn't matter. If your heart is not in it, all the money in the world won't make a difference."

Morgan had a point, but he thought a woman as worldly as Emma might look at things differently. "He seems like a decent fellow."

"I'm sure he is. Do you like him so much that you want him to take Emma with him?"

Clay laughed. "Point made. I'll come to dinner."

"Prepare to spend the night." Morgan looked up at the sky. "It's going to snow some more."

"That'll give the townsfolk even more to talk about." Clay told Morgan about the conversation with Bob. "I'm going to go talk to him now. He was rude to Emma, and I won't stand for that. I may not be the pastor of the church after today."

"Nonsense. Bob Reed is worse than an old gossipy woman. Did you tell Granny about this?"

"No. I didn't want her to feel like she had to take my

side. She's done enough for me, and I can handle Bob. If he doesn't change his mind after I quote some scripture, then I'll give him a gentle squeeze of the shoulder until he sees things my way."

Morgan barked with laughter. "I wondered what that squeeze of the shoulder was supposed to do."

Clay laughed with him. "I tried it on you, but it didn't work. Your shoulders are too thick."

"I thought a gnat landed on me," Morgan teased.

"You'd best be thankful God didn't add His muscle to mine. I guarantee Bob won't think a gnat landed on him."

The determined look on Clay's face convinced Morgan that Clay was really upset over Bob's attitude toward Emma. "Don't let him get to you."

"I thought my last sermon made an impact on people passing judgment. It's disappointing."

"You've heard the saying about old dogs and new tricks. You just have to keep reminding us to be better men."

By the time Clay made it back to Morgan's that night, he was tired and grouchy. His meeting with Bob had not gone well, and some of the other parishioners in town had given him the cold shoulder. To top off the frustrating day, Leigh King had cornered him on the sidewalk. In passing, he mentioned seeing Frank at the Grand Crystal Palace with Ruth. Leigh asked him if he would take her to Denver. He politely declined, telling her that he didn't think that was a good idea. He wasn't worried about what Frank would say; he was more worried about what Emma would think.

Leigh had tucked her arm through his just as two of the church members passed by. Clay figured this inopportune encounter would be the icing on the cake with his congregation. He'd already decided that he wasn't going to worry about being forced from his position. If that happened, he'd go back to Kansas, sell his ranch, and bring Jonas to Whispering Pines and buy a new place. He didn't question why he would come back to Whispering Pines; this was where he wanted to build his life. He considered Morgan and Jack good friends, and he loved Granny. Then there was Emma. He was interested to see how she interacted with the prince tonight. It might give him some insight as to her feelings for him. It bothered him to think that she might care for the prince, but if she did, he would never interfere by confessing his feelings.

Morgan answered the door when Clay knocked. "He's been here almost an hour."

"Good evening to you, too," Clay said.

"Henri's in the kitchen making headway with Emma while you're taking your sweet time," Morgan responded.

Clay removed his hat and hung it on a hook. "Morgan, if she wants him, there's not much I can do to compete with a prince."

Morgan shook his head at Clay. "I can't believe you would give up that easy. If you think she's worth it, then you've got to put in some effort."

"If she already cares about him, why should I interfere?"

Morgan removed Clay's hat from the hook and shoved it at him. "Fine. You're right. You have no reason to at least find out the lay of the land. Just get on with living like you have been. Don't take a chance."

The two men stood there looking at each other for a few seconds, until Clay took his hat and hung it back on the hook. "You're right. Let's eat."

Morgan slapped him hard on the shoulder. "Now you're talking. I hope you're hungry. If you remember correctly, Rose picked me because I could eat more flapjacks than you." Everyone knew Morgan liked to tell that story, but in all truth Rose was already in love with Morgan before the two men engaged in an eating contest. Morgan saw it as a contest of wills, and there was no way he was going to lose if it made him look bad in Rose's eyes. He wanted to see if Clay had the same fortitude when it came to winning Emma's affection.

"I keep telling you I wasn't in a contest that morning. If I had known, you would have lost, hands down," Clay teased.

Morgan grinned. "Why don't we see if the prince can keep up tonight? I have a feeling the prince doesn't know the way to a woman's heart."

Clay laughed at Morgan's plan. "Do you really think women are impressed by the amount of food a man eats?"

Morgan looked at him as if he'd just uttered sacrilegious words. "Yes. It tells them they did a fine job preparing the meal. It would be an insult to pick at your food like a bird. You want to compliment them, don't you?"

"Why can't I just say that was a fine meal?" Clay knew he'd forgotten how to impress a woman.

"Aren't you the one always saying people should read their Bibles and not just listen to what it says? Put your words into action, eat heartily and tell her it was a fine meal." Morgan leaned to his ear and whispered, "Just so you know, Emma's cooking the chicken."

Clay figured he wasn't one to argue with Morgan. After all, his friend had a beautiful wife and a happy marriage, so it seemed logical he knew how to capture a woman's heart. Clay reminded himself he'd done it once, he could do it again. "Lead me to the lion's den."

* * *

Instead of sitting beside Emma like Henri, Clay was seated opposite the couple. And that's what they looked like to him: the happy couple. He couldn't help but notice how comfortable they were with each other, indicating they'd spent a lot of time together in France. Emma was giving Henri her undivided attention.

He decided to take Morgan's advice and enjoy the meal, and he even had a second helping of everything on the table. He didn't need to worry about outeating Henri; the man ate less than the women. But Clay had to hand it to the prince. While he was shoveling food in his mouth, Henri was the one talking with Emma. Naturally the whole family seemed taken with the prince, and why not? He was a foreigner, and the women seemed to find his accent charming, as well as his stories about his home country. Clay wasn't able to get a word in edgewise with all of their questions. He figured the only thing in his favor was Sweetie, who hadn't left his side since he walked through the door. Henri may have Emma's attention right now, but Clay definitely had the affection of her dog. To make certain Sweetie didn't desert him, he slid chunks of his chicken to him every few minutes.

"Clay, you've been very quiet tonight," Granny said.

"I'm just enjoying this fine meal. This is the best fried chicken I've ever eaten."

Granny beamed with delight. "Emma prepared the chicken."

Clay glanced at Emma to make sure she was listening to their conversation.

Emma was staring at him. "I think Sweetie has enjoyed it as much as you have."

So much for giving Henri her undivided attention. She had been watching him feed Sweetie under the table, and that thought gave him some hope. Clay arched a brow at her. "I don't want him going hungry."

Emma laughed. "There's no danger of Sweetie going hungry."

"You're a fine cook, Emma," Clay said.

"Thank you."

"If she accepts my proposal, she would never have to cook. She will have servants at her beck and call," Henri said.

Emma's eyes widened at Henri's comment. "Henri, we haven't discussed this." She noticed everyone had stopped eating, and they seemed to be waiting for some sort of explanation or announcement.

Henri smiled and reached for her hand. "I know there is much to discuss, my dear, but I'm merely saying you will have a palace full of servants. Your life will change if you decide to accept my hand in marriage."

Emma pulled her hand away. She was aggravated that he had put her in a position of offering an explanation to her family. He'd arrived too early for dinner and pressed her to talk with him a few minutes before she started cooking. He'd told her that he had traveled to Denver specifically to ask for her hand. The only reason he hadn't made a formal proposal was he thought it was customary to speak with Granny first, as she was the senior family member. Emma politely attempted to discourage a conversation of a forthcoming marriage proposal, but Henri persisted. Finally, she told him they would discuss the topic later when they had more time. She thought he deserved to be heard since he'd traveled so far, and by postponing the discussion, it would give her time to think of a way to politely refuse. "Please everyone, finish eating. Henri and I have much to discuss, but I'm afraid now is not the appropriate time."

Clay placed his fork on his plate. He'd lost his appetite.

If Henri had already proposed, and obviously Emma hadn't turned him down, then it made no sense to pursue his course of action. He wasn't even certain what his course of action was going to be, but he'd planned to find out how she felt about Henri tonight. It seemed he had his answer. She hadn't rejected the prince.

Chapter Nineteen

At dusk, Indian Pete returned to his isolated one-room shack built into the side of a ledge high up in Purgatory Canyon. It had been there so many years that it was indistinguishable from the rocky terrain. You could look directly at the sun-faded wood and fail to realize it was not part of nature. He lost count of the years he'd spent in the canyon, but it was where he knew he would die. He came and went without fear of being detected. He never had to watch his back, and his days were spent walking the canyon. He liked to know who was in his canyon, and when they left. That's how he thought of Purgatory—his canyon—and no white man had a reason to be there. So when they came, if he could, he relieved them of their supplies. In his estimation, they deserved it for invading his land. Most who ventured here were outlaws, and they'd come by their goods stealing from others.

There was no back door to his cabin, and only a few small holes in the front door afforded little outside light. Pete walked in and struck a match to light the only oil lamp. Once the wick flared, he blew out the match and carried the lamp to the small table.

"How are you doing, Pete?"

Pete nearly dropped the lamp. Collecting himself, he held the lamp higher so his old eyes could see the man straddling the solitary chair. Frank Langtry. "What are you doing here?"

"I came to see you."

Pete saw the pearl-handled pistol dangling in Frank's hand. He wondered how Frank rode into his canyon without his knowledge. He'd been sitting at the most strategic location today to see all riders. He was getting old. He'd fallen asleep. "Why do you want to see me?"

"You know everyone coming and going in this canyon. I want to know if you saw two hombres by the name of Culpepper and Taggart."

"There were two men, but they rode out a few days ago," Pete said. "How did you get in the canyon?"

Frank laughed. "You think you know something about this canyon that I don't? How about my men? They been here?" Frank had already been to the cabin where they stayed. Someone had been there recently.

"I haven't seen them," Pete said.

"Here's the thing, Pete. I don't believe you." Frank pointed his pistol directly at Pete's chest.

"I was sick for a few days and didn't leave the cabin," Pete said.

"The two hombres you saw, where did they stay?" Frank asked.

Pete told him the location of the cabin. "I never saw those two before."

Frank had searched Pete's small space, and he saw the old man was set for supplies. "Where did you get all of the supplies?"

"Those two left them behind, so I took them."

"And you didn't see my boys?"

Pete shook his head. "They could have been here when I was sick."

"Uh-huh." Frank stood and used his pistol to motion toward the door. "Let's go."

"Go where?" Pete didn't want to go anywhere with Langtry; he'd heard too many men say he couldn't be trusted.

"We're going to the cabin where Culpepper and Taggart stayed."

"It's getting dark; we can't see now. It's dangerous out there on those ledges."

Frank walked closer and glared down at him. "Get moving."

"You know the shack I'm talking about. Why do I have to go with you?" Pete asked.

"I haven't been there in a while." Frank knew exactly how to get to the shack. If he decided Pete was lying to him, he better be able to do some fast talking, or he'd make his death slow and painful. Frank never trusted fellow outlaws, but something told him Culpepper was telling the truth when he said someone took the money from them. The way Frank saw it, it was either Indian Pete, or his gang was in the canyon at the same time as Culpepper and Taggart. Frank nodded toward the lantern by the door. "Light that lantern."

Giving him no choice, Pete lit the lantern and walked out the door with a gun in his back. Pete moved slowly, trying to maintain his footing as he climbed over rocks in the waning light. When he wasn't moving fast enough to suit Frank, he was nudged in the back with the barrel of the pistol. They finally reached the shack where Culpepper and Taggart stayed, and Frank told Pete to sit on the floor while he searched the place. Frank quickly rummaged through the meager contents inside the cabin, but he found nothing of value. Remembering his brother's favorite hidey-hole at home, Frank pulled away the remaining few floorboards. Nothing. Frustrated that he came up empty-handed, he looked at Pete and said, "You cleaned them out good. And you're telling me you didn't find money?"

"No money. I took food and whiskey."

Being an outlaw himself, Frank knew Culpepper and Taggart wouldn't have hidden the money far from their reach. He wouldn't have. Frank opened the door, and motioned for Pete to leave the cabin. With dread, Pete followed Frank's instruction to walk to the back of the cabin. A light dusting of snow covered the ground that hid any possible footprints that might have been left behind. But Frank saw something that looked suspicious. Dried brush was stacked at the base of an overhanging ledge. The perfect place to stuff something inside and cover it with the dead debris. Kneeling down, Frank peeked beneath the ledge. Nothing. Wait. He thought he saw something. "Bring that lantern closer."

Pete set the lantern near the overhang, and Frank held it inside.

"Well, I'll be." Frank reached to the back of the hole and pulled out a currency wrapper. When he held it to the light, he saw the print on top. BANK OF DENVER. "It looks like Culpepper and Taggart did hide their money in here."

He stuffed the wrapper in his shirt pocket and stood. "Pete, let's go have a look around at my cabin."

They made their way to the cabin where Frank and his gang always hid out. Just as in the other cabin, Frank tore the place apart. Once again, he came up with nothing to show for his efforts. "I reckon the only thing to do now is go to your cabin, Pete. If you are hiding any money, it won't go well for you."

"Why do I need money? I have no money," Pete said.

Thankfully he was telling the truth, so he hoped Frank would leave him alone when he found nothing in his cabin.

Once they returned to Pete's cabin, Frank destroyed his room. Finding no money, he sat Pete in the chair and proceeded to remove all of the cartridges from his pistol, save one. "Pete, it's time you told the truth." Frank spun the cylinder, and placed the end of the barrel against Pete's temple. "I want to know if my men were in the canyon recently."

"I said they could have been here when I was sick. I was in my cabin for days," Pete replied, trying to remain calm.

Frank pulled the trigger. Click. "Want to try again and see how lucky you are?"

"Why are you doing this? I told you I was sick," Pete said.

"The thing is, Pete, I've seen you in this canyon for years, and I've never known you to be sick." Frank pulled the pistol from Pete's temple and twirled the cylinder.

Pete breathed a side of relief. "I'm getting to be an old man. I get sick."

Frank pressed the end of the barrel against Pete's temple again. Click.

"Pete, old boy, you are one lucky son of a gun." Frank laughed. He held the pistol in front of Pete's face. "You think you'll be that lucky a third time?"

Pete's eyes were on the barrel of the pistol as Frank spun the cylinder again.

"Of course, if you'd rather I take you outside and stake you out like your kin used to do, just let me know. If you're lucky, you'll freeze to death before the critters finish you off."

When Pete didn't respond, Frank pulled back the trigger.

Pete held up his hand. "I saw them. They took the money from those two men."

"When?" Frank asked without removing the pistol from Pete's head.

"I can't remember."

Frank roughly nudged the barrel into his skin. "When?"

"Maybe ten days ago," Pete said.

"Why did you lie to me?"

"They told me to say I did not see them. Another man was with them, and he found the money under the ledge," Pete admitted.

"Who was the man?"

"I don't know. I've never seen him before," Pete said.

"What did he look like? Did they call him by name?"

Pete tried to remember if he heard his name. His old mind couldn't recall. He shook his head. "I do not remember."

"What did he look like?"

Describing the man as best he could, Pete knew it wouldn't be enough for Frank. Suddenly he remembered one detail that he hoped would get him out of this situation alive. "He rode a Paint."

Frank pulled the trigger.

Riding to Whispering Pines in the middle of the night, Frank went directly to the hotel, ran upstairs, and tapped on the door to Leigh's room.

"Who's there?" Leigh asked.

"Frank."

Leigh cracked the door, and Frank pushed it open and walked inside and pulled her to him.

"Who were you expecting?"

Pulling away, Leigh tugged her robe tighter around her. "What do you care?"

"What do you mean?" Frank reached for her again.

Leigh wiggled away from his hands and walked across the room. "You leave me stuck here while you're squiring that older woman around Denver. I'm tired of it. I'm tired of sitting here all alone while you go to dinner and shows at the Grand Crystal Palace. You've never taken me there."

Frank walked to the table and picked up the decanter filled with whiskey. "Who told you what I'm doing?"

Leigh put her hands on her hips and glared at him. "What does it matter? Are you, or are you not escorting that woman around Denver while I sit here with nothing to do all day and night?"

"That woman happens to pay my salary," Frank reminded her.

"What does that include? Is part of your job being her escort? Doesn't she pay you to work at the mine?" Leigh countered.

Frank poured himself a drink and tossed back the contents. "Watch yourself." Frank leaned against the table and stared at her. She was wearing a silk nightgown with a matching robe. Frank thought it was strange she was wide awake in the middle of the night. "Who's been here?"

"No one has been here."

Frank walked to the window to see if it was locked. He pulled back the curtain and saw the latch was hooked. "Why are you all dolled up in the middle of the night?"

"What are you talking about? I wear this all of the time at home. If you were here more you would know that," Leigh countered.

"Your hair is combed. You weren't in bed."

"I couldn't sleep. I don't do anything to get tired in this flea-bitten town. There's nothing to do here like there is in Denver. I want to go to Denver. I'm not staying here any longer. I want you to take me today," Leigh demanded.

Frank stalked across the room and took her by the arm,

pulling her to him. "Who have you been talking to? That preacher again? Has he been in here with you?"

Leigh tried to pull away. "Let me go! You're hurting my arm."

Frank twisted her arm behind her. "What are you doing with that preacher?"

"Why would you care if he was here? You're leaving me alone all of the time. At least he's interested, and he thinks I'm pretty."

Frank released her arm and shoved her on the bed. "When was he here?"

Leigh didn't answer; she turned her face away from him.

Frank kneeled on the bed beside her, trapped her face in his hand. "I asked you a question."

"You don't care, you're never here." Leigh wanted to make him jealous. "He likes being around me."

"What else does he like that you're offering?"

Leigh didn't like the look in his eyes. She didn't think she should carry the lie too far. "He's a pastor."

Frank released her face. "If I find out he's been here, you'll both be dead."

"He told me he saw you with that woman at the Grand Crystal Hall listening to your sister sing. You won't take me, but you'll escort her around as though she's your woman."

"I told you, Ruth and I have a lot of business to discuss." Frank strolled back to the table for another whiskey.

"I don't think that is all you're doing. Why are you worried about the pastor when you have that older woman for a girlfriend?"

Frank tossed back another drink before he returned to the bed. He sat down and removed his boots. "You jealous?"

"I have no reason to be jealous of that old woman. Don't you think other men want me?" Leigh was angry she hadn't been able to interest the pastor. If she had, he might be taking her to Denver, instead of her sitting here waiting on Frank all of the time. She was young, and she wanted to enjoy her life. It was bad enough living in Black Hawk, but at least Frank was there at night. There were times she wished she hadn't left the judge. He had big plans to travel the world and show her off. All Frank wanted to do was leave her while he went off and had a good time. "If you don't want to take me to Denver, I'll go by myself."

Leigh started to get off the bed, but Frank pulled her back. "You'll do as I say, and right now I'm saying you need to stay here. The judge is going to be back in Denver any day now." Ruth had told him she'd received a telegram from the judge informing her that he was on his way home.

"Why did you want me to leave the judge? He liked taking me places and showing me off. You just want me to sit here all alone. Well, I'm not doing it anymore."

Frank stood, removed his holster, and hung it over the bedpost.

"I asked the preacher to take me to Denver and he's going to," Leigh spouted.

Frank wrapped his hand around her throat and squeezed. "You aren't going anywhere with that preacher. I'll make certain of that. You can go back to Black Hawk if you want."

Leigh clutched his hand, struggling to remove it before he crushed her windpipe. "Let me go! You're hurting me."

Frank loosened his grip, but he didn't let go.

Feeling his fingers relax, Leigh took that opportunity to place some doubt in his mind. "If you don't stop treating me this way, I'm going to go to Denver and tell that old woman your part in the robbery. I bet the judge won't let you get out of prison again."

Enraged, Frank grasped her neck and squeezed as hard as he could. "Don't you ever threaten me!"

Leigh was on the verge of passing out, but she managed to whisper her last threat. "I already gave that preacher a letter and told him if anything ever happened to me, he was to give it to the judge."

Her words filtered through Frank's mounting rage and he released her. "What do you mean you gave that preacher a letter?"

Leigh turned on her side, coughing and gasping for air. When she was finally able to respond, she said, "Just what I said. If something happens to me, the judge is going to know your part in the robbery. He'll know it was your fault his daughter died that day, just like I could have died."

Frank couldn't believe her duplicity, if she was telling him the truth. But how could he find out? Knowing that pastor, if he was confronted by a man with a gun, he'd tell him anything he wanted to know. "Why would you double-cross me? Haven't I given you everything you wanted? You were stuck with that old man pawing at you day and night. Now you have a real man."

Snapping her head around to face him, she could tell by the doubt in his eyes that her bluff had worked. At first, she had trusted Frank, even when he'd double-crossed his gang. But when he left her alone in Whispering Pines, she began to understand how little he thought of her, and real-ized she was as indispensable as his gang. For the moment, she wasn't worried he would hurt her, and that emboldened her to say what she really thought of him. "Real man? That's what you call a man who leaves his woman in a strange town for days on end until he decides to come back. At least the judge took me everywhere with him. He knew how to please me. He was more of a man than you'll ever be, Frank Langtry." She was already formulating a plan to give the preacher a letter just as soon as Frank left town again.

Frank wanted to kill her. Suddenly everyone was turning on him. Well, no man or woman threatened him and lived to tell about it. Not his gang and not this woman. He envisioned wrapping his fingers around her neck and squeezing until there was no breath left in her. He wanted to see the light go out in her eyes. *Calm down,* he told himself. He'd take care of her once he found out if she was telling the truth. If she had given a letter to that pastor, he'd need to kill both of them. He'd like to kill them at the same time, but unless he found them together, he didn't know how that was possible. He needed to come up with a plan.

Chapter Twenty

Frank spent two days with Leigh, and managed to appease her demands by promising to take her to his sister's last performance in Denver. If everything worked out as he planned, Leigh wouldn't be around by the time that performance took place. He had tired of her anyway and he wanted to move on. Now all he had to do was find out if she was telling the truth about giving a letter to the pastor.

Leaving Leigh's room at dawn, Frank walked behind the buildings, making his way to the church. Once inside, he hurried to the back door and cracked it open so he could see the pastor's home. From this vantage point, he had a clear shot if he caught the pastor leaving his home. But the church was too close to other buildings, and he wouldn't have time to escape unseen. He'd have to find a way to search the pastor's home when he was not in town.

"What can I do for you, Frank?" Clay asked.

Frank whirled around to see the preacher sitting in the front pew. "Where did you come from?"

"I saw you come in," Clay said. He'd had a restless night thinking about Emma and Henri, so he decided to walk to the restaurant for an early breakfast. He was just returning home when he saw Frank entering the church. When he quietly slipped inside, Frank was standing at the back door.

"I just came in to see if the place still looked the same," Frank said.

"Does it?"

Frank looked around the room with a smirk on his face. "I reckon it does. It never looked like much." He turned to stare at Clay. "Why did you come to Whispering Pines?"

"They needed a preacher."

"You don't look like the typical preacher," Frank said.

"Really?" Clay had heard that statement so many times, he wasn't surprised.

"Nope, most preachers are older. You look more like a gunslinger."

"Sorry to disappoint you," Clay said.

Frank laughed. "It don't mean anything to me one way or the other."

"Do you want to renew your faith, Frank? You know it's never too late to repent."

"Me? I got nothing to repent." Frank walked to the pew where Clay was sitting, leaned over until he was mere inches from his face. "I came to tell you to stay away from Leigh. She said you were going to take her to Denver. I wouldn't recommend that."

Clay couldn't believe Mrs. King told Frank such a blatant lie. "What I do or don't do is none of your business."

"That's where you are wrong." Frank straightened and intentionally rested his hand on the butt of his pistol. "You wouldn't want Whispering Pines to have to find another new preacher, would you?"

Clay stood and used the difference in height to force Frank to look up at him. "Frank, you don't scare me."

"No? Maybe I should. Don't forget what I said, Preacher." He turned, strolled down the aisle, and out the door.

Clay didn't know if Frank had intended to waylay him that morning, but he knew he was up to no good. He wondered why Leigh told Frank he was going to take her to Denver. Of course, it was possible Frank wasn't telling the truth. As soon as Frank left town, Clay planned to talk to Leigh and find out what was going on.

While Clay waited for Frank to leave town, he stopped in to see the sheriff and tell him about his meeting with Frank.

"You better watch your back. He may be planning on waylaying you," Jack said.

"Mrs. King told him I was going to take her to Denver." Jack arched his brow. "Are you?"

"She asked me to take her, but I told her it wasn't a good idea." Clay was almost tempted to take her just to show Frank his threats wouldn't keep him from helping Mrs. King if she needed help.

"Clay, you need to stay away from that woman," Jack said.

"Jack, I really think she's in trouble," Clay said.

"It's trouble of her own making, and she's going to draw you into her dangerous schemes." Jack didn't trust Mrs. King, and he didn't want Clay to be taken in by a pretty face with a sob story. "She's going to go to jail for her part in that robbery just as soon as the judge gets back to Denver. Frank's gang already told the part she played. Don't forget that. It's possible the marshal would want her to testify against Frank along with his gang."

"Isn't it possible Frank's gang are saying whatever they can to save their own hides?" Clay said.

Jack could tell that Clay didn't want to think the worst of Mrs. King. "It's possible. But don't you think it would be quite a coincidence for Frank and his wife to be in front of that bank at the exact moment Mrs. King walked out?"

Clay silently debated Jack's question. Morgan had said the exact same thing to him, but still he hesitated to pass judgment. "It's possible it was accidental."

Jack shrugged. He figured Clay would come to the logical conclusion once he had time to think it through. "If Frank's smart, he'll keep Leigh far from Denver. But I can guarantee you when Judge Stevens hears his girlfriend helped Frank in that robbery and she's been holed up with him all this time, things are going to get mighty interesting."

Later when Clay walked into the restaurant to have lunch, he saw Emma seated at a table with Henri. They were so engrossed in their conversation, they didn't even notice him. Throughout his lunch, he couldn't help glancing at their table. He never thought he was a jealous man, but he did feel some envy. He wanted to be the one laughing and smiling with Emma instead of Henri. He wanted to be the one planning a future with her. If Henri and Emma had found happiness together, he told himself if he were a better man, he would be happy for them. At the moment, he wasn't certain he'd reached that selfless pinnacle.

While Clay had been at Morgan's ranch, he hadn't had the opportunity to spend one moment alone with Emma. Henri dominated her time, and Clay was frustrated since he'd allowed it to happen. All he'd thought about for two days was Emma, and whether or not she was going to marry Henri.

By the time he finished his lunch, Emma and Henri were still talking. Frustrated, he decided to go home.

Leigh was walking down the staircase when she saw Clay leaving the restaurant. She glanced around to see if Frank was lurking about before she called out to the pastor.

Recognizing Leigh's voice, Clay turned to see her beckoning him to an area under the staircase. "What is it?"

"Shh," she whispered when he approached. She took his hand and led him to the back of the alcove, out of sight of anyone walking into the hotel. "I need to see you."

Even though Clay thought there was a desperation in her tone, he remembered Jack's warning. "What do you need?"

Tears filled Leigh's eyes. "I have no one else to help me."

No matter how much he told himself to remember Jack and Morgan thought she was a criminal, Clay's tender heart won the battle over reason. The young woman obviously needed his help. "What do you need?"

"I can't talk now. I'm not certain Frank has left town, and I don't want him to see me talking to you. I will come to see you." She didn't give him time to respond. She hurried from the alcove and walked directly to the restaurant.

If Frank was about, Clay didn't want to cause Leigh problems, so he waited a few moments before he left the alcove. At the same moment, Emma and Henri were walking from the restaurant.

"Hello, Clay," Emma said. She'd seen Clay leave the restaurant, and she wondered why he hadn't stopped to speak. She passed Leigh as she was walking from the restaurant, so she assumed Clay had been talking with her. After Clay revealed the reason he'd seemed interested in Leigh, Emma wondered if he might be developing a romantic interest in her. Leigh reminded him of the woman he still loved, and it made sense he could be vulnerable to her for that reason alone. In some ways, Emma wished she had romantic feelings for Henri. Henri was in love with her, and though his proposal was flattering, her heart was elsewhere. Even though she knew she may never receive another offer of marriage, she had to reject Henri's offer.

Clay removed his hat and said, "Emma."

"Did you enjoy your lunch?" What she wanted to ask was what he was doing with Leigh.

"Yes." Clay glanced at Henri, who was not smiling, nor was he as congenial as he was at dinner the other night. "Henri, Emma should bring you to church on Sunday. We'd love to have you as a guest."

"I may be back in Denver," Henri said.

Clay didn't know how to respond. He couldn't say he was sorry Henri was leaving Whispering Pines, but he wondered if Emma was going with him. He glanced Emma's way. "Are you giving another performance?"

"No. We only plan one more performance before Christmas."

Clay thought about asking if she was going to Denver with Henri, but he didn't want to sound like a jilted suitor.

Emma took a step toward the door, saying, "I must be on my way. I told my family I would be back in time to work on Christmas presents."

Henri took Emma's hand in his, giving her his usual kiss. "My dear, until tomorrow." Henri said good-bye to Clay and walked up the staircase.

Seeing an opportunity to spend a few moments with

Emma, he accompanied her outside. "Did you come to town alone?"

"Morgan's foreman is waiting for me now at the mercantile." Clay kept pace with her as she turned toward the mercantile.

"Why is Henri going back to Denver?"

"I'm afraid he is disappointed with me," Emma said.

Clay couldn't imagine anyone being disappointed with her. "Why would you say that?"

"I told him I'm not ready to marry," Emma said.

Clay wondered if she meant she wasn't ready to marry, or she wasn't ready to marry Henri. There was no time like the present to ask. "Are you not ready to marry, or is it the man asking for your hand?"

Emma stopped and turned to look at him. "Does it matter?"

They stared at each other, and Clay knew now was the moment for him to say what he wanted. "Yes, it matters."

Emma didn't know what to say to him. She couldn't exactly tell him she'd fallen in love with him, and no other man would do. "Why does it matter?"

Clay took her hand and pulled her to the side of the hotel, out of sight of prying eyes.

Surprised by the unexpected move, Emma said, "What are you doing?"

"Emma, answer my question," he said softly.

"Why?" She wasn't prepared to profess her feelings to a man still caught up in the web of his past.

"Emma . . ." Clay hesitated, but he told himself not to think about the past. "Emma . . ." He couldn't find the words, so he took her face in his hands, lowered his head, and kissed her tenderly. When he pulled back, he gazed into her eyes, and he knew this was the right moment to ask what he wanted to know. "Could I be the right man?"

Emma's heart was pounding as she searched his eyes. "What are you asking?"

"I love you, Emma. I think I fell in love the first time I saw you, but I didn't think I was ready to move on." He had finally confessed the truth. When he first saw her in that hotel lobby in Denver, he remembered thinking he'd never seen such an impressive woman.

"Truly?" Emma said softly.

"Yes. I love you, and I want you to marry me." It was a relief when he shared what was in his heart. His past was just that—past. He wanted Emma to be his future. "Would you marry me?"

Emma wrapped her arms around his neck. "Yes, I will marry you."

"Do you love me, Emma?" He wanted to hear those words from her.

"Yes, I love you."

"Do you want to continue singing on tour?" Clay didn't know how he would handle it if she did, but he'd find a way.

"No, the only singing I want to do is in your church," Emma whispered in his ear.

Clay hugged her tightly. "I love you, Emma."

Aware they might call attention to themselves, they reluctantly pulled apart.

"I do want a ranch though, and a family," Emma said.

Clay felt a happiness he hadn't known in a long time. He couldn't wait to begin his life with her. "I want the same things. I'd like to marry soon, or would you prefer a long engagement?"

"Let's get married right away." Emma knew what she wanted, and she wanted this man. There was no sense being coy about it.

"Good. What do you think about the Sunday before

Christmas? We will have our normal church services, and then we can have our marriage ceremony afterward."

Emma's eyes filled with tears, and Clay noticed. "What's this? We can do something different if you prefer."

Emma wiped her tears away. "No, it all sounds perfect to me. I'm just so happy."

"I'll do my best to always make you happy." He'd had one happy marriage, and he was confident he would have another one with Emma. He kissed her again before he took her by the hand and led her back to the sidewalk. He kept his arm firmly planted around her waist as they walked. He didn't care who saw them. He was with the woman he loved and he wanted everyone to know.

Emma was anxious for her family to know about their plans. "Will you come to dinner tonight?"

"Yes. We'll tell your family during dinner." Clay wanted to properly ask for her hand and to give her his mother's diamond ring. His mother was alive when he'd married Violet, so he had bought Violet a ring.

"I don't know if I can keep the news to myself until then," she admitted.

He remembered Henri said he would see Emma tomorrow. "Why are you seeing Henri tomorrow?" He hoped he didn't sound jealous, but he was.

"He invited me to dinner tomorrow night," Emma said. Thinking she might not like it if he were having dinner with Leigh King alone, she added, "You can join us, and we can tell him together about our plans."

Clay appreciated that she wanted to include him. "I like that idea."

They said good-bye at the mercantile, and Clay walked back to the church. He'd just opened the door when a young boy approached him and handed him a piece of paper. "Pastor Hunt, I was told to give this to you."

"Clay, please meet me one mile east of town at the turnoff to Denver at four o'clock. Leigh."

Clay was going to be headed in that direction to go to the ranch for dinner, so he decided he would leave a little early to find out what Leigh wanted.

Chapter Twenty-One

Rose noticed Emma seemed to be in fine spirits after she returned from her lunch with Henri in Whispering Pines. Knowing Emma hadn't looked forward to rejecting the prince's proposal, Rose expected her to be upset. "You've done nothing but hum all afternoon. Did you and Henri have a nice lunch?"

"Yes, very nice. He tried to change my mind about marrying, but he was very decent about my refusal." Emma was deliriously happy, and it was difficult for her not to tell Rose about Clay's proposal. She could hardly believe she had received two marriage proposals in one day.

"Henri is a nice man, and I'm sure he will make someone a fine husband," Rose said.

"Yes, he will." Emma hadn't yet told Rose she'd invited Clay to dinner. She was afraid if she even said Clay's name, she wouldn't be able to keep her secret. "I saw Clay in town and I invited him to dinner."

"Oh?" Rose was surprised that Emma invited Clay. The last time Clay joined them for dinner, Emma had very little to say to him. Of course, Henri had surprised everyone when he'd asked for Emma's hand.

"Do you mind?" Emma asked.

"Of course not. I like Clay very much. We all do." Rose eyed her sister. There was something she wasn't saying, but she wasn't going to pry.

"I think I will walk over to Addie's and leave a note on her door that they should come to dinner tonight." Emma wanted her whole family at the ranch when she and Clay told them their news.

"Perfect." Rose was certain something was going on, something important enough that Emma wanted the whole family to be at the dinner table tonight. "It will be a nice night with everyone here. It will make Granny's evening. There's nothing that makes her happier than to have all those she loves together."

"She does love Clay, doesn't she?" Emma asked.

"Just as much as she loves Morgan and Jack." Rose smiled. Her sister wasn't very good at keeping a secret.

Jack reined to a sliding halt in front of Morgan's house. He'd been holding the reins of the horse pulling the buggy for miles. When he jumped from his horse, he saw Morgan walking from the stable and called out. "Morgan, I need your help!"

Morgan heard the urgent tone in Jack's voice and ran to him. "What is it?"

"Clay's been shot, and Mrs. King is in a bad way." Jack was already helping Clay from the buggy.

"What happened?" Morgan asked, taking Clay from Jack's arms so he could lift Mrs. King from the buggy.

"I'm fine, Morgan. I can walk," Clay said, but his voice sounded weak. Morgan supported most of Clay's weight onto the porch, opened the door and yelled for Granny.

Jack held Leigh in his arms and ran to the porch. "I was

riding home and I heard a shot ahead of me. I found Clay and Mrs. King on the side of the road. Mrs. King was inside the buggy and Clay was on the ground. I think Mrs. King was strangled."

Granny, Emma, and Rose came running from the kitchen when they heard the commotion in the front room.

"What is it?" Granny asked.

Emma saw the blood on Clay's jacket and ran to him. "Clay! What happened?"

Granny said, "Get them upstairs." She asked Rose and Emma to boil some water and prepare some bandages.

Emma didn't even hear Granny speak; she ran up the stairs behind Morgan and instructed him to put Clay in her room. After Morgan lowered Clay onto the bed, Emma helped remove his coat. She could tell by the blood on his shirt that he'd been hit in the shoulder. Morgan tore Clay's shirt off and Granny shooed them out of the way so she could get a good look at his wound.

"Emma, don't look so worried. I'm okay," Clay said.

Emma clasped his hand. "Thank goodness."

Clay smiled at her. He was in pain but he didn't want her to fret. "Don't worry. You're going to be stuck with me."

Emma couldn't stop her tears from flowing. "I want to be stuck with you."

Granny looked at Morgan and winked. "Told you."

"You were right from the start, Granny. Emma was the one for me," Clay said. "Now get me on the mend so I can marry your granddaughter."

Granny fought back her own tears as she peered at Clay's shoulder. "I guess this means you found a way to keep my granddaughter in Whispering Pines?"

"Yes. My last performance will be in Denver before

Christmas." Emma glanced at Clay, and asked, "Do you want to tell them now?"

"We're going to be married the Sunday before Christmas," Clay said.

"Congratulations, but first things first," Morgan said. "Who shot you?"

"I don't know. I didn't see anyone. A young boy gave me a message from Mrs. King asking me to meet her. Earlier in the day she said she needed my help, but I tried to ignore her. When I received her message to meet her at four o'clock on the trail near the turnoff toward Denver, I intended to find out what she wanted. I found her unconscious on the trail, and that was the last thing I remember, until I heard Jack's voice."

"I saw you talking to her at the hotel," Emma said. "What kind of help did she want?"

"She didn't say. She was afraid because Frank was still in town." He pointed to his coat on the chair. "The note should be in my coat pocket."

Rose appeared in the room with some boiling water, and Morgan took it from her and carried it to the bedside table. While he cleaned the wound, Granny left to check on Leigh, and to fetch her medical bag. Emma took that moment to tell Rose of her impending marriage to Clay.

While the women talked, Clay whispered to Morgan, "Would you get the small box out of my coat pocket?"

Morgan found the small box and handed it to Clay. When Granny returned with her instruments, Clay opened the box and pulled out the ring. "Emma."

Emma turned to him, and when he motioned for her to sit beside him on the bed, she didn't hesitate.

"I wanted to do this proper in front of your family." He took her hand in his, and said, "This ring was my mother's, and no one has ever worn it but her."

Emma knew he was saying that the ring wasn't worn by his deceased wife, and that made it all the more special.

He held the ring to her finger. "Would you do me the honor of becoming my wife?"

Emma was so emotional she could barely speak. She nodded and said softly, "Yes."

Clay slid the ring on her finger, and brought her hand to his lips. He placed a kiss on her ring finger. "Forever."

"Forever," Emma repeated, her heart filled with an over-whelming love for this man. When she finally looked down at the ring on her finger, she saw it was designed with sapphires surrounding a center diamond. "It's beautiful."

"My father had it made for my mother. It looks beautiful on your hand," Clay said.

"We can celebrate when I get this slug out of your shoulder," Granny said. "Rose, go see if Jack needs anything. That young woman has not come around, and I'm not sure what I can do for her."

Granny removed the bullet from Clay's shoulder quickly, and she left Emma and Morgan to bandage him while she hurried to check on Leigh.

"She's still unconscious, Granny," Jack said.

Granny lifted Leigh's eyelids and looked into her eyes before she examined the marks on her neck. "It looks like someone almost choked her to death."

"She fought whoever did this. There is some skin under her nails." Jack figured Clay must have interrupted who-ever was intent on killing Mrs. King, and they'd tried to kill him. Frank Langtry was most likely the culprit. Why would anyone else want to kill Mrs. King?

"Clay said Mrs. King sent a note to him asking that he meet her on the trail," Granny told Jack.

"Did the note say why she wanted to meet?" Jack asked.

"No."

"There was a pistol on Leigh's lap. It looked like she

may have shot Clay," Jack said. "But I think that is what someone wanted us to believe.

Jack walked to Emma's bedroom and told Clay about the gun. Clay was surprised by that revelation. "You mean they wanted it to look like I was choking her, and she shot me?"

Jack nodded. "I think that was the plan."

"There was no gun when I found her," Clay said.

"Jack, are you going to look for Frank?" Emma asked.

"I'm thinking he'll be back in Denver by now," Jack said.

"I'll go with you." Morgan walked to the kitchen to find Rose to tell her he was leaving with Jack. "We'll bring Addie and the kids over here to spend the night before we leave."

Frank arrived in Denver and went straight to Ruth's house. He slipped in through the back door, and first walked to the library where he expected to find Ruth sipping her brandy. Seeing the room was empty, Frank quietly walked upstairs, hoping to avoid the housekeeper. Reaching Ruth's bedroom door, he walked inside without knocking.

Ruth gasped when a dark figure entered her room. "What do you want?"

"Shh. Ruth, it's me, Frank."

"Frank? What are you doing in here?" Ruth was in her nightclothes sitting in front of the fire on the other side of the room. She was nursing her second brandy for the evening.

Frank hurried to her chair and kneeled in front of her. "I had to tell you what happened."

Ruth set her brandy aside. "What happened? Are you hurt?"

Clutching her hands in his, Frank said, "No, I'm not hurt, but I hurt Leigh."

"Tell me what happened."

Frank leaned over and pulled her into his embrace. "She threatened to tell everyone my true feelings about you. I lost my temper, and I'm afraid I couldn't control what I did."

Ruth didn't pull away from him. "What do you mean she was going to tell everyone about your true feelings?"

"She guessed how close we are, and threatened to ruin your reputation," Frank said.

"Frank, we have nothing to hide," Ruth said.

Frank pulled back and looked into her eyes. He knew what Ruth wanted to hear, what would convince her of his innocence. "Don't you see, we are not related, our relationship might be misunderstood? I couldn't stand the thought of someone trying to hurt you because of me."

Frank had a point, but she was of an age, and had enough wealth, that she didn't care what people thought. People would never shun her. Her money and influence carried more weight than gossip. "Tell me what happened."

"I lost my temper and I choked her, but I don't think I killed her."

"Did anyone see you?" Ruth asked, noticing the scratches on his face.

"No, but the pastor saw me early this morning. He knew I was in Whispering Pines." Frank didn't mention he'd shot the pastor.

"Then no one can prove it was you. It will be your word against hers." She didn't give a thought to the young woman Frank may have choked nearly to death. "I will tell anyone who inquires that you were here from early afternoon and had dinner with me. But I do think it wise that you leave Denver right now, at least for a while. Go back to Black Hawk. If the marshal goes to Black Hawk, tell him you broke off your relationship with Leigh that morning." She rose and walked to her bureau and removed several bundles of cash. "Here," Ruth said, shoving the money into Frank's hands. "This is all I have at home. You need to leave before my brother returns tomorrow. He will certainly hear about this, and if that young woman survives, he will know you have seen her."

Frank stuffed the cash inside his shirt. "You're right. The judge will be out for blood." Of course, Frank had already realized that the judge would be enraged as soon as he found out Leigh was living with him in Black Hawk since leaving Denver. No man liked to be played a fool. It wouldn't be long before the judge would have the marshal searching for him. Still, he had to remember it was his gang's word against his. No one could prove he was part of the robbery. Unless Leigh survived he figured he didn't have anything to worry about.

"I'll handle my brother. I'll tell him that young woman gave you a sad story and asked for your help to get away from him."

"Thank you, Ruth. You are the only person I trust." She was the only person who still believed his lies.

"This will all blow over soon. I don't think many people will care about the rantings of an immoral woman. If she's not dead, then it would be little more than a lover's spat."

"People will think you are protecting me," Frank said.

"Let them think what they please." Ruth knew Frank had a dark side, but something about his dangerous lifestyle was electrifying. He brought an excitement to her life that she hadn't experienced before. Her privileged life had always been predictable and mind-numbingly boring with committee meetings, hosting parties, luncheons, and her game nights with women whose lives were as pathetically humdrum as her own. Yes, she was much older than Frank, but in many ways he made her feel desired. He whispered forbidden comments in her ear, he ignored propriety and held her too close in public, he'd indiscreetly brush his lips over hers; all of these little moments triggered her repressed passion. For the first time in many years, she felt alive, and she wanted to cling to those brief moments as long as she could. She knew he enjoyed her money, her prestige, all of the status he'd never have without her as a benefactor, but she didn't care.

Frank pulled her into his arms. "I don't want to leave you."

"You must." Ruth allowed him to hold her tightly. She wasn't surprised when he kissed her on the lips.

Frank pulled back and looked down at her. "I hope to see you soon."

"Good-bye, Frank. I'll wire when you can come back, or I'll come to Black Hawk."

"Don't wait too long, Ruth." He left the room, hurried down the staircase and out the back door.

He needed Ruth and he hoped she didn't learn the depth of his deceit. He didn't tell her he'd sent Leigh a note that said the pastor wanted to meet her, and he had the same boy take a similar note to Clay. He'd set Leigh up and she'd taken the bait. When he'd appeared at the designated spot instead of Clay, he could see the surprise on her face. He'd confronted her, told her what the note said, and when she realized the truth, she laughed and told him he was acting like a jealous lover.

Her laughter sent him into a killing rage, and the next thing he knew, his hands were around her neck. He started choking her, and she started fighting back. Though she had marked his face and hands with her fingernails as she struggled, she was no match for him. He didn't release her until he felt her body go limp.

He was so enraged that he barely heard the rider coming

down the trail. Seeing Leigh's reticule on her wrist, he ripped it off and jumped on his horse and rode into the brush. Just as he expected, it was the pastor coming to meet Leigh. He watched as Clay felt Leigh's neck for a pulse, and decided then and there to shoot him. Pulling out the extra pistol he carried in his saddlebag, he pulled the trigger, and watched Clay slump to the ground. He ran to the buggy to make certain Clay was dead, but he heard him groan. He glanced at Leigh and he thought she was still breathing. Pulling his gun, he was ready to pull the trigger when he thought he heard another rider. He dropped the gun he'd used to shoot the pastor on Leigh's skirt before he ran back to the brush. Reaching his horse, he held his muzzle so he wouldn't reveal his hiding spot.

Within seconds, Sheriff Roper rode around the bend. He briefly thought about killing the sheriff, but he didn't think he should take that chance. The sheriff jumped off his horse and checked for Clay's pulse, then checked Leigh's. He lifted Clay inside the buggy beside Leigh before he tied the pastor's horse to the back of the buggy. Mounting his horse, the sheriff reached for the reins of the horse leading the buggy and headed toward Morgan's ranch at a fast pace. Frank figured if he'd killed them, the sheriff would be going back to town, not taking them to Morgan's where Granny could doctor them.

Frank sat in the trees debating his next move. He searched Leigh's reticule and found a letter she'd written to the pastor.

If anything happens to me, Frank Langtry is responsible. He planned that bank robbery in Denver. Leigh King

She'd told him she'd already given the letter to the pastor. She had lied. He cursed himself for not killing her that night in the hotel. Leigh was the only one who could corroborate Dutch's and Deke's version of the bank robbery.

If they all testified against him, he'd surely go to prison. He wasn't about to allow that to happen. There was no way anyone would ever lock up Frank Langtry in a cage. The preacher didn't know who shot him, but Frank knew Leigh could point to him in a courtroom and say he tried to murder her. Fallen woman or not, people would believe her before they'd ever believe him.

"We can't prove it was Frank," Jack said to Morgan once they were on the trail to Denver.

"No, we can't. But the least we can do is let the marshal and the sheriff know what is going on. If the judge is back in town, we may be able to finally convince him of Frank's guilt. I think he'll be more inclined to believe us now that Leigh King is in such a bad way."

"I wish you'd hung that sorry son of a gun that day," Jack said.

"I try not to look back. But I can tell you this much; Frank should thank his lucky stars that Rose happened by on that stagecoach. He'll never have another chance like that in his lifetime."

Morgan and Jack reached Denver and went straight to the sheriff's office where they found both Marshal Holt and Sheriff Trent. After explaining what had happened to Clay and Leigh, the marshal said, "This should put the nail in the coffin with the judge. Surely he won't believe Frank now."

"He may not, but his sister is still convinced Frank is the injured party. I think he could commit murder in the middle of the street and Ruth would continue to defend him," Sheriff Trent said.

"Well, I guess there's no time like the present to see if Frank is at Ruth's home right now," Marshal Holt said.

* * *

Frank rode behind the buildings in town, but he'd seen Morgan's and Jack's horses in front of the sheriff's office. He figured there was only one reason they were in Denver. Leigh must have told them he tried to kill her. Since Morgan wasn't home, Frank decided it would be the perfect time to sneak onto his ranch and take care of Leigh and anyone else who got in his way. Frank figured if he got lucky, Morgan might return to the ranch and he could exact his revenge on the man he hated most.

"How may I help you, Marshal?" Ruth asked when she walked into the library where the housekeeper had asked Marshal Holt to wait for the lady of the house.

"I'm looking for Frank Langtry," Marshal Holt said.

"I'm sorry, but Frank is not here." Ruth walked to the sideboard and picked up a decanter. "May I offer you a brandy?"

"No, thank you. Where can I find Frank?"

Ruth took a sip of brandy before she responded. "What is this about, Marshal?"

"It seems the young woman traveling with Frank was nearly choked to death earlier, and the pastor in Whispering Pines was shot," Marshal Holt said. "There's a witness who places Frank in Whispering Pines today, and he was seen with Mrs. King. I'd like to question him."

"If Frank was in Whispering Pines today, it had to be very early."

"Why do you say that?" Marshal Holt asked.

"He was with me today. He arrived just after lunch, and he had dinner with me," Ruth said.

"Where is he now?"

"He left earlier for Black Hawk. He needed to get back to the mine." Ruth finished her brandy and stared at the marshal. "Is that all I can do for you?"

Marshal Holt twirled his hat in his hand, trying to figure out what kind of game Ruth was playing. He didn't understand why this wealthy woman was so intent on protecting Frank. "When will Judge Stevens return?"

"Tomorrow."

"Please ask him to stop by the sheriff's office when he arrives." Marshal Holt settled his hat on his head. "Good evening."

Chapter Twenty-Two

Frank cut through the edge of the pine tree boundary separating the Langtry farm to Morgan's ranch. He hadn't been in the pines alone since he was a young boy. His gang was always with him. Even though he always made light of his gang being scared to death when they rode through the pines, he was just as frightened of the eerie sounds echoing through the trees. They were the very same sounds he was hearing tonight. Thankfully he didn't have far to ride to reach Morgan's ranch, but he kept looking over his shoulder to make sure no one was behind him. When he reached his hiding spot where he could see any movement on the ranch, he settled in, waiting for the right time to sneak inside the house. There was only one light coming from the house, and the bunkhouse was dark and quiet.

Unbeknownst to Morgan, Frank had been inside Morgan's house several times, and he was familiar with the layout. He even knew which room was Morgan's bedroom, and he figured with Granny and Emma staying there, Leigh would have to be in one of the back bedrooms. Everything was quiet when he slipped inside the back door and headed to the back staircase that led to the second floor. Stopping long enough to remove his boots, he then pulled his pistol and made his way to the top of the staircase. He hid in the shadows as he listened for sounds that might indicate someone was still awake. Silence. He quickly reached the room closest to the back staircase. He eased the door on the right open and peeked inside. Once his eyes adjusted to the darkness, he saw the bed was empty. Silently moving to the room on the opposite side of the hallway, he leaned his ear to the door. Hearing nothing, he slowly turned the doorknob and inched the door open until he could see the bed. With the aid of the moonlight shining through the curtains, he saw a form in the bed. He knew it was Leigh.

Slipping inside, he quietly closed the door behind him before he made his way to the bed. Leigh wasn't moving, but he could see she was breathing. He holstered his pistol and grabbed the pillow beside her.

"Frank, what are you doing here?"

Frank whirled around to see Granny sitting in a chair in the corner of the room behind him. She was pointing a pistol directly at him.

"I heard you had Leigh here, and I wanted to see her."

Granny tried to sound calm, but she was visibly shaking. "How did you hear that? Who told you?"

Frank ignored her question. "What happened to her?"

"I think you know," Granny replied.

Frank threw his hands in the air. "How am I supposed to know? I was in Denver."

Without hesitation, Granny said, "I think you choked this young woman and left her for dead."

"Why would I do that?" Frank countered.

"Frank, I stopped trying to understand why you do the things you do a long time ago. The devil got his hooks into you at an early age and he hasn't let you go. You've never wanted to be out from under his control, and you've never wanted to redeem your soul."

Moving toward Granny, Frank said, "Why are pointing that pistol at me? You know you aren't going to shoot me."

"I will if I need to. You are through hurting people in this family." Granny stood and pulled the hammer back on the pistol. "You need to leave this room, Frank."

Frank grinned at her. "Are you going to shoot me, Granny? Are you forgetting I'm your grandson? The only grandson you have left."

Granny tightened her grip on the pistol. "You're the reason I only have one grandson left. For the last time, you need to leave, Frank."

Frank reached out and quickly wrapped his hand around the barrel, aiming to wrestle the gun from Granny's hands. Granny held on tight. They struggled, and Frank elbowed Granny in the shoulder, but Granny refused to release the gun. The gun exploded, and in her shock, Granny dropped the gun. The bullet grazed Frank's arm. He ran from the room and down the back staircase. Hitting the bottom stair, he grabbed his boots before he ran for the back door. He heard the doors upstairs opening and people running down the hallway. By the time he reached his horse, he heard someone riding in. He didn't wait around to see if it was Morgan; he headed toward the pines, riding fast.

Morgan was headed toward the stable, but he saw men running from the bunkhouse toward the house. He turned his horse toward the house and he saw someone on the front porch holding a lantern. All of the commotion told him something was very wrong. Emma was running toward the pines, yelling for Sweetie who was several yards in front of her. Clay was trying to keep up with Emma, and he was carrying a pistol.

"Frank was here," Granny said as soon as Morgan reached the porch.

"When?" Morgan's eyes moved to his pregnant wife, and seeing the fear in her eyes made him furious.

"Just now. Morgan, I know he was going to kill that girl, but he didn't know I was in the room. I had a pistol on him, but he grabbed it and we struggled. It went off, and I think he was hit, but I don't think it was serious. He was able to run out of here." Granny's hands were still shaking from her encounter with Frank.

Morgan glanced around to see if he saw Joseph, but he wasn't with the other men.

"I'll saddle up," Murphy said.

Morgan appreciated his foreman's offer. "No, I'll go. Murph, you need to stay here and keep watch on the house. I want a man at the front and back. If you see Joseph, tell him I'll be in the pines."

Rose ran to her husband. "Please don't go after him alone." She pointed to the trees. "You hear those sounds? Those are the sounds I always heard when Frank was in there with me. He'll be waiting to kill you." From a young age, Rose never believed it was the wind that made the sounds in the pines as Granny had always tried to convince her. She believed what Joseph Longbow told her. He always said the great spirits echoed warnings with alarming sounds. The pleasing sounds said the great spirits were at peace with the visitors on their land.

Morgan heard the disturbing sounds, but it wasn't going to stop him. He understood his wife's fear of Frank; she had good reason to be afraid. He leaned over in his saddle and kissed the top of her head. "Honey, the men have work to do in the morning. I'll be fine. Now you need to get some rest."

Emma and Clay walked back to the porch with Sweetie.

Afraid Sweetie would go after Frank, Emma had a firm grip on his fur.

Clay heard Morgan say he was going after Frank.

"I'm going with you," Clay said.

"Not in your condition. You should be in bed," Morgan responded. "I'm just going to see what direction he's headed." He glanced at Murph. "Have someone go tell Jack what's going on, and tell him to wire Sheriff Trent to let them know what happened here. The judge is supposed to be back in Denver tomorrow, so tell Trent to inform the judge his girlfriend is here."

Morgan rode through the pines alone. He knew Frank well enough to know that the area frightened him, and he'd try to get out of there as fast as he could. After searching for a few hours, Morgan couldn't find his trail and he turned for home. He'd spent too much of his time dogging Frank through the years, and he didn't want to add to Rose's worry in her condition. Morgan had already come to accept that Frank would get his due, and he no longer needed to be the one to dole out justice. His life had changed. It was more important to him to be a good husband to Rose, and a father to their child than it was to seek vengeance.

As expected, when Morgan reined in at the ranch, Rose hurried outside to meet him.

"I knew you wouldn't rest until I came home." Morgan picked her up and carried her inside and up the stairs to their room. Once he put Rose to bed, he walked to the kitchen where Granny had a steaming cup of coffee waiting for him.

"I've already started breakfast. The biscuits will be ready in a minute," Granny said.

"Are you okay, Granny?" Morgan knew her well enough

to know she would have been fretting over Frank being shot, whether he deserved it or not.

Granny sat down beside him. "I'm okay. It was Frank's fault. He shouldn't have been here in the first place."

Morgan reached over and placed his arm around her frail shoulders. "I'm sorry I wasn't here, Granny."

Granny patted his hand. "Nonsense. You can't be here to protect us all of the time."

"It's my job to look after the women in my life," Morgan said.

"You do a fine job of that, but we can't live our lives expecting Frank at every turn," Granny replied.

Logic told him Granny was right, but it didn't settle well with him that he wasn't at home to protect his family. "Did Murph see Jack?"

"Yes, and he sent a telegram to Denver. I expect Marshal Holt will be tailing Frank again." Granny left her seat to crack four eggs in the iron skillet. She pulled the biscuits from the oven and lifted six from the pan and placed them on a plate. Once the eggs were done, she added them to the plate with a stack of bacon. "Eat your breakfast, then go upstairs and get some rest."

"Yes, ma'am." Morgan dove into his breakfast. "How's Mrs. King doing today?"

"I'm praying she wakes today. She's been moving around more and I think that is a good sign."

"It would be nice for her to be able to tell us who did this to her," Morgan said.

Granny refilled his cup. "We both know the answer to that."

"I'm surprised with Sweetie being upstairs that Frank was able to sneak in," Morgan said.

"Clay was sleeping, and Emma had fallen asleep in the chair. I was walking back and forth checking on Mrs. King and I didn't want to disturb them, so I closed the door. I did notice that Sweetie seemed restless."

"Too bad Sweetie wasn't in the room with you. It would have saved Marshal Holt a trip," Morgan said.

Judge Stevens was on Morgan's porch before lunch. When Granny answered the door, he introduced himself and said, "I understand Mrs. King is here."

Granny invited him inside. "I'm Granny Langtry. Yes, Mrs. King is here. I've been caring for her."

"That is very good of you. If you don't mind, I'd like to see her," the judge said.

Granny led the way upstairs. "I'm sorry to tell you that she hasn't awakened. It's in God's hands."

"I understand that Frank Langtry is your grandson," the judge said.

"Yes, he is."

"Sheriff Trent told me Frank was here last night," the judge said.

Granny stopped outside the door to Leigh's room, and explained to him what had transpired last night. "I think Frank was going to make sure she was dead. Morgan tried to trail him, but he didn't find him."

"Mrs. Langtry, I have spoken with Frank's gang in the Denver jail, and I assure you that my vision regarding your grandson is no longer clouded. I was in hopes of talking to Leigh to confirm what those men told me."

"I know you believed in Frank's innocence, and I can't tell you how much I wish that were true, but it isn't. Frank is guilty of everything Morgan told you, and much more. He needs to pay for his crimes."

The judge acknowledged her words with a shake of his

head. "It seems I owe Morgan an apology for not taking his word. I came here to find out if Mrs. King was involved with the bank robbery. As you may know, my daughter was killed that day."

"I'm so sorry for your loss. All I know is Mrs. King was involved with Frank, and that didn't bode well for her."

"Yes, I learned of their relationship when I arrived back in Denver. My sister was also privy to their deception. But I am unclear if Mrs. King was coerced in any way." The judge wanted to believe Leigh was forced by Frank, but his sister told him Leigh gave Frank a sad story and that was why he'd helped her. No matter what had transpired, he still loved Leigh, and he didn't want to believe she had deceived him.

Granny opened the bedroom door. "I hope she awakens so she can tell you the truth." She walked to the bed with the judge, and said, "I'll leave you alone for a few minutes." She glanced up at him and saw the tender look on his face as he stared at Leigh. Knowing he was a man who had been betrayed by the woman he loved, Granny couldn't help but feel sorry for him.

Granny left the judge alone with Leigh, and walked back to the kitchen where Rose was preparing lunch.

"I heard part of what he had to say," Rose said.

"He's still in love with her," Granny said.

"I'm sorry for that," Rose said, and picked up the tray of food she'd prepared. "I'll take this tray up to Emma and Clay, and I'll ask the judge to join us for lunch."

"I think he would appreciate the offer."

"Morgan, I owe you an apology," the judge said when he sat down at the kitchen table.

"Judge, you weren't the first person who was fooled by Frank Langtry. No apology is necessary."

"All the same, I do apologize for not taking your word for the problems he caused you. If there is anything I can do, please let me know." The judge recognized he'd been foolish to ignore the warnings of good people who had been harmed by Frank.

"There is one thing you can do," Granny said.

Morgan and Rose looked across the table at Granny. It was rare Granny would ask a favor of anyone. She was the one always giving to others.

"What's that?" the judge asked.

"When the marshal finds Frank, I want you to make certain he never hurts anyone again."

The judge stared at Granny. He understood what she was asking, and he admired her for her courage. "I give you my word on that."

"Judge, if you would like to stay here until Mrs. King comes around, you're welcome," Morgan told him.

"That's generous of you, Morgan. You sound confident she will survive," the judge said.

"Granny is the best doctor there is," Morgan replied.

The judge smiled at Granny. "I expected as much."

"I've never seen anyone stay unconscious this long though," Granny said. "I wouldn't mind if Joseph had a look at her."

"Joseph?" the judge questioned.

Realizing Granny didn't think before she spoke, all eyes slid to Morgan. Morgan didn't hesitate to respond. "Joseph Longbow."

"That would be the Sioux Indian on your ranch," the judge stated.

Morgan and the judge had had words about Joseph in the past, but Morgan wasn't going to lie. "That would be him."

The judge stared at Morgan and nodded. "If you think he could help Leigh, please ask him."

Morgan knew that was the judge's way of saying he would accept Joseph staying on his ranch without asking questions. "I'll find him right after lunch."

True to his word, Morgan brought Joseph to Leigh's room where Granny and the judge were sitting beside the bed. Granny had already told the judge of Joseph's ability to heal with herbs. Leigh didn't have visible wounds, so she couldn't promise Joseph would be helpful in this case.

Joseph approached Leigh and placed his hand on her head and closed his eyes. As was his way, he spoke some words quietly in his language. He opened his eyes, looked Granny's way, and gave a little imperceptible nod of his head.

Granny walked with him to the door where they spoke softly to each other. Granny turned back to the judge and said, "He says she will live."

The judge took a deep breath. "Thank God."

Chapter Twenty-Three

Two days later Leigh awoke in the evening with the judge and Granny beside her. She tried to speak, but her throat was so dry, words would not come out. Granny held her head while she sipped some water.

"Where am I?" Leigh asked.

"You're at Whispering Pines Ranch," Granny said.

"Why am I here? Have I been ill?" Leigh asked.

Granny glanced at the judge. "I'll let Judge Stevens explain."

"Judge Stevens?" Leigh said. "Who is he?"

The judge stood and leaned over her. "Leigh, don't you recognize me?"

Leigh drew her brows together as though she were trying to recall his face. "I'm sorry, I don't know you."

The judge looked across the bed at Granny, and she looked as confused as he did.

"Do you know who you are?" Granny asked.

"No. He just called me Leigh. Is that my name?"

"Yes, it is. Mrs. Leigh King." The judge took her hand

in his. "Don't you remember, we were going to travel the world together?"

Leigh's eyes darted to Granny. "Why don't I remember anything?"

Granny leaned over and patted her shoulder. "There is no need to be frightened. The judge knows you well. He means you no harm."

"Do you remember Frank Langtry?" the judge asked.

Leigh shook her head. "No, I'm sorry I don't."

"You've been unconscious for several days. Your memory may come back slowly," Granny said, trying to reassure her.

"Why was I unconscious?"

"Someone tried to kill you by choking you," Granny responded.

Leigh's eyes widened. "Why would someone try to kill me?"

"We think Frank Langtry tried to kill you, but we don't know why," the judge replied.

"That's the name you asked if I remembered," Leigh said.

"Yes. He was part of a bank robbery, and we didn't know if you were involved or not."

Leigh's gaze met the judge's. "Why would I be involved in a robbery? And why would he try to kill me if we were involved in a robbery together?"

"That is a good question." The judge was determined to hold on to a thread of hope that she wasn't a party to the bank robbery.

"You called me Mrs. Leigh King. Am I married?"

"No, you are a widow. I was going to ask for your hand."

"Have we known each other very long?"

"A couple of years." He gently squeezed her hand. "It was a special time."

"Why don't you rest now? Dinner is almost ready and I'll bring you a tray." Granny looked at the judge. "Judge Stevens, you come on down for dinner. I'm sure Mrs. King needs a few minutes to herself."

As much as he didn't want to leave, the judge understood Leigh needed some time. He squeezed her hand. "Rest now, my dear. I will check on you later."

While Granny brought Leigh her dinner, the judge sat with the family and told them of her condition. "I've never seen anyone who has lost their memory. Of course, I've heard of such conditions, but never saw it firsthand."

Emma and Clay had joined the family at the dinner table, and once they heard what the judge had to say, Emma said, "Perhaps she might remember Clay. He spoke with her that day."

"It's worth a try. We'll go up right after dinner," Clay said.

Morgan didn't voice an opinion, but it occurred to him that Mrs. King may be playacting. She'd been implicated in the bank robbery by Frank's gang, and she had to know the law was on to her by now. He hated to think a woman would be so devious, but she'd left the judge fast enough when Frank came along, so he didn't think she was particularly trustworthy.

The judge, Clay, and Emma finished dinner and walked upstairs to visit with Leigh, leaving Rose and Morgan alone at the table.

"Do you think she's really lost her memory?" Morgan asked Rose.

"I asked Granny the same thing, and she said she couldn't say for sure she was telling the truth. I guess the only thing we can do is believe her. If her memory doesn't return, it will be very frightening for her. I wonder what the judge will do with her."

"He will find a way not to bring charges against her. His feelings for her will overrule his good judgment." Seeing firsthand how the judge protected Frank, Morgan expected him to do the same thing for Leigh.

"Leigh, this is Pastor Clay Hunt. Do you remember him?" Judge Stevens asked.

Leigh glanced at Clay. "No, I'm sorry. Were you the pastor of my church?"

Emma was certain Leigh almost smiled when she saw Clay walk into the room. She couldn't very well call Leigh a liar, but she knew she recognized Clay. Emma glanced across the bed at Granny, and she could tell by the look on Granny's face that she'd noticed the same thing.

"No, I wasn't your pastor, but we spoke the day you were injured. You sent me a note to meet you," Clay said.

"Clay was shot when he stopped at your buggy," Judge Stevens said.

Leigh's eyes widened. "I'm so sorry." Her gaze landed on Emma. "Who are you?"

Clay put his arm around Emma's waist. "Emma is Granny's granddaughter, and my fiancée."

"Fiancée?" Leigh questioned.

"Yes, I am a fortunate man. Emma has agreed to become my wife."

"Why would I send you a note to meet me if we were not . . ." Leigh let the question hang in the air.

"You said you had something to give me," Clay responded.

Emma didn't miss Leigh's obvious insinuation. "We'll leave you alone now. I hope your memory returns soon."

Granny left the room with them, and the judge sat on the bed beside Leigh. "Leigh, I hope you remember our time together. We were very happy once, and I think we could be again."

"Have they caught this man who tried to kill me?" Leigh asked.

"No, but the marshal is looking for him. You have nothing to fear here, my dear. You are well protected."

Leigh reached down to clutch his hand. "Thank you for caring about me. I can't remember our past, but I hope the memories will come back to me." She recognized that the judge was the only one who could keep her out of prison, and she needed him to believe she had no knowledge of the robbery, or of Frank Langtry. She had to continue to pretend she couldn't remember anything. "Can you tell me why we weren't together when this happened?"

The judge brought her hand to his lips and placed a tender kiss on her skin. "You were in the clutches of Frank Langtry. I'm afraid that was also my fault for allowing that scoundrel into our lives. He had me fooled all along and it cost me my daughter and almost cost me you."

"What do you mean?" Leigh hoped she sounded confused and sincere.

"I think Frank coerced you into going with him." His sister had told him Leigh willingly left with Frank, but the judge no longer believed his own sister. Ruth had known all along that Leigh was at Black Hawk with Frank and hadn't told him. His own sister had allowed him to suffer not knowing what had happened to the woman he loved. No, he no longer knew whom to trust.

* * *

Marshal Holt visited the ranch early the next morning, and he was having coffee in the kitchen with Morgan. "I haven't found Frank's trail. I can't believe he covered his tracks that well."

"I found no sign of his trail through the trees. I've never known Frank to be adept at diversion." Morgan had chased Frank for days before, and he'd never failed to find his trail, until now.

"I agree. I'm not giving up. I just wanted to stop by to have a talk with Mrs. King." Marshal Holt wanted to arrest her for her part in the Denver bank robbery. After Morgan filled him in on her condition, and of the judge's hesitation to believe she was involved, he had a feeling he was going to butt heads with Judge Stevens once again. "It won't be the first time the old man and I go at it."

Morgan arched a brow at him. "He hasn't left her side. I'm afraid he's as smitten as ever, if not more so. He'll not allow you to charge her with anything is my guess."

"Maybe so, but I'm talking to her all the same. I'm prepared to get another judge in Denver if I need to." Marshal Holt intended to hold all of those responsible for the bank robbery accountable. "The judge's daughter died sense-lessly, and you'd think he'd want everyone involved held to account."

"I'm sure he does, but he doesn't want to believe the worst of the woman he loves," Morgan said.

Marshal Holt shrugged. "I'd never feel that way about a woman who was responsible for my daughter's death. If Mrs. King helped with that robbery, she is as guilty as the men inside that bank."

"I'll take you upstairs, and try to get the judge to leave you alone with her for a few minutes," Morgan said.

* * *

"I'm staying with her." The judge wasn't about to allow Marshal Holt to speak to Leigh alone. He thought Leigh was in a fragile condition, and shouldn't be forced to answer questions until she recuperated. He wasn't going to allow Marshal Holt to intimidate her.

"I'd like to speak to her alone," Marshal Holt reiterated.

"I'm staying," the judge repeated.

"Judge, I made some fresh coffee. Why don't you join me," Morgan suggested.

"I appreciate the offer Morgan, but I'm staying with Leigh."

Morgan glanced at Marshal Holt and shrugged.

"Have it your way, Judge," Marshal Holt said.

"What do you want to ask?" Leigh questioned.

Marshal Holt fixed his eyes on Leigh. He wanted to see if her expressions gave her away since he expected her to lie. "I have two men in the Denver jail who are willing to testify in a court of law that you were involved in the bank robbery along with Frank Langtry. When did you and Frank plan the robbery?"

When the judge started to object to his question, Marshal Holt held up his hand indicating that he should allow Leigh to respond without interrupting.

"Who are these men? How do they know me? Why would I be involved in a bank robbery?" Leigh asked.

"They are Frank Langtry's gang," Marshal Holt responded.

"That's the man everyone says is trying to kill me. If I participated in a bank robbery with him, why did he try to kill me?" She turned her pleading eyes on the judge. "This doesn't make sense to me. You don't believe I was involved in a robbery, do you?"

The judge immediately came to her defense. He wanted to believe she had no part in the robbery unless Frank had coerced her in some way. Not only that, but she'd been shot and almost died. He figured she was under some duress to leave town with Frank. "I certainly do not." The judge looked at the marshal. "She has a point. It makes sense that those men are lying."

"You thought Frank was innocent," Marshal Holt countered.

The judge took offense at the marshal's tone. "Now see here. I don't have to explain myself to you. These questions can wait until Mrs. King is feeling better."

Marshal Holt wasn't going to back down. "Judge, why would they lie? It will do nothing to lessen their complicity."

"They may be trying to offer more information hoping it will benefit them when it comes time for their judgment."

Marshal Holt wasn't buying the judge's reasoning. "I'm prepared to call for another judge in this case. I don't think you can be impartial."

The judge stood and pointed to the door. "You've said quite enough. You need to leave this room."

The marshal looked at Leigh. "I'm not finished with you. You were involved in the robbery, and even though the judge seems to have forgotten that his own daughter's life was taken, I haven't forgotten."

"Out!" the judge yelled.

"I guess that didn't go well," Morgan said when Marshal Holt came down the stairs. "Come on in the kitchen and have some more coffee."

The marshal followed him to the kitchen. "You heard him?"

Morgan nodded. "Everyone in the south pasture heard him."

"I told him I was going to request another judge. I don't think he liked that."

Morgan grinned. "I guess not. Have a seat. Emma and Clay have something to tell you."

The marshal took a seat at the table. "I hope someone has good news for a change."

"I feel certain Mrs. King recognized Clay when we walked in the room," Emma said.

"Really? Are you saying she hasn't lost her memory?"

"I think she knows without the judge on her side, her goose is cooked," Emma replied.

"I agree with Emma," Granny said. "She definitely recognized Clay."

The marshal looked at Clay. "What did you think? Do you think she recognized you?"

Clay hated to think the worst, and he didn't think there was anything amiss, right up to the point where Leigh insinuated to Emma that they had planned a tryst. "I don't think she's lost her memory."

The marshal leaned back in the chair. "Well, I'll be. So she's trying to get back in good graces with the judge so he can save her bacon."

Morgan placed a steaming cup of coffee in front of the marshal. "Sounds like it."

The marshal sipped his coffee. "If that's the truth, she is a real schemer. How do we prove she's lying?"

"All we can do is wait for her to make a mistake," Emma said.

"The judge said he's taking her back to Denver tomorrow if she's up to it," Granny said.

"What are you going to do?" Clay asked the marshal.

"I'm going to keep looking for Frank. If I find him, I'm certain he'll sing like a bird if he thinks it will save his hide. He would incriminate Granny if he thought it would keep him from going to jail."

"That's the truth of it," Granny said.

Chapter Twenty-Four

Once Ruth heard that her brother was at his ranch with Leigh King, she marched into Sheriff Trent's office to demand some action. She assumed Mrs. King would have already identified Frank as her attacker. She had already told Marshal Holt that Frank had dinner with her that night, and she planned to swear to that if necessary.

"What can I do for you, Ruth?" Sheriff Trent asked.

"I want to know why you don't have Mrs. King in jail. The marshal said she was involved in the bank robbery. As you know, my niece was killed as a direct result of that robbery."

"Yes, ma'am, I'm aware," Sheriff Trent replied. "Frank Langtry was also involved, and yet you didn't hold him accountable."

Ruth waggled her finger at the sheriff. "Frank told me he had nothing to do with that robbery. I think that woman was in cahoots with those men locked in your jail at this very minute, and they are all trying to place the blame on Frank when he had nothing to do with it. It's time you did your duty, or perhaps the people of Denver will need to find your replacement."

Ruth's superior attitude didn't faze the sheriff. "You are

welcome to believe what you want, but I know Frank Langtry, and he led that gang. Those men are going to testify against him."

"Has Marshal Holt found Frank?" Ruth was worried about Frank. She'd telegraphed the mine in Black Hawk asking if he had returned, but they had not seen him.

"No, ma'am, but he's still out there looking for him," Sheriff Trent replied. "I guess you know your brother brought Mrs. King back to Denver."

"Yes, I've heard. He is as big a fool as ever," Ruth said. "Are you as big a fool, Sheriff? Or do you intend to arrest that woman?"

"When Marshal Holt gets back, we'll talk about what we intend to do with Mrs. King. She supposedly has lost her memory."

Ruth was surprised by that revelation. "What do you mean, lost her memory?"

"Someone tried to kill her by choking the life out of her, and she was unconscious for days. She says she can't remember anything. She didn't even know her name."

"You can't be serious!" So they didn't know Frank was involved. "Who tried to kill her?"

"We think it was Frank."

"As I've already told Marshal Holt, Frank was with me that day. I am his alibi."

"Well, he wasn't with you when he went back to finish the job on Mrs. King at LeMasters's ranch. Granny Langtry was the one who stopped him at the end of a pistol. Apparently Frank was wounded in a struggle over the gun, but he was able to run away."

Ruth could hardly believe what the sheriff was saying. Surely Frank didn't go back to Whispering Pines. Why would he be so foolish? She'd told him to be careful, and to go directly to Black Hawk. "Was he badly injured?"

Sheriff Trent was taken aback by her concern for Frank. "He ran away, and he's evaded Marshal Holt, so I'd say he wasn't badly injured."

Ruth hurried from the sheriff's office. She could hardly breathe thinking that Frank might be dead. She'd accepted that she was infatuated with Frank Langtry, and the thought of never seeing him again saddened her beyond belief. No matter their age difference, she still felt that spark of femininity when she was around him. Of course, she knew Frank was aware of her feelings, but she didn't care. She'd grasped what remaining time she had left on this earth with both hands, trying to ignore the march of time. She was so caught up in her fantasy with Frank that she didn't recognize the irony in her disapproval of her brother's relationship with a much younger woman.

She was tempted to go to her brother's home and insist on speaking with Mrs. King. But toward what end? If the woman lost her memory—Ruth stopped walking. What if she was feigning her memory loss? According to Frank, she was a woman who knew how to protect her own survival. Ruth understood that meant she could be conniving to further her own goals. The question was if Leigh was pretending to have memory loss, what was her goal? The answer seemed obvious. She wouldn't have to explain to the judge why she willingly became Frank's paramour. If she admitted that she left with Frank of her own free will, she would have a lot of explaining to do. It seemed logical she was feigning memory loss. Having no memory, she couldn't explain her relationship with Frank. The judge would see to it she wasn't charged with a crime.

* * *

Sheriff Trent had another surprise in store when Judge Stevens walked through his door just a few hours after Ruth left. "Hello, Judge."

Forgoing any pleasantries, the judge said, "I would like to speak to your prisoners."

Sheriff Trent was surprised, but he had no valid reason to deny the request. "Which prisoners?"

"Dutch Malloy and Deke Sullivan."

The sheriff opened the door that led to the cells and allowed the judge inside. When the sheriff turned to leave, the judge shut the door behind him. He approached the cell where Dutch and Deke were sitting and spoke quietly to them for several minutes.

The judge stopped at the sheriff's desk before he left the jail. "The trial will be held in the morning for Dutch and Deke."

"But Marshal Holt won't be back by then," Sheriff Trent said.

"We don't need Marshal Holt to hold court. I'll be leaving for Colorado City soon, and I want this behind us." The judge didn't wait to hear further objections from the sheriff. He turned to walk out the door, saying over his shoulder, "Court at nine in the morning."

As soon as Judge Stevens returned to his home, he walked to his bedroom where Leigh was resting. "Leigh, we need to talk."

Leigh sat up and the judge propped a pillow behind her. "I spoke to those men in the jail, and they are prepared to swear that you were involved in the robbery."

Leigh reached over and took his hand in hers, urging him to sit beside her. "I told you that I don't know those men. You say you knew me and we were close. Why would I be involved in a robbery?"

"To be honest, I can't prove one way or the other that you have truly lost your memory."

"But . . ."

The judge held up his hand for her to stop talking. "Hold on. Let me finish what I want to say. I hope you are telling me the truth. I'd like to believe that you were coerced by Frank to go with him, but I need to make certain. It is within my power to give those men their freedom if they agree not to testify against you."

"How can I ever thank you?" Leigh asked, clutching his hand between her breasts.

"I'm getting to that. I have one condition for my assistance."

"What is your condition?" Leigh asked.

"You must marry me today. I will have the preacher come here tonight if you agree. As my wife, you will always have my protection. If not, I can't guarantee what will happen to you."

"I'm sorry you aren't confident that I'm telling you the truth about my memory. I'm taking your word that we were once very close. I know you are an honorable man and you wouldn't lie to me."

"You haven't answered my question," the judge said.

"Naturally, I wanted some time to get to know you again," Leigh equivocated.

The judge pulled his hand from hers and started to stand. "I take that to mean you have no interest in my proposal."

Leigh reached for his hand again and urged him to sit back down. "I didn't say that. I will marry you today." She had quickly weighed her options. She had none. While she didn't really want to be tied to him for the rest of her life, it seemed like the only viable way out of her present dilemma. She knew she wouldn't be safe as long as Frank was alive, unless she was with the judge. There was also the chance the judge wouldn't live a long time. He'd already had one heart attack. If he did die, she would be a wealthy young widow. "Go get the preacher."

The judge leaned over and kissed her. "I promise you, we will be happy again. We will travel the world and do all of the things we planned before all of this nonsense."

True to his word, the judge was in his one-room courthouse ready for the defendants by nine the next morning. No one in the town was aware of the proceedings, so the judge, the sheriff, and the defendants were the only people in the room. The judge had the sheriff go to the bank and ask Mr. Rivers, the president of the bank, to join them. The judge wanted him to be questioned about the shooting under oath. The judge thought Mr. Rivers's appearance would lend the proceeding some credibility to justify his ruling.

Dutch and Deke both stood before the judge while he asked the questions. "Tell me what happened when the shooting started."

"We were standing with our backs to the window when the man in the bank pulled a gun from a drawer and started shooting," Dutch said.

The judge's eyes slid to Deke. "Is that your memory of the incident?"

"Yes, sir. It wasn't our bullets that hit those women. We weren't facing the windows. The man in the bank shot out those windows."

"Who planned this robbery?" the judge asked.

"Frank Langtry," Dutch said, and Deke nodded.

"You were prepared to say that Mrs. King was involved," the judge said.

"We never met the woman," Dutch said. "We just knew Frank knew her."

Again, Deke nodded his agreement.

Once Mr. Rivers, the bank president, entered the room, the judge asked him his recollection of the robbery.

"I was facing the windows when I fired, and I'm sorry to say it was my bullets that hit your daughter and Mrs. King," Mr. Rivers confirmed.

"Did these two men shoot at the windows?" the judge asked.

"No, sir."

"You may go back to the bank." The judge dismissed Mr. Rivers.

"Tell me what happened to the money from the robbery," the judge asked Dutch.

Dutch relayed how the killers, Culpepper and Taggart, robbed them in the middle of the night and took all of the money.

"When Marshal Holt brings Frank Langtry in, are you two prepared to face him in court and testify to of all of his misdeeds?" The judged peered at them over his spectacles. "And I mean everything he's done."

"Yes, sir," Dutch and Deke said at the same time.

The judge asked them about rustling on Morgan's land, and the men told him the truth.

"Mr. LeMasters told me after the stagecoach accident, which left Frank's sister in a bad way, he credited you with releasing his horse so he could get her some help. Was that the way of it?" the judge asked.

"Yes, sir. Frank almost shot me because I released two horses. Dutch and I felt real bad that Morgan wouldn't have a way to help Frank's sister without those horses," Deke said.

The judge looked at the sheriff. "You have anything to add?"

"I think you should wait on Marshal Holt before sentencing," Sheriff Trent said. He knew that wasn't going to happen, but he asked all the same.

"I don't think the marshal can add anything to what I've heard." He glanced back at the prisoners. "What do you two plan to do with your lives if you're given a second chance?"

Dutch didn't hesitate with his response. "I plan to marry Harper Ellis's sister, sir. That is, if you'll declare her husband dead. He left her years ago with four children to raise alone, and she's not heard hide nor hair from him in all these years. She needs help on that farm."

The judge's expression indicated his surprise by Dutch's response. He was aware of the situation with the woman who barely eked out a living on her small farm. If not for her brother, her children would have starved to death long ago. "A worthy endeavor to take on another man's responsibility."

"I figure I need to make up for all the wrong that I done," Dutch said.

The judge looked at Deke. "What about you?"

"If Dutch will have me, I'll work with him on that farm. Maybe we can even run some cattle," Deke said.

Dutch looked at his friend. "We've been closer than brothers for years. I'd be happy to have you work with me."

Sheriff Trent believed them. He'd always thought Dutch and Deke weren't bad men; they'd just made bad decisions.

The judge stood and brought his gavel down. "Court will be adjourned for fifteen minutes while I deliberate on this case."

* * *

The judge paced the sidewalk for the fifteen minutes while Sheriff Trent waited with Dutch and Deke. When the judge returned to his courtroom, he asked Dutch and Deke to stand.

"For your testimony against Frank Langtry when the time comes, I'm dropping charges in this case. If you fail to appear to testify against Langtry, I will find a way to send you to the territorial prison for twenty years. Do I make myself clear?"

"Yes, sir," Dutch and Deke said simultaneously.

"Judge," Sheriff Trent said.

Judge Stevens held up his hand. "The matter is settled, and that's my decision. These men are free to go. Court is adjourned."

Chapter Twenty-Five

Emma, Carlo, and Andre were glowing from the appreciative response of their audience. Judging by the deafening applause, they knew their performance was one of their best. To quiet the boisterous crowd, Carlo held his hands in the air, motioning for quiet to make his announcement. He told the crowd of Emma's impending marriage and her retirement from the stage, which started another round of applause.

After a lengthy good-bye from well-wishers, it was quite late by the time the family made it to the restaurant. Carlo and Andre joined the family, and Carlo ordered champagne for everyone at the table. He filled their glasses and offered a toast to Emma and Clay. "Congratulations. We wish you a long and happy marriage."

"We should be angry with you, Clay, for taking Emma from us," Andre said.

"I would understand if you were, but I won't change my mind. You two will be coming to the wedding, won't you? I spoke to the pastor here in Denver and he will come to Whispering Pines to marry us after my sermon." After hearing Emma sing tonight, Clay had a moment when he questioned if he was doing the right thing. Was he taking Emma from her life's purpose? Seeing how the people responded tonight, he almost felt guilty that large crowds may never hear her again. She didn't just sing beautiful songs, she brought joy to the lives of people who struggled, people who often had little to smile about. On their walk to the restaurant, he'd mentioned his thoughts to her. She assured him she wanted him and a family, and that was her purpose now.

"We wouldn't miss the wedding," Andre said. "But our lives will never be the same without Emma."

Carlo and Andre were both happy for Emma, but they had come to love her like a sister, and they knew they would have a difficult time finding another soprano with her amazing talent.

"You must plan on staying with us when you come this way again," Emma said. "Who knows? You two may decide to settle down in the West."

"We will come here again if you promise to sing with us when we do," Andre told her.

"Of course I will," Emma replied.

"If we could find wives as beautiful as you and your sisters, I might consider living in Denver," Carlo teased. He started to say something else, but he was interrupted when Prince Henri stopped at their table.

Emma hadn't seen him at the performance, and she assumed he'd already left Denver. "Henri, I didn't know you were still in Denver."

"I'm leaving tomorrow. I wanted to see your last performance." Henri acknowledged everyone at the table.

Clay stood and extended his hand. "Please join us."

Henri smiled and shook Clay's hand. "No, but thank

you for asking. I offer you my congratulations." He glanced back at Emma. "I wish you the very best."

Emma figured Henri heard of her marriage along with everyone in the hall when Carlo made his announcement. She'd totally forgotten about their planned dinner when Clay was shot. She and Clay had planned to tell him of their engagement that night. "Thank you, Henri. That means a great deal to me."

Henri said good-bye to everyone and left the room.

Clay leaned close to Emma's ear. "Are you certain you don't want to marry a prince?"

Emma smiled at him. "I am marrying a prince."

Clay's chest swelled with pride. If there was a better feeling in life than knowing his soon-to-be wife considered him a prince, he didn't know what it would be.

Sheriff Trent walked into the restaurant and saw the celebration, so he stopped to offer his congratulations.

"Please join us," Clay said.

Sheriff Trent sat beside Morgan and Jack, and he told them of the judge's decision to free Dutch and Deke.

"Why didn't the judge wait on Marshal Holt to see if he captured Frank?" Morgan asked.

"I asked him to wait, but he refused," Sheriff Trent said.

"Dutch and Deke should have steered clear of Frank from the beginning," Morgan said.

Sheriff Trent told them about Dutch and Deke's plan to stay in Denver. "Dutch says he's going to marry Harper Ellis's sister."

"Harper Ellis?" Clay asked, overhearing their conversation.

The sheriff nodded. "You know him?"

"Yes, he's related to a man who works for me in Kansas. I saw Harper the other day," Clay said.

"Doc told me he's in a bad way," Sheriff Trent added.

"Harper is a fine man. I asked him to come to church." Clay wished the hour wasn't so late, or he would call on Harper to see how he was doing. "If you see him, tell him our congregation will be praying for him."

Everyone was leaving the restaurant when they saw Marshal Holt riding into town. Sheriff Trent waved to him, and the marshal reined in at the hotel.

"Sorry I missed your performance," Marshal Holt said to Emma.

"I wish you could have been there. It was beautiful," Granny said. "Emma and Clay are marrying tomorrow, so it was her last performance."

Marshal Holt extended his hand to Clay. "Congratulations."

Clay shook his hand. "If you're up to it, we'd like to have you there."

Before the marshal responded to Clay, Sheriff Trent asked, "Any luck with Frank?"

"I couldn't find his trail," Marshal Holt said.

The marshal's admission surprised them. He had a reputation for his exceptional tracking skills.

"If you can't find them, then I don't hold out hope he'll be found right now," Sheriff Trent said.

Marshal Holt was as baffled at the sheriff. "It's like he never came out of those pines on Morgan's land."

"I have more news for you," Sheriff Trent said.

Marshal Holt expelled a loud breath. He was tired and he didn't want to hear bad news, but the look on Sheriff Trent's face said he was about to get it. "What?"

"The judge held court this morning. He freed Dutch and Deke in exchange for their testimony against Frank."

"What about Mrs. King?"

"He didn't charge her with anything. Dutch and Deke testified they had never spoken to her."

"Judge Stevens made that decision because I told him I planned to ask for another judge for this case."

Sheriff Trent whistled. "That explains everything."

"You're right about that."

"What about Culpepper and Taggart?" If the judge had let those killers go free, then Marshal Holt was going to put the judge in jail for impersonating an officer of the law.

"They didn't go on trial," Sheriff Trent said.

"Good."

"I would like to be at their trial," Clay said. He glanced down at Emma. "Would you mind?"

Emma linked her arm though his. "We will both be at their trial."

"I'm sorry we can't charge them with those murders." Sheriff Trent understood Clay wanted justice for his family. "We don't have witnesses to that crime."

"I know. I still want to be there," Clay said.

"I'll let you know as soon as we have a date," the sheriff replied.

"What do you think happened to the bank's money? Who is telling the truth about that?" Marshal Holt asked.

Sheriff Trent had heard Culpepper and Taggart accuse Dutch and Deke of taking the money, but he didn't know if they were telling the truth. How could a lawman believe murderers? "I don't know what to think. But no matter who is telling the truth, I don't think we will ever see that money."

"Yeah, I've had the same feeling. I guess we'll know if Deke and Dutch have it if they start living high off the hog.

And if Culpepper and Taggart stashed it somewhere, then it'll be of no use to them where they're going."

"There is some solace in that," Sheriff Trent agreed.

Marshal Holt picked up his reins. "I think I'll go have a talk with the judge tonight." He glanced at Granny and asked, "Are you cooking the wedding feast?" When Granny had nursed him after he'd been shot, he'd found out the Langtry women were mighty fine cooks.

"I am. You'll have a fine meal and some wedding cake," Granny said.

Marshal Holt smiled. "That's the best offer I've had since I was shot. I'll be there in time for the service."

It was past midnight when Marshal Holt reached the judge's ranch. He knocked on the door and waited for several minutes before the judge's housekeeper cracked open the door.

"I want to see Judge Stevens," Marshal Holt said.

"He's not here. He left for Colorado City this morning," the woman told him.

"What about Mrs. King? Is she here?"

"She went with him."

Marshal Holt jumped back in the saddle and rode toward Denver. He thought about the judge not holding Leigh King responsible for her part in the robbery. He remembered what his father always said about letting sleeping dogs lie. The judge lost his daughter, and Mrs. King nearly died from her injuries during the robbery. Marshal Holt figured there was some sort of justice in that if she was guilty. He felt she'd probably paid a hefty price for her duplicity. Frank nearly choked her to death, and if she did truly suffer memory loss, then he figured her penance was from the Almighty. He'd found it wasn't always necessary for the law to deliver justice.

By the time the family reached the ranch, the women were asleep in the back of the buckboard. Morgan could tell something was amiss as soon as he saw the lights on in the house and in the bunkhouse. The men jumped from the buckboard, and Morgan's foreman came outside to greet them. "The kids are fine," Murph said before the men thought the worst. "It's Judge—he's missing."

The women came awake at the sound of the men's voices. "What's going on?" Rose asked when she saw all of the men milling about.

"Judge is missing." Morgan turned back to Murph and asked, "Did he jump the fence again?"

Murph lifted his arms in the air indicating his frustration. They had seen Judge jump the paddock fence before, but he always returned before night. "No one knows. I brushed him down and put him in his stall. I know I secured the stall, but when Joseph went to check on all of the horses tonight, his stall was empty. Joseph's been in the pines looking for him for hours. I stayed with the children in case someone was lurking about."

Morgan knew Murph expected Frank must be about causing mischief. "Murph, stay with the women, I'll help Joseph. Judge is more likely to come to me than to anyone else."

"I'll go with you," Jack said.

"So will I," Clay added.

"Who is Judge?" Emma asked, confused by the conversation.

"Morgan's horse," Rose said.

Morgan turned to help the women from the buckboard. When he lifted Rose to the ground, she held on to his arm. "Don't you hear that?"

Morgan noticed she was staring toward the pine trees. "What, honey?"

"The trees. The wind wasn't blowing all of the way home. Listen?"

Everyone stopped talking and listened. At first it sounded as if people were speaking in whispers. Within seconds, the volume increased until it was almost deafening.

"It's just the wind picking up," Morgan assured his wife.

The women looked at each other, and Granny said, "I've never heard the wind so loud."

"It's louder than the other night when you went to look for Frank. He must be close," Rose said.

"It's unnerving," Emma added. She glanced at Clay. "Maybe you should wait until morning."

"Honey, just like the other night, it's just the wind." Clay remembered the first time he'd heard the noises in the pines. The sounds were indeed startling, but he wasn't one to believe in superstitions.

"I don't like the thought of you riding through there again," Rose said to Morgan.

He hugged her to his chest. "When we find Joseph, there will be four of us. We'll be fine."

"Let's go." Clay kissed Emma on the cheek.

Jack told Addie not to wake the children. "We'll be staying the night."

Emma was baffled why everyone was so concerned about a missing horse. She thought if a horse got loose, he would return home when he was good and ready, or when he was hungry. "Why didn't they just wait for the horse to come back?"

"Let's go inside and I'll tell you all about it," Rose said.

They reached the kitchen with Murph right behind them. "You ladies take a seat and I'll make us some fresh coffee."

When the coffee was ready, Murph poured each woman a cup and sat with them.

"Someone please explain what is going on," Emma said impatiently.

Everyone turned their eyes on Granny, so she took charge of the explanation. "Emma, you remember years ago when Morgan gave Frank a job on his ranch?"

"Yes."

"I didn't realize it back then, but now that I look back, I think Frank was consumed with hate toward Morgan even when he was much younger."

"But what does that have to do with a missing horse?" Emma asked impatiently.

Granny held her hand up. "Do you remember that big black stallion Morgan used to ride?"

Emma nodded. She'd always thought it was the most beautiful animal she'd ever seen.

"I think Frank was smart enough to realize how he could hurt Morgan. Anyone who saw Morgan with that horse knew he loved him. Frank whipped Morgan's horse so badly, he nearly killed him. When Morgan saw what Frank had done, Morgan beat him badly." Granny glanced at Murph, and added, "Murph and Joseph had to pull Morgan off of Frank, or he would have killed him."

"I tried to tell Morgan to put the horse down, but he refused. He nursed that horse back to health, and now Judge only allows a few people to touch him." Murph glanced in Rose's direction, and said, "Your sister is one of the few. Judge is as crazy about her as he is about Morgan.

I've never seen anything like it. For years, Morgan was the only one who could approach him without the horse going into a frenzy."

"How could Frank do such a thing to a poor animal?" Emma asked.

"Honey, I told you—Frank is evil," Granny replied. "There's no explaining the mind of an evil person."

Chapter Twenty-Six

Morgan tried whistling for Judge, but the wind in the trees drowned out all other sounds.

"Have you ever heard it like this before?" Jack asked, looking up at the trees.

"Never."

"The women were right. It's downright eerie," Clay said.

Eerie was the perfect word for the strange spine-chilling sounds. Morgan had heard strange noises in the pines over the years, but nothing compared to what he was hearing tonight. "That's why most people don't want to come through here."

"I can almost understand why people would steer clear, particularly if they aren't right with their Maker," Clay replied.

The men found no trace of Judge's hoofprints, and they saw no sign of Joseph. After searching for over two hours, and seeing nothing that would lead them in a particular direction, Morgan suggested they head back to the ranch.

"We can stay out as long as we need to," Clay said.

"Tomorrow is your wedding day, Clay. You need to get some rest," Morgan said.

"I'll be fine. Don't turn back on my account." Clay knew Morgan was worried about his horse, and he wanted to do what he could to help find him. He felt the same way about Moonrise, and if he had a lead on his horse, he would keep going until he found him.

"I don't even know which way to go," Morgan said. "There's no sense staying out here with nothing to go on."

They rode back to the ranch, cared for their horses, and were walking from the stable, when Joseph came riding in.

"I've been looking," Joseph said.

"We found no sign of him," Morgan said.

"I have other men looking."

Morgan figured Joseph meant he'd talked to some of the braves that sought refuge in the trees. "Get some rest. There's nothing more we can do right now."

Once in bed, Morgan stared out the window at the moon, trying to make sense out of Judge's disappearance. Morgan knew the horse liked to roam, and the last year he'd jumped the fence fairly frequently, but he never failed to return to his paddock or stall. Morgan didn't think it was a problem allowing Judge some freedom as long as he ran on the ranch. Morgan tried to think if Judge's habits had changed over the last few days, but nothing came to mind. He didn't think it was possible that someone Judge didn't trust led him from his stall. Most people thought Judge was dangerous so they steered clear of him. Morgan didn't try to dissuade them of that notion. He wondered how Judge would react if he ever saw Frank again. When sleep continued to elude him, Morgan crept downstairs and made some coffee.

It was just a few hours before dawn, but Morgan walked to the stable to saddle his horse. He wanted to find Judge before the day began. Clay would need to get to town and prepare for his Sunday morning service, and the wedding was planned afterward. It was going to be an exciting day for the family, but Morgan knew if he didn't find Judge, he would have a difficult time celebrating. Slowly Morgan rode to the pines, using his lantern to search the earth for any sign of his beloved horse. He'd owned many horses, but he had a special bond with Judge. His large strong body belied his gentle heart. Morgan had often thought that Judge understood every word he said. There was a trust between them that Morgan had never found with another horse. The day he saw what Frank had done to that beautiful animal, he wanted to kill him. Morgan had never seen such horrific injuries on an animal in his life. Rage consumed him, and he went after Frank with a fury he didn't know he possessed. No doubt he would have killed Frank if not for Murph and Joseph. Goodness knows he tried.

Morgan had stayed with Judge in his stall for days as he cared for him. He remembered how Judge would rest his head on his shoulder, conveying his trust in Morgan to do what was best for him. There was no way Morgan would have let him down, nor would he listen to his men who said Judge should be put out of his misery. Judge was scarred for life on the outside, and Morgan often wondered if he was forever traumatized on the inside. Thinking his horse was lonely, Morgan tried to spend as much time as he could with him. Once Morgan saw how Judge had taken to Rose, he knew he had the capacity to trust another person. At least he knew he could trust the people on the ranch. That's why it didn't make sense that Judge would leave the safety of the ranch. But then, Judge didn't know Frank was roaming free.

The longer Morgan searched, the more discouraged he

became. He decided he needed to get back to the ranch, but he fully intended to resume his search after the wedding. As he cleared the pine tree boundary on his ranch, Joseph was riding toward him, with Clay and Jack following.

"Judge is in the paddock," Joseph said.

"What? How? Did you find him?" Morgan asked.

"We were in the stable saddling our horses, and when we came out, there he was in the paddock." Before Morgan asked, Joseph said, "He has no injuries."

"Morgan, I'm glad he came back. I'll be leaving for town, so I'll see you later at church," Clay said.

The relief Morgan felt over Judge returning unharmed was written on his face when he smiled wide. "We'll be on time with your bride." Morgan rode to the paddock, and Judge was standing there looking at him. Morgan dismounted and walked inside the paddock. "Where have you been?" The horse came to him and hung his head over his shoulder as he usually did in greeting. Morgan stood there gently stroking his neck for a long time. Before he led him to the stable, he checked him over, and as Joseph said, there was not a scratch on him.

Morgan walked into the kitchen and Jack handed him a cup of coffee. The women were getting ready for the big day, but Jack's children were at the table and full of questions.

"Where is your Christmas tree, Uncle Morgan?" Jane asked.

"Rose and I were waiting for you to help us decorate," Morgan answered.

"We can do it tonight since Ma and Pa said we are staying here, so Aunt Emma can stay at our house for her wedding night," David said.

"I think that sounds perfect," Morgan said.

Claire climbed in her father's lap. "Can I help?"

Jack kissed the top of her head. "Of course."

"It's going to be a fun day. We get to see a wedding today. We've never been to a wedding," Jane said.

"One day I'll be attending your wedding," Jack said, leaning over to give Jane a kiss on her cheek.

"It'll be a lucky man who snags one of you two beautiful girls," Morgan said. He stood and excused himself to get dressed for church.

"I'm never getting married," David said.

Jack laughed.

"What's so funny?" David asked.

"Morgan and I said the same thing, son," Jack said. "But one day you'll change your mind quick enough when the right young lady comes along."

Carlo and Andre arrived at the church just as the service was about to begin. Clay ushered them to the first pew to sit with the family. As he walked back to the door to greet the arriving parishioners, he was surprised to see Harper Ellis dismounting in front of the church.

Clay greeted him warmly. "Harper, I'm so glad you came."

"Clay, it's good to see you. I figured it couldn't hurt to make peace with my Maker before it's too late."

"Harper, as I told you, it's never too late to seek God." Clay wasn't going to push Harper, but he fully intended to ask the congregation to pray for him today. "Have you heard I'm getting married today after the service?"

"No, I didn't know. Congratulations. Who is the lucky bride?"

Clay told him about Emma and their plans to buy a

ranch. "I've already wired Jonas and asked him to join me out here. We are going to buy a small ranch."

"What did Jonas say?"

"He said he's excited to see the West." Clay wasn't certain Jonas would ever leave Kansas, and he was thrilled when he'd received his telegram agreeing to come to Colorado.

"It will be good to see him again," Harper said.

Sheriff Trent and Marshal Holt rode up to the church, and after Clay greeted them, it was time for the service to begin.

Before Clay ended with his prayer, he introduced Carlo and Andre to the congregation. He started to introduce Harper, but he saw Harper's slight shake of his head. Instead, Clay said a friend of his was joining them for services this morning, and he asked them to pray for his healing. He finished with his prayer, and reminded everyone they were welcome to stay for the wedding, and the reception following at Morgan's ranch.

Granny, Rose, Addie, and Emma left the church by the back door to go to Clay's home so Emma could change into her wedding dress. The gown had been designed in Paris for one of her performances. The white silk and lace dress made the perfect wedding gown.

"Emma, you are beautiful," Granny said.

"For the first time, I really feel beautiful." It was almost impossible for Emma to believe how her life had changed in the short time since she'd arrived in Whispering Pines. Her plans hadn't included marriage, but now that she'd found Clay, she couldn't imagine a life without him. She prayed she could bring him the happiness he'd found in his first marriage.

"I just hope Clay can talk once he gets a look at you," Addie said.

The pastor from Denver arrived thirty minutes after Clay's service ended. Carlo and Andre were walking the bride down the aisle, so it was their responsibility to fetch her.

Morgan and Jack stood near the altar with Clay, trying to calm his nerves. The men laughed each time Clay tugged at his tie.

"You aren't nervous, are you, Clay?" Morgan asked.

"Just a bit," Clay admitted.

"You don't want to leave by the back door, do you?" Jack asked.

"No." That wasn't even a thought in Clay's mind. He wanted to marry Emma, but there had been times he was tempted to worry something might happen to her. But he'd made a decision not to live in fear; he chose to live in faith. His feelings for Emma had developed quickly, and though he'd fought the notion of marrying again, thankfully he'd come to terms with the past. He looked forward to a long and happy life with her.

Finally Granny appeared at the door of the small church. Morgan and Jack took their seats in the first pew and Clay moved to the center of the altar. Granny, Rose, and Addie took their seats, and all eyes turned to the door, awaiting Clay's bride.

Emma entered the church, her arms linked with Carlo's and Andre's. Murmurs could be heard from the women in the congregation when they saw how beautiful Emma looked in her exquisite gown.

Clay couldn't stop smiling as he watched Emma walk down the aisle. He thought she was the most stunning bride he'd ever seen. When their eyes locked, they were the only two people in the room.

After the wedding almost everyone in town arrived at Morgan's ranch for the reception. Granny, Rose, and Addie had baked several cakes to serve a large crowd, and they weren't disappointed. It looked as though all of Whispering Pines were in attendance. Carlo and Andre entertained the guests, which allowed Clay and Emma to have a few brief moments to themselves.

"I haven't seen Joseph. You know how much he loves cake," Granny said to Morgan.

Morgan had already noticed Joseph's absence. "I was just getting ready to go look for him." Morgan caught Murph's eye, and inclined his head to the door.

Murph made his way to the door, and said, "What's up?"

"Have you seen Joseph?"

Murph looked over the crowd. "I hadn't realized he wasn't here. I'll go look for him."

"I'll go. Have some more cake, and keep an eye on things." Morgan walked to the stable and Judge wasn't in his stall, so he checked all of the stalls. Not finding Judge in any stall, Morgan knew the horse was missing again. He saddled his horse and walked from the stable when Joseph came riding in.

"You need to come with me," Joseph said.

Morgan could tell by his tone that something was wrong. "Is it Judge?"

Joseph looked puzzled, and his eyes slid to the paddock. "Where did he go? He was there earlier."

Morgan was relieved that Joseph wasn't going to give him bad news about Judge. "I don't know. I was going to look for him. What's going on?"

"I found Frank Langtry," Joseph replied.

Joseph didn't have to say Frank was dead; Morgan read it on his face. Mounting his horse, Morgan followed Joseph through the trees.

Morgan noticed there was little wind today, and there was a peacefulness in the pines that was absent last night.

Leading the way through the trees, Joseph rode to the area where the Langtry girls played as children. It was also the place where Morgan and Rose were married. Morgan dismounted and walked to Frank's body with Joseph right beside him. Morgan could hardly believe what he was seeing. Frank's mangled body was a gruesome sight. It was difficult to tell if Frank had been attacked or trampled by an animal.

"No gunshot," Joseph said.

Morgan looked at Joseph, and said, "Do you think Judge did this?"

"No."

Morgan wished he had the same confidence, but where was Judge?

"Are you thinking a bear?"

Joseph shook his head. "I don't think so."

Morgan examined Frank's body again. It certainly looked like he'd been attacked by an animal. He glanced at Joseph and said, "It has to be an animal."

"I have seen men like this before in the trees," Joseph said.

"Well, if you don't think it was a bear, what do you think it was?"

"Some things we can't explain," Joseph replied evasively.

Morgan wondered if Joseph really did think Judge could have killed Frank but hesitated to tell him. On the heels of that thought, Morgan knew Joseph would never tell him a lie. "You really don't think Judge did this, do you?"

"No."

Morgan had asked the same question twice, and twice he received the same answer. "If you go get the buckboard, I'll keep looking for Judge."

Before Joseph rode away, Morgan said, "Don't tell anyone about Frank. I'll let everyone celebrate today and tell them in the morning. If anyone wants to know why you are taking the buckboard, tell them I'm looking for a Christmas tree. Bring an ax with you." Morgan didn't want to ruin their day by telling them about Frank. Even though he knew they wouldn't be surprised by Frank's demise, that didn't mean they wouldn't take the news hard. Frank had been on a path of self-destruction for a long time, and everyone tried to warn him to no avail. But family was family, and Frank's family would grieve his passing.

Morgan figured Frank's horse might also be in the pines somewhere. He searched for any hoofprints around Frank's body, but he found nothing. No prints of any kind, man or animal. While he waited on Joseph, Morgan searched the surrounding area. Seeing nothing, he was making his way back to Frank's body when he spotted the perfect Christmas tree. At least this night would bring some joy watching the children decorate the tree.

Morgan and Joseph returned to the ranch with Frank's body, and drove the buckboard into the barn without stopping. Morgan pulled the tree from the buckboard and hoisted it over his shoulder. "Joseph, come on in the house and get some cake. We'll take care of Frank after the party ends."

Together they walked to the house and Morgan placed the tree on the back porch. As soon as he walked in, the children converged on him.

"As soon as the guests leave, you can start on the tree." Morgan saw Rose walking his way, and he figured she'd ask him about leaving the party.

"I see you found Joseph," Rose said.

"We decided to get the tree while we were out, so the children could decorate it tonight." Morgan had never lied to Rose, but he thought right now it was best to only tell her a portion of the truth.

Rose eyed him suspiciously. "What are you not telling me?"

Thankfully Claire interrupted, and asked Rose if they could pop some corn later and string it for the Christmas tree.

Rose turned her attention on Claire. "Of course we will. That will be a lot of fun."

Morgan took that opportunity to speak to Jack, Sheriff Trent, and Marshal Holt. Once he told them about Frank, Jack agreed that they should wait to tell the women.

"I don't think we should tell Clay until we tell the women, so he can enjoy his wedding night," Morgan said.

"They'll be leaving soon for the farm, so there's no sense in telling them tonight," Jack said.

"It's too bad that this happened right before Christmas," Sheriff Trent said.

"There was never going to be a good time." Morgan walked to the door and grabbed his coat. "Joseph and I are going back out to look for Judge."

"You're thinking your horse did that to Frank?" Marshal Holt asked.

Morgan stood there a minute with his hand on the

doorknob before he responded. "I don't want to think so, but something happened to Frank out there, and he didn't get shot."

"I'll take care of building a coffin," Jack said.

"Thanks, Jack."

"We'll go with you, Morgan," Marshal Holt said.

The time came when Emma had to say good-bye to her two friends. Both she and Clay had tried to talk Carlo and Andre into staying for Christmas, but they had already booked passage on the next stage for San Francisco.

With tears in her eyes, Emma hugged both men. "I'm going to miss you so much."

"No tears on your wedding day. What will the groom think?" Carlo teased, trying to mask his own emotions.

Clay shook hands with the men. "Come for a visit when you can."

"Make certain she is practicing, and so she will be ready when we come to Denver again," Carlo told Clay.

"I will."

After the good-byes, Emma and Clay left for the farm. Emma was both nervous and excited to spend time alone with her new husband. She'd never given much thought to a wedding night, but she knew she would remember this night forever.

Later that evening, Granny and Rose were in the kitchen popping corn for the tree, while Addie and the children worked on the decorations at the kitchen table.

"Where did the men go?" Granny asked.

"Judge is gone again, and Morgan went to look for him," Rose said.

"Jack said he needed to do some work in the barn," Addie said.

"Maybe I should go help Pa," David said.

Addie wanted David to enjoy the evening working on decorations with his sisters. She knew it wouldn't be long before he was going to think he was too old to do things with his sisters. "Your pa will be in soon. Let's get the decorations done so we can surprise everyone when they get back."

Morgan, Joseph, Marshal Holt, and Sheriff Trent returned to the ranch without finding a sign of Judge or Frank's horse. Morgan couldn't figure out what was going on with Judge, but it worried him. At first, he'd thought it possible Frank was the one who had led Judge away, but he dismissed that thought. Frank would have killed Judge on the ranch if he had the chance. He hoped Joseph was right, and Judge didn't kill Frank.

Marshal Holt and Sheriff Trent left to return to Denver, and Morgan walked into the stable.

Jack looked up and said, "Just in time to help me lift the coffin onto the buckboard."

"We will tell the women in the morning after breakfast. Afterward I'll ride to the farm and tell Clay and Emma," Morgan said.

Jack agreed with Morgan's plan. "I guess we'd better get to the house to help with that tree, or the women will be out here looking for us."

"Yeah." Morgan knew he had to put aside the sad news he'd have to deliver in the morning so everyone would enjoy the evening. "This is the first Christmas the children have a family, and I want this to be the best one yet."

"Addie and I are as excited as the children," Jack said.

"Christmas is always more special with children." Morgan couldn't wait to experience his child's first Christmas.

Chapter Twenty-Seven

Before dawn Morgan was downstairs making coffee when Jack joined him.

"The women will be down soon," Jack said.

Morgan nodded and set out coffee cups for everyone. When he heard the women walking down the stairs, he started pouring coffee.

"You've been up for hours, husband. I know you have something on your mind, so you might as well tell us what it is," Rose said.

Morgan told them how he found Frank in the pines. Wanting to spare them from the gruesome details, Morgan just said Frank wasn't shot, but may have been attacked by an animal.

Granny wiped her tears away and said, "I can't say I'm surprised. We all knew Frank was going to come to this kind of end. I prayed for his redemption, but it was something he didn't want for himself."

"We should see him and say a proper good-bye," Rose said.

"No, honey, we've already nailed the coffin closed."

Rose didn't question her husband; she knew he had a good reason for what he had done.

"We should go tell Emma," Granny said.

"I thought I would ride over and tell them, and we can take the coffin over later," Morgan said.

"Morgan said the children can stay here with Joseph and Murph while we bury Frank. There's no sense in them facing such a sad event. This is their first Christmas with us, and we all want it to be a happy occasion," Jack said.

Rose walked outside with Morgan when he was ready to leave for the farm. She glanced at the paddock and saw Judge. "He's back."

"What the devil?" Morgan said.

Together they walked to the paddock, and Morgan opened the gate to join Judge inside to look him over. Once again the horse looked fine.

"Is he okay?" Rose asked.

"Perfect."

"Why do you think he's doing this?" Rose asked.

"I don't know." Morgan had to tell her he thought it was a possibility that Judge could have killed Frank. He walked toward her and braced his arms on the top rung of the fence. "Rose, I think I should put him . . ." He couldn't bring himself to finish the sentence. Judge walked to him and dropped his head on his shoulder.

"No, you will not!" Rose said vehemently, causing Judge to raise his head and look at her. Seeing she'd caused Judge to be alarmed, she held her hand out to rub his nose as she did every time she gave him treats. "I know what you are thinking, and you are wrong, Morgan. Judge didn't hurt anyone. He's the gentlest horse I've ever seen." When

Morgan mentioned Frank had been attacked by an animal, she knew he thought it was a possibility Judge had hurt him.

"What if he did? What if one of the children approach him and he's taken by surprise?" Rose hadn't seen how the horse responded to people right after Frank whipped him. It took Judge a long time to be around people without being a danger to them.

"The children have been near him, and he loves them."

This was news to Morgan. "When have they been around him?"

Rose stuck her chin in the air. "When you are not here."

"Rose . . ."

"Don't you dare say a word! Judge has always behaved admirably around the children. You seem to be the only one who thinks he could do something wrong. Where is your faith in this animal?"

Morgan reached out and placed his palm on her cheek. He loved that she was defending the animal he loved so much. It brought back memories of the day she'd defended her brother. She was the reason he didn't hang Frank when he had the chance. And look how that turned out. Frank went on to cause more trouble. But now wasn't the time to remind his wife of that fact. "Honey, there's faith, and then there's common sense."

Judge stuck his head over the rail and nudged Rose's shoulder, as if thanking her for defending him.

"Well, husband, I'd say you are the one lacking in common sense if you think this animal could hurt anyone."

Morgan stroked Judge's neck. Maybe his wife was right. He'd found no blood on Judge, or anything to indicate he'd had contact with anyone or anything. "I hope you're right, honey."

"I know I'm right. Now get the buckboard. I'll ride . . ."

Morgan waited for her to finish what she was about to say, but when she didn't, he glanced her way. She was looking toward the pines. "What is it, honey?"

"Don't you hear it?"

Morgan looked at the trees and saw the limbs swaying in a gentle wind. He heard what Rose was hearing. "It's what I've always heard. Sounds like singing."

Rose smiled. "I know. Everything is peaceful again."

"It's sad, but not unexpected." Once Emma had learned of Frank's deeds, she knew his death would never be a surprise. Yet it didn't lessen the sadness she felt over the life her brother had lived. She mourned the brother she once knew, or thought she knew.

Clay stood with his arm around his new wife, comforting her as she received the sad news. He glanced at Morgan. "How's Granny handling this?"

"Granny's faith always sees her through," Morgan said.

"Clay, would you say a few words over Frank when we bury him?" Rose asked.

"Of course." Clay didn't know what it would do for Frank's soul, but if he could bring comfort to the family, he would do whatever they asked of him.

Clay and Morgan walked to the family cemetery to dig the hole for Frank's coffin. They didn't think it proper to place him beside his brother. Frank had been responsible for Stevie's death, so they chose a spot near an unmarked grave on the opposite side of the graveyard.

Rose and Emma sat at the table and reminisced about the brother they knew as children.

"What do you think happened to Frank?" Emma asked.

"Morgan said he hadn't been shot. I think he thought

an animal attacked him." Rose told Emma that Morgan worried Judge might have killed Frank.

"From what you've told me about that horse, there's no way he has it in him to be vicious," Emma replied.

Rose was thankful her sister was of the same opinion about Judge. "That's what I told Morgan."

While the men were working on the grave, Morgan told Clay how they'd found Frank, and how he was concerned Judge may be involved considering his recent absences.

"I think it was probably a bear," Clay said. "What did Joseph think?"

"He didn't really say, but he didn't think Judge killed him."

"If anyone would know, it would be Joseph," Clay said, hoping to relieve Morgan's mind.

Morgan knew Clay was right; Joseph usually knew what went on in those trees. Morgan moved on to discuss something else on his mind. "Clay, I know you don't usually celebrate Christmas, and I was wondering how you feel about it now."

"I'm looking forward to it. I've come to accept the past, and believe God had a plan for my life. It's not up to me to question why my wife and son were killed. I had a dream before my wedding, and Violet appeared at the lake where I proposed to her. She said she wanted me to be happy, and she wouldn't be back, but she would send me a message. I think she was telling me I was free to go on with my life. I felt that she wanted me to marry and she let me go. I won't cheat Emma out of all of the celebrations we should enjoy together."

"I'm glad to hear that, Clay. I know you and Emma will have a good future. She's something special, just like her sisters."

"Yes, she is. I'm a fortunate man."

"I can't wait to see the children's faces on Christmas morning."

"And next year, you and Rose will have your own child," Clay said.

"You know if you get started right away, you and Emma could have a child by next Christmas," Morgan teased.

"I've already thought of that. Wouldn't it be wonderful if we all had children by next Christmas?"

"I can't think of anything better," Morgan agreed.

The men finished their work at the cemetery. Morgan told Clay they would be back with the coffin in an hour for the burial.

Morgan and Rose returned to the ranch to find Judge had taken off again. Morgan told Rose he was going to look for him, but he'd be back in time to take Frank to the farm. Once again, Morgan started searching for a trail. This time he found fresh tracks leading him through the pines. He followed for some distance before he lost the trail. Just as he turned back toward the ranch, Judge came galloping up to him. "Why do you keep leaving, boy? And where are you going?"

Judge trotted alongside Morgan all the way back to the ranch. This time Morgan led Judge to a stall in the stable, hoping he would stay put for the rest of the night.

When the family returned to the farm with Frank's body, Morgan, Clay, and Jack lowered the coffin in the ground before the women joined them at the gravesite.

Clay stood at the head of the grave, and Granny, Emma,

Addie, and Rose held hands as they bowed their heads in prayer. Morgan and Jack flanked the women as Clay began speaking.

"We don't know what happened to Frank," he began. "We can only hope Frank prayed for forgiveness before it was too late." He asked for comfort and peace for Granny and her granddaughters during this difficult time. "Let us pray for Frank's soul." Clay ended with an emotional prayer, and silently asked that his words offered the women some peace.

While the men covered the grave, the women walked back to the house.

"Frank always thought he'd go out in a blaze of glory. Instead, he died all alone in a place that scared him to death," Granny said.

The sisters exchanged a glance, then Emma asked, "Frank was afraid of the pines?"

"He was scared to death to go in there alone. When he saw you girls weren't afraid, he wasn't about to let you know." Granny looked at Rose, and said, "Like the other night. Those were the sounds you heard with Frank."

"Yes, I was afraid when Frank was with me. Morgan told me it surprised him that Frank rustled on his land knowing he had to ride through there."

"I had never heard those sounds until the other night. It was the scariest thing I've ever heard," Granny admitted.

The entire family came to the ranch for dinner, and the adults made every effort to be joyful for the children's sake.

All through dinner, the children asked questions about how they would celebrate Christmas Eve and Christmas.

"We will cook all day, and then tomorrow night we will read about the birth of Jesus, and sing some carols," Addie said.

"And when you wake up the next morning, it will be Christmas," Jack said.

"Uncle Morgan, do you like the Christmas tree?" Claire asked.

"I believe it is the prettiest Christmas tree I've ever seen," Morgan said.

"I would like to hear Aunt Emma sing for Christmas," Jane said.

"Me, too," David agreed.

Emma was touched by the children's request. "I will sing as much as you want."

"Would you sing one song tonight?" Jane asked.

"I most certainly will," Emma said.

Clay winked at the children. "Carlo and Andre told me Emma needs to practice, so now that she has a willing audience, we'll make certain she does."

"We could be your audience every week," Jane said.

"And what a fine audience that would be. I shall look forward to it."

As soon as the last dish was dried, everyone gathered in the parlor to hear Emma sing. She'd chosen to sing "Silent Night" for them, and the children, like the adults, were in awe of her inspiring rendition. The children begged her to sing one more song, so Emma gladly complied.

Each time Clay heard Emma sing he felt guilty that he was taking her away from something she loved. When they retired for the evening, he asked her once again if she was certain she would be content if she weren't singing professionally.

"I will sing for the people I love most. Tonight I brought joy to my family and that makes me happy. I'll always sing, so you have nothing to worry about."

Clay pulled her in his arms and kissed her. "All I want is your happiness."

"As long as I'm with you, I am happy."

Chapter Twenty-Eight

On Christmas Eve, the women spent the day in the kitchen cooking, and after the men finished working, they took the children riding. When they returned before dinner, Judge was once again missing from the paddock.

David pointed to the trees. "There he is."

Morgan watched as Judge jumped the fence to get back inside the paddock. He figured he was either going to have to build a taller fence, or find out where his animal was going.

They led Judge to the stable and the children showered him with attention, and Morgan knew he had Rose to thank for that. She'd been right; Judge was gentle with them just as he was with her.

"Where do you think he goes, Uncle Morgan?" David asked.

"I don't know. What do you think?"

David looked puzzled. He remembered he and his sisters ran away when they were separated. "He must have a good reason to run off. But he always comes back. Did he have brothers or sisters?"

"Nope." Morgan knew what David was thinking. "He's been with me his whole life, from the time he was born."

"I guess that what's important is he comes back," David said.

"That's what I keep telling myself." Morgan thought David sounded wiser than his twelve years.

"Maybe he wants to roam for a while," Clay said. "See what else is out there."

"And he always knows he has a home to come to," David said.

Jack was listening to their conversation. "It's important to know a home is always waiting for you. When you kids grow up and get married, you'll always have a home here, too."

"We know," David said.

Jack ruffled his hair. "Good. Don't ever forget that."

"I hope Aunt Rose has a boy. It'd be nice to have another boy in the family," David said.

"I imagine we are going to have a lot of boys in the family," Jack said. "And just look at all the things you've learned that you will be able to teach them."

David smiled. "Yeah. It'd be fun to teach him to ride."

"We want some girls too," Jane said.

"We'll see what we can do," Jack replied. Addie had told him she might be in the family way, but not to say anything until she was certain.

The children left the stable to clean up before dinner, and the men were finishing the chores when Joseph walked in. He approached Morgan and said, "White Cloud and Little Elk said Frank killed the old man everyone calls Indian Pete in Purgatory Canyon."

"Who's Indian Pete?" Clay asked.

"A Sioux. He's lived in that canyon for many years," Joseph said.

"Why did Frank kill him?" Morgan asked.

"Little Elk and White Cloud had taken the old man some meat. He told Little Elk and White Cloud that two men had been in the canyon with much money. He said four men had also been in the canyon looking for the two men. The braves spent several days in the canyon with the old man, and when they were leaving, they saw Frank riding in." Joseph told them the braves decided to follow Frank and see what he was up to. "They watched Frank take Pete from shack to shack before they ended up in Pete's cabin again. They heard a gunshot, and Frank came out of the cabin drinking whiskey. When Frank rode away, the braves went inside and found Pete. He was shot in the head."

"Aren't those the braves who found the children in the pines when they ran away?" Jack asked.

"Yes," Joseph said.

"Did they see Frank in the pines recently?" Morgan thought the braves may have killed Frank in retribution for killing one of their own.

Joseph nodded. "They saw Frank several nights ago and followed him. He drank a lot of whiskey for two days. They saw him fall off his horse, but his boot was caught in the stirrup. His horse spooked. It took the braves a long time to catch up to them. When they found Frank, he was dead."

Morgan was relieved that the braves confirmed Judge had nothing to do with Frank's death.

"Granny said Frank was scared to death of riding in the pines," Jack said.

"Whiskey makes some men brave, or careless," Clay said.

"I guess justice was served to Frank in the end," Morgan said.

"Do you think that means that Frank's gang did steal that money from Culpepper and Taggart?" Jack asked.

"But why would they turn themselves in if they did steal that money? They could have taken off to Mexico and never returned," Morgan said.

"Joseph, you said four men stole the money from the two men who had the money, right?" Clay asked.

Joseph nodded.

The men exchanged a glance. "There was only Deke, Dutch, and they said Reb had been killed by Culpepper and Taggart. I know Corbin Jeffers met up with Deke and Dutch, but he wasn't in on the robbery at the bank. There was no wanted poster on him," Jack said.

"Do you think Reb was killed?" Morgan asked.

"Marshal Holt said he rode to the cabin to see the grave for himself. He thought Deke and Dutch were telling the truth," Jack said.

"Then who was the fourth man?" Morgan asked.

"The only person who could describe him is dead," Jack said.

Morgan looked at him and nodded. "Indian Pete."

"You know Harper Ellis told me his sister was marrying Dutch Sullivan," Clay said.

"Do you think Harper would be involved in the bank robbery?" Jack asked.

"I don't think Harper ever did anything illegal," Clay said. "I sure can't see him robbing a bank." Clay didn't want to betray a confidence, but he saw no harm in telling them about Harper's health. "He's very ill."

"Is that the friend you mentioned during your last sermon?" Morgan asked.

"Yes. Harper has always helped to support his sister since her husband ran out on her and those children," Jack said. "A portion of that bank money could go a long way to help feed and clothe them."

"A man will do what he has to for the people he loves," Morgan said.

"I'd hate to think he was involved," Clay said.

The men grew quiet. They all liked Harper, and didn't want to accuse him without some proof.

Jack finally broke the silence. "It's not like we have evidence of anything. I see no reason to suspect Harper of anything."

"If he's done something illegal, then I guess it will come to light," Clay said.

They all agreed.

Christmas morning

The adults pretended to be asleep when they heard the children running down the hallway. They couldn't contain their excitement as they opened the bedroom doors, shrieking, "It's snowing, it's snowing!" Sweetie added to the melee with his deafening deep howl.

Joining the children in the hallway, the adults followed them down the stairs. Everyone ran to the windows to see several inches of glistening snow covering the ground, and the pines sparkling like a magical white forest.

"It's so beautiful," Emma said.

"Just perfect for Christmas morning. I'll get the coffee going," Granny said.

"I'll handle the coffee, Granny," Morgan told her.

The children ran to the parlor, and seeing the presents under the tree, they started squealing again. After the presents were opened, Morgan and the men walked to the stables to feed the horses. Chores done, they all returned to the house where the women had a large breakfast waiting for them.

"Can we play in the snow?" Jane asked.

"We'll all go out after breakfast and build a snowman," Addie said.

"Can you help, Pa?" David asked Jack.

"We'll help for a while, but we need to get out to the range to help the men with the chores," Jack replied.

When breakfast ended, the children ran upstairs to get their coats and gloves. The men spent an hour with the children building snowmen before they left to work.

When the men returned from the range, Morgan noticed Judge was not in the paddock, nor was he in his stable. Morgan knew their Christmas dinner would be ready, so he decided not to search for him. The horse had come back on his own before, and Morgan hoped he would do so today.

"Aunt Emma, can you sing outside after dinner?" David asked during dinner.

"Of course," Emma replied.

"Why do you want her to sing outside?" Clay asked.

"Everything sounds different with snow on the ground," David said.

After dinner, everyone grabbed their coats and headed outside again. Morgan looked toward the paddock, but Judge had not returned. As Emma sang, everyone noticed the wind seemed to increase. Her song ended, but the sounds coming through the pines sounded like people singing.

"Emma, do you hear that? Those are sounds I always heard in the pines," Rose said to Emma.

"I hear it now, Rose," Emma said. "Addie and I always heard laughter before."

"It does sound like angels singing." For the first time, Granny understood what Rose was talking about when she was a child.

Just then, Judge came running through the trees and jumped the paddock fence.

Morgan watched as the horse gracefully leaped over the fence. "I would build a taller fence, but I don't think that would keep him in," he said on his way to the paddock.

"Look, Uncle Morgan," David said.

Morgan turned to see David pointing to the pines. Slowly walking from the trees was a very thin, white horse, followed by a small black and white colt. They looked skittish as they stood at the boundary, longingly looking at Judge in the paddock, yet ready to bolt through the trees if necessary. As soon as Morgan opened the gate to the paddock, Judge ambled over to him and nudged his shoulder in his usual greeting. "Is that your baby, Judge?" Morgan could tell by looking that the mare hadn't eaten properly for a while. That told Morgan the colt probably wasn't receiving the nourishment he required. "Let's see if they'll come in the paddock on their own." Morgan stroked Judge's neck as they watched the mare and colt. He didn't want to make any sudden moves that might frighten them away.

Clay stared at the white horse who was standing a good forty feet from him. His first thought was something about the animal seemed familiar. Taking a few steps in the direction of the horse, the horse turned to look at Clay. *It couldn't be.* Surprisingly the horse took a few tentative steps toward him.

"Moonrise?" Clay said, more to himself than aloud.

"What is it, Clay?" Emma asked.

Clay didn't respond; he started running toward the horse, and at the same moment the horse took a few hesitant steps toward him. Reaching the weakened animal, Clay wrapped his arms around her neck. "Moonrise! I never thought I would see you again."

The colt timidly followed his mother, and Clay reached out to stroke his neck.

"Does Uncle Clay know that horse?" David asked.

"I think he does," Morgan replied.

Emma and Sweetie joined Clay beside the horses, and Clay said, "Honey, this is my horse, Moonrise."

"The one Culpepper and Taggart stole from you?" Emma remembered Clay telling her about the horse the night they captured the two killers. She had a difficult time believing it was possible the horse was Clay's.

"I told you in my dream Violet said she would send a sign. I think this is her sign that she wanted me to be happy," Clay said.

"Clay, how is it possible this horse came this far?" As much as she wanted to believe this was Clay's horse for his sake, she had doubts.

Clay pointed to Moonrise's hindquarter at the visible half-moon brand. "I don't know how she did it, but that is my brand. Jonas had it made when I named the ranch."

Emma had to admit that his brand was unique. Still, it was difficult to believe after four years of being apart, the horse would recognize Clay. But once she saw how the horse was responding to him, her doubts began to diminish.

"Would you look at that," Granny said. "Sweetie is as big as that colt."

Everyone laughed as they watched Sweetie and the colt playfully nosing each other. Sweetie had found his own playmate.

The entire family had gathered around Clay and Moonrise. He explained how he'd looked for Moonrise for four years in every town he'd traveled through. He tried to hold on to his belief that he would see her again, but after so much time had passed, he started to lose faith.

"I think this is a Christmas miracle, Uncle Clay," David said. "Did you notice the colt has a half moon on his forehead?"

Everyone looked at the colt, and noticed his head was all black hair, with the exception of an interrupted blaze in the shape of a half moon.

"David, I think you are right. It is a miracle," Clay said.

"Moonrise is starving. Let's get her in the paddock with Judge," Morgan said.

David ran to the kitchen to gather some apples and carrots to feed the horses as their Christmas treat. Clay walked Moonrise and her colt to the paddock to join Judge. Everyone gathered around the paddock and watched as the horses ate their fill.

"They are so beautiful together," Emma said, admiring Morgan's black horse beside Clay's white horse.

"Once Moonrise is cleaned up and gains some weight, she'll be even more beautiful," Clay said.

"How do you think she found you here, Uncle Clay? It's a long way from Kansas," David said.

"David, I don't know. The Bible tells us love is the most important thing. I'd say this proves that you'll never be separated from those you love, no matter how much time passes."

"I think they heard your singing, Aunt Emma," David said.

"I bet they thought angels were singing," Jane said.

"This is the best Christmas. I guess you're right, Uncle Clay," David said.

"Right about what, David?" Clay asked.

"You always thought you would find your horse, and you did," David said.

"I'm not sure I found her. I think God led her to me," Clay said.

"I'm glad Judge has a family, just like us," David said. "I think we should name the colt, Christmas."

"That sounds perfect," Clay replied.

Morgan choked up at the thought of his beautiful animal having a partner. Judge had suffered so much, and it warmed Morgan's heart to see him in the paddock with his family. It wasn't lost on Morgan how all of their lives had been richly blessed in a few short months. He reached for Rose's hand and held her to him. "We have all been blessed."

Clay pulled Emma into his arms. "You're right Morgan. We've all been richly blessed. I never thought I would believe in miracles again, but I was wrong."

"We should always believe in miracles. How else will we recognize one if we don't believe?" Granny asked.

Visit us online at
KensingtonBooks.com
to read more from your favorite authors, see books
by series, view reading group guides, and more.

Join us on social media

for sneak peeks, chances to win books and prize packs,
and to share your thoughts with other readers.

facebook.com/kensingtonpublishing
twitter.com/kensingtonbooks

Tell us what you think!

To share your thoughts, submit a review,
or sign up for our eNewsletters, please visit:
KensingtonBooks.com/TellUs.